I0776666

The
Mean
Street

a 509 Crime Story

by Colin Conway

The Mean Street

Copyright © 2021 Colin Conway

Original Cover Design by Zach McCain
Updated Cover Design by Rob Williams

Amazon ISBN: 9798709161689
Mass Market ISBN: 978-1-961030-10-7

Original Ink Press, an imprint of High Speed Creative, LLC
1521 N. Argonne Road, #C-205
Spokane Valley, WA 99212

Visit the author's website at www.colinconway.com

What is the 509?

Separated by the Cascade Range, Washington State is divided into two distinctly different climates and cultures.

The western side of the Cascades is home to Seattle, its 34 inches of annual rainfall, and the incredibly weird and smelly Gum Wall. Most of the state's wealth and political power are concentrated in and around this enormous city. The residents of this area know the prosperity that has come from being the home of Microsoft, Amazon, Boeing, and Starbucks.

To the east of the Cascade Mountains lies nearly two-thirds of the entire state, a lot of which is used for agriculture. Washington State leads the nation in producing apples, it is the second-largest potato grower, and it's the fourth for providing wheat.

This eastern part of the state can enjoy more than 170 days of sunshine each year, which is important when there are more than 200 lakes nearby. However, the beautiful summers are offset by harsh winters, with average snowfall reaching 47 inches and the average high hovering around 37°.

While five telephone area codes provide service to the westside, only 509 covers everything east of the Cascades, a staggering twenty-one counties.

Of these, Spokane County is the largest with an estimated population of 506,000.

*If you don't deal with your demons,
they will deal with you.*

And it's gonna hurt.

\-   Nikki Sixx

The Mean Street

1

I struggled to concentrate over the loud music.

A woman lay in the middle of the sidewalk as the song played. Blood pooled around her head, and her body was a broken mess.

After leaping over the eastern edge of the Western Bank Building, she fell eighteen floors to the concrete below. When she hit, she landed on her back. I wouldn't know for sure until her autopsy, but I imagined she broke every bone in her body.

The guitars screamed louder and interrupted my thoughts. I pressed a thumb into my temple to alleviate some of the pain the music caused. Blinking several times, I refocused on the woman.

Up and down both legs, her pant seams had exploded upon impact. A dirty tennis shoe lay several feet away—thrown clear by the sudden and violent stop from terminal velocity.

The lead singer of the heavy metal band, Megadeth, belted out "High Speed Dirt." I squinted in hopes of blocking the music from my consciousness. It didn't work. The guitars and lyrics continued their frantic pace.

The bones in her face and skull caved in at inhuman angles, and her hair splayed out above her. She no longer looked like a woman. Instead, she resembled a demented Troll doll—the ugly child's toy.

Megadeth's song about jumping to one's death looped inside my brain. I closed my eyes and lowered my head. Guitars squealed. Clenching my fists, I inhaled deeply. Drums pounded, and cymbals clashed.

A hand shook my shoulder, and I opened my eyes.

"Dallas?"

Letting out my breath and relaxing my fists, I turned to my partner, Detective Glenn Higgins. He tucked his hands into his brown, knee-length wool coat, and concern registered in his eyes. Draped around his neck was a tan scarf.

"You okay?" he asked.

"Yeah."

"I said your name—*twice*."

"Sorry," I mumbled. "Didn't hear you."

Glenn watched me closely now. He'd been doing that a lot lately.

He'd gotten this call and was the lead investigator. Every suicide was treated as a homicide—the unlawful killing of a person. There's only one shot at a death investigation, so that's the attitude with which we must approach it.

I shoved my hands into my pockets and pulled my coat tighter. Even though the sun was out and the sky clear, the November chill signaled the approaching winter.

The dead woman wore a gray button-up work shirt over a white turtleneck and faded black pants. A sewn-on patch with the name *Carlotta* was above her left breast.

"Patrol found a note," Glenn said.

"Where?"

"On the roof. Under a brick."

"Think she worked in the building?"

"Maybe she was a janitor. We can confirm with the property manager."

Glenn fell silent as I glanced toward the top of the building—the tallest in Spokane. If she were part of a janitorial crew, that would explain how she gained access to the roof. My eyes traced the path of her descent to where her body lay.

I wondered if I would have the guts to jump like her—*assuming* she jumped. Inside my head, a new song stuttered to life and quickly reached a crescendo.

Ted Nugent's "Dog Eat Dog" looped inside my brain. The lyric about swan diving from the hundredth floor turned my stomach as I wondered what Carlotta looked like before her fall.

A group of onlookers assembled beyond the outer perimeter. The faces in the crowd showed a mixture of curiosity and horror. Among the public, a news crew filmed our actions. The body wouldn't usually be left exposed like it was. The forensic team was still on its way, and they would erect a tent over it. Once they did, the looky-loos would leave. Privacy for the dead wasn't as exciting as having it openly displayed on a downtown sidewalk during the Friday noon hour.

Glenn's movements caught my attention. He gestured while he spoke, but I couldn't hear him. Instead, I listened to the song's main chorus, circling over and over, almost chanting now.

My partner waited for a response, then shook his head and walked away. Ambling as if his knees hurt, he headed toward the lieutenant and captain who had arrived on the scene.

"Dog Eat Dog" looped over and over inside my head.

Turning my attention back to Carlotta, I recentered my focus. The music receded slowly into the back of my mind like a wave pulling out to sea.

Why would a person jump to their death rather than taking pills and drifting off quietly? Statistically, women are more likely to harm themselves in ways that won't damage the body as severely.

"Dog Eat Dog" returned on a wave and crashed onto the shore of my consciousness. I waited a moment for it to leave before continuing.

Reexamining how bad her head injuries were, I wondered if she regretted her decision to jump the moment she leaped. It would be impossible to regret it at impact.

The music played louder and pushed all thoughts from my head. I closed my eyes and pressed a knuckle into an eye socket, hoping to lessen the associated pain. It didn't.

"Dog Eat Dog."

"What?"

I opened the eye without my finger shoved into it. Captain Gary Ackerman stood at my shoulder. Quickly, I dropped my hand and blinked the other eye into focus.

"Dog eat dog?" he said. "Why say that?"

I hadn't realized I had. To cover my mistake, I said, "Thinking about life." There was no way I could tell the captain about the songs. The chaplain knew about them, and that was already one person too many.

"You look like hell, Nash."

"I'm okay."

Ackerman's gaze ran my length. "You don't look it."

I shrugged again. There wasn't any point in arguing with the captain. Doing so, especially at an active crime scene, was only the stuff they did in the movies. Besides, such behavior would only prove his fears to be right.

Ackerman looked around before leaning in. "You drinking?"

"Occasionally," I lied.

"I meant today."

"No, sir. Not at all."

He leaned back and studied me again. "Late nights, then?"

"Some." It was another lie.

Ackerman slowly nodded as if the pieces fitted together. An alcoholic cop, no matter how cliché, was something he understood. He could deal with that concept. Better to have him worry about me and a bottle than what was happening inside my head.

"Maybe you should take some time off."

"I'm good."

He opened his mouth to say something, but the music started again. "Dog Eat Dog" repeated at full blast between my ears. Ackerman moved his lips, but I only heard the chorus of the Ted Nugent classic.

When he stopped speaking, he cocked his head as if waiting for an answer.

The music inside my own blocked out the real world, so I nodded. It was either that or shake my head. I guess I could have stared dumbly at the man. Accepting whatever he said seemed the least likely to blowback.

Ackerman's eyes softened, and he patted my shoulder. He said a couple more words I couldn't hear, then headed toward the news crew.

The music faded, and silence echoed inside my skull.

2

"Ever think of jumping?" Glenn asked.

"What?"

We were on the roof, leaning on the parapet wall, looking over its edge. On the sidewalk below, the forensic team assembled a white tent over the body. They moved around the dead woman with practiced efficiency.

"Dog Eat Dog" stuttered to life again. I waited for it to overwhelm my thoughts, but it hung in the background, softly chanting its chorus.

"Sometimes I hear a voice," Glenn said, "whenever I get near a ledge like this."

"A voice?"

My partner nodded.

"What's it say?"

"Jump."

I studied him. I wasn't sure if he was yanking my chain.

"It sorta whispers," Glenn said. Then he murmured, "*Jump,*" in a spooky sort of way.

"Don't do it."

My partner smirked. "I'm not going to, but it sorta freaks me out, you know? Happens whenever I get up someplace high."

"I didn't know you were afraid of heights."

"A little maybe. It's not a big deal."

"This voice—it doesn't tell you to do anything with your gun, does it?"

Glenn rolled his eyes. "Jesus, Dallas. I was sharing something. It's not like I want to off myself."

We fell quiet as we watched the activity below. The lunchtime crowd should have thinned by now, but the group of onlookers remained thick. Several people gawked from the windows of nearby buildings.

The music inside my head played at a tolerable, almost comforting, level. Over the last six months, though, it rarely stayed like this. Now, whenever the songs came, they dominated my thoughts and became so loud it turned painful.

I studied the note contained inside a plastic evidence bag.

Ask him why.

Someone had written the three words on the back of a daily log sheet for Lilac City Janitorial.

Glenn said something I didn't catch. "Huh?"

"Quite the show," he repeated and motioned toward the crowd below.

"It's not every day those people are faced with mortality."

"Lucky for them."

"Excuse me," a feminine voice said.

We turned to see a woman with dark auburn hair in a black wool coat. Her gloved hands held a manila file. A patrol officer stood near the roof entrance, but he had let her pass for some reason.

"Colleen Jamison," she said, extending her right hand. "I manage the property."

We shook hands, then she and Glenn did the same.

"The woman who jumped was Carlotta Winkler." Her words and tone were cold and efficient.

She handed me the folder. Inside were several papers regarding Carlotta's employment with Lilac City Janitorial, as well as a copy of an employment security check. Also included were a copy of a work visa and an Employment Authorization Document. Her country of birth listed Germany.

"She worked for you?" Glenn asked.

"No," Colleen said. "She worked for the janitorial company that we contract with." Irritation flashed in her eyes, and I tilted my head in response. She tapped the file in my hand. "That's the info her employer emailed us to give to you. If you need any more—"

"Did she normally have access to the roof?" I asked.

The property manager frowned. "She wouldn't need it, but there's a key to the roof in the maintenance office. She had access to that. She probably took it without asking."

I closed the folder and handed it to Glenn. "Who else had access to that key or the maintenance room?"

Colleen rolled her eyes. "Our maintenance staff. And the rest of the janitorial team, I guess. The elevator vendor uses it when they're here."

"Can they all go up unaccompanied?"

The property manager's face soured further. "I suppose so, but they shouldn't be."

Glenn glanced at me before saying, "We'll need a contact name and number for the woman's employer. Also, we need a list of everyone who has had access to that key."

"Why?" Colleen asked. "I thought she jumped."

I put my hands in my coat pockets. "We can't be sure of that until we're finished with our investigation. Until then, it's a homicide, and we investigate it as such."

Colleen's demeanor seemed to waver between disappointment and frustration. She audibly sighed.

"Is everything okay?" I asked.

"Besides the dead woman on my sidewalk? And the assembled news crews? Or the angry calls I'm getting from tenants about problems getting in and out of the building? Yeah, everything is perfectly okay. Couldn't be better. Thank you for asking."

Glenn discreetly touched my arm before asking, "Was Carlotta having problems with anyone at work or home?"

"How would I know? She wasn't my employee, so I didn't know the woman. She came in, did what was asked of her, then she left. Beyond that, you'll have to ask her employer."

3

While Glenn returned to the station to prepare a search warrant for Carlotta Winkler's apartment, I drove to the administrative office for Lilac City Janitorial. It was on East Trent Avenue, a stone's throw from Felts Field, the small airport that once served as the primary air hub for this region until the mid-forties.

The small brown-brick building stood out in the diverse industrialized area. Inside, the aroma of cinnamon enveloped the workspace. The desktops were sloppy with files and papers.

Verne Calbert, the district manager, led me into his office. In his late fifties, Verne seemed a genial man with smiling eyes. Photographs of picturesque golf locations adorned his office walls.

I explained my reason for being there.

"That's terrible," he said remorsefully.

"It is," I agreed. I could have given other platitudes about suicide being sad anytime it happens, but I didn't have the energy. Instead, I hurried into the background questions. "How was Carlotta as an employee?"

"Fine."

"Only fine?"

Verne spun to a wide oak cabinet and opened a drawer. His fingers tumbled over a series of folders before he tugged one out. He removed several pieces of paper that he laid on the desk.

"Her performance reviews," he said. "She's been with us for almost a year, so that's her ninety-day—" Verne pointed to one piece of paper "—and that's her six-month. She was a good worker but never really stood out. Don't mean to speak ill of the dead, but, well, you know. She was sort of middle of the road."

I pulled the reviews closer to see. "You didn't email these to the property manager."

"Colleen asked for Carlotta's hire info, so that's all we sent. I didn't think you'd want this kind of stuff."

Verne put the folder on the edge of the desk, and I grabbed it, too. Inside was Carlotta's initial employment information that we reviewed on the roof of the bank building, the size she wore for her uniform shirts, and a copy of the acknowledgment of receiving both a Human Resources policy manual and a training binder.

I set the file and papers back on the desk. "Did she have problems with anyone?"

Verne shook his head. "She worked almost exclusively at the Western Bank Building. Occasionally, she'd cover for someone on a nearby property we handle. But *problems*? I've never heard of any."

"What about her home life? Was she married?"

"She was for about a year—to a soldier. Did you know she was from Germany? It's in the file if you didn't. Anyway, I guess they met while he was stationed over there. She came to the states with him after he got out. I don't know the full story behind it, but I guess he decided to re-up and was shipped back overseas. Not Europe, if I remember right. Anyway, she didn't want to travel the world with him. She wanted to stay here."

"In Spokane? As a janitor?"

Verne's face slackened. "There's nothing wrong with being a janitor. I started as one. Now I oversee the entire region."

I raised my hand in apology. "I didn't mean any offense. I was saying it doesn't seem like a job and city to break up a marriage over."

The manager nodded a couple of times, and his smile slowly returned. "I get it. She wasn't working here when she was married, though. She came to us after. What happened to that relationship, I have no idea. Anyway, when they divorced, she changed her name back to Winkler, which she pronounces with a V like Vinkler. It sounded better when she said it. We all said Winkler around here. She never complained none."

When we finished talking about Carlotta's work history, I said, "She left a note."

Verne's eyes softened. "What did it say?"

"Ask him why."

His face scrunched. "What does that mean?"

"I don't know. I was hoping you could tell me."

The manager stared at me for a moment, then his brow furrowed. "Wait a minute. You don't think I'm *him*? The one in the note."

"Are you?"

"*No*. At least, I don't think so." He swallowed, and his eyes darted around. "I don't think I ever said anything to upset her."

"Did you and she—"

His eyes widened. "What? You mean—*No!* We never. I would never do that. I've got a wife and kids. Besides, I'm her boss. If I did that, I would get fired, and I've worked too damn hard to get to this level. No woman is worth getting canned over. Not a chance."

He never looked away.

"What about a boyfriend?"

Verne shrugged. "Heck if I know. I don't fraternize with the workers. To be honest, most of them stay here an average of ten to twelve months. If they make it beyond that, I start to warm up to them because I think they'll be with us for the long haul."

"She never mentioned any health issues?"

He shrugged. "We don't provide health insurance, but she never called in sick. As I said, she was a good worker."

"You said she was middle of the road."

"She did good work, but a lot of our people do good work. She never stood out is what I said—never went above and beyond. She always did what was asked and did it on time, but never more than that. She was good at following directions."

I waggled my finger between the performance reviews and the employment folder. "Can I get copies of everything?"

Verne stood and collected the items. "Anything else?"

"She didn't list an emergency contact."

"I asked her about that when she first filled out her paperwork. She said she didn't have any family, so there wasn't anyone to list."

He walked off toward a copy machine.

4

Carlotta Winkler lived in the basement of a converted apartment-house off the corner of Ruby Street and Augusta Avenue. Its access was on the east side of the property, away from the busy northbound arterial.

The upper units' entrance was on a porch, and a stained, blue couch sat near its edge. Around its perimeter ran a dilapidated white railing with several missing spindles.

Glenn and I met there after he completed the search warrant and got a judge's signature. We found Carlotta's purse and keys in her locker at the Western Bank Building.

At the door, Glenn knocked three times, each time loudly announcing, "Spokane Police Department. We have a search warrant." This was as much for the possibility of another occupant as it was for anyone watching what we were doing.

When there was no answer, he tried several keys before finding the one that granted us access. After we both slipped on latex gloves, we entered.

Inside, the ceilings were low, and it smelled of cigarettes and incense. A quick search revealed it to be an orderly and relatively bare one-bedroom unit—Carlotta Winkler didn't have many possessions.

The bed was made, and there was a nightstand with a reading lamp. The red cloth draped over it provided the room with a rosy hue. A dark blanket with a moon design hung on the far wall. A paperback with a shirtless man on the cover rested near an empty wine glass. The novel was written in German.

Various bottles of perfume clustered together on top of the dresser. In the drawers were the typical types of clothing and sundries.

"Check this out," Glenn said. He stood in front of the closet.

A single dress hung on the left side. On the floor below, a single set of high heels perfectly lined up underneath.

"Nice, huh?"

"She can't dress up?" I asked.

"But only one dress? You'd think she would have more."

"Maybe that's all she could afford."

In the small living space, a tattered brown couch faced a small flat-screen television. Between the two sat a glass coffee table with a couple of pieces of folded paper, along with torn-open envelopes.

With a gloved finger, I spread the papers apart. The first was a church schedule. The second was a letter from U.S. Citizenship and Immigration Services signed by Lynn Slater.

"She was denied citizenship."

Glenn stepped over and picked up the letter. "I thought she automatically got it after marrying a service member."

I flicked the paper he was holding. "She had a green card, remember? If it were automatic, everyone would marry a soldier to bypass the system."

"I guess."

"I wonder why she was denied."

"Something in her background, most likely. I'll call and find out." He put the paper on the coffee table and photographed it.

"Not taking it?" I asked.

"You want it for evidence?"

I shrugged.

"I only wanted the number of the person to call at Immigration."

"Then leave it."

Carlotta didn't have a dining table, but the small kitchen area provided enough room for one. I imagined she ate her meals on the coffee table.

Nothing hung on the walls in the kitchen or the living room. Except for the blanket with a moon that hung in the bedroom, all the walls were bare. "No pictures," I said.

"That's weird. You'd think she'd have something up."

"Maybe we'll get something from her phone."

"Doubt it."

He was probably right. Her cell phone was in her back pocket when she landed, and Forensics found it after they moved the body. It exploded on impact. Extracting any information now was iffy at best.

When we finished searching the apartment, Glenn locked it and jotted the time in his notebook.

Outside, a woman sat on the porch couch, smoking a cigarette. She wore a tattered housecoat, pajamas, and red cowboy boots. She appeared sickly with sunken cheeks and sallow skin. It was hard to determine her age.

"You the police?"

"That's right," Glenn said.

The woman inhaled on her cigarette. When she asked, "What'd she do?" smoke escaped with each word.

"She died."

"Too bad."

"You knew her?" Glenn asked.

Another inhale. "As neighbors."

"What can you tell us about her?"

"Pretty thing with an accent. Not from around here." She pursed her lips. "She entertained occasionally."

Glenn stepped forward. "Entertained?"

"A man."

"A boyfriend?"

She inhaled again, then exhaled a long plume of smoke. "I guess so."

"You guess so?"

The woman thought about it. "Didn't seem romantic."

"How did it seem?" he asked.

"Business-like."

"Over how long a period?"

Her eyes rolled up. "I don't know. Few weeks maybe. She'd get dressed up for him."

"Would they go out?" Glenn asked.

The woman laughed, then coughed. "Don't think so. Never saw them leave. He would show up alone, then leave alone."

"But you saw her dressed up?"

"A couple times when I was coming back from the store." Her cigarette dangled between her lips as she spoke. "She was in the doorway. The same dress both times."

"Can you describe him?"

"White. About your age."

"Was he dressed up?" I asked.

"Not necessarily, no. He looked a businessman type. Like a clock puncher."

"Ever see his car?" Glenn asked.

"Nope."

"And you're sure he wasn't a boyfriend?"

She shrugged. "Not really, but that's not the feeling I got. Listen. I don't want to say anything bad about the dead."

"Nobody does," he said.

Glenn jerked his head toward Carlotta's apartment, and I fell into step behind him.

Back inside, I viewed her bedroom with a different eye—the red cloth over the lamp, the various perfumes, the long dress, and the neatly positioned pair of high heels.

A new song started inside my head, and I stuck a knuckle in my right eye to alleviate the pain. "Flesh for Fantasy," Billy Idol's ode to man's lust, wailed loudly for no one but me.

Glenn said something, but I couldn't make it out.

"What?" I said louder than necessary.

"You going deaf?"

I shook my head, and the music faded slightly.

"I said, do you think she might have been a working girl?"

"We're jumping to conclusions."

"Her husband wouldn't be the first serviceman to go to Europe and fall in love with one. Is it still legal over there?"

"I have no idea."

Glenn moved his position to get another look at the single dress. He lifted it out of the closet with its hanger. "Maybe he married her, brought her home to meet mom, and then saw all the homegrown girls he could have wed. The kind of girls who hadn't slept with hundreds of men for money."

"Her boss said he re-upped, and she didn't want to follow him. That implies she wanted the divorce. Besides, she's been alone for over a year. Nothing was stopping her from seeing someone. None of this," I said, waving my hand around her room, "makes her a prostitute."

He returned the dress to the closet. "No, it doesn't."

"And if she was hooking, why clean toilets?"

Glenn put his hands on his hips. "Yeah."

The music disappeared entirely from my head.

My partner glanced around the apartment. "This suicide feels hinky."

"Don't they all?"

"Not like this one. A woman denied her citizen status commits suicide but leaves behind a cryptic note like some *National Treasure* movie. 'Ask him why.' What the hell is that supposed to mean? Do you think maybe she did it to yank our chain? Kind of a screw with the cops from the grave type of thing."

"Serious?"

"No, Dallas. That was sarcasm."

"But to your point, if she were going to leave a note, you'd think she'd say something more direct."

"Exactly," Glenn said. "So her words wouldn't be misinterpreted."

"*If* they were her words."

***

Glenn and I visited some of the neighboring businesses lining Ruby Street. Due to their locations, we expected most of them to have security cameras. We hoped one of those retailers might have had one pointed at Carlotta's apartment.

About half a block away, a convenience store had multiple cameras. Unfortunately, all were pointed either at the gas pumps or at the cashier stand inside the store. Unless we already knew who we were looking for and what day and time he visited Carlotta, there was no way we could find him on those cameras. And if we already knew who Carlotta's visitor was, why would we need footage of him stopping in for a candy bar and fill-up?

We found two security cameras at the neighboring travel agency, but they were only pointed over the front and rear entries. They weren't worried about what was happening across the street.

Several smaller businesses had no cameras. They seemed either temporary in nature or positive in attitude. Either way, they wouldn't be around long enough to warrant installing the security devices.

Like canvassing frequently turns out to be, our efforts were a bust. But the only way we could know for sure was to do it. That was the job, and we knew it.

5

At the department, I entered Carlotta Winkler's information into the reporting software—single, white female, thirty-four years old—and started my portion of the report.

I picked up the evidence bag and reviewed the suicide note. Hell, it wasn't a note; it was a suicide sentence.

Ask him why.

I stared at it for a while. Why would she write a note like that? I reminded myself that why she chose to write a cryptic message wasn't a necessary component to close this case. I slid it to the side and opened my notepad.

According to the neighbor, she entertained a man in her apartment. So what? She was a single woman and alone for over a year. It wasn't unreasonable to think she could have a man in her life by now—several, maybe more than several—in that time.

But her note amped up the urgency to find *him*. There was only one him we knew about right now—her ex-husband.

She left Germany to follow him to the United States, then died alone on a Spokane sidewalk. What a waste.

A new song burst to life inside my head—Rammstein's "Du Hast."

My head bowed, my eyes snapped shut, and my teeth ground together. My hands hovered over the keyboard even though my arms wanted to pull in tight to protect my body.

The song was loud, mean, and powerful and the initial drumbeat pounded inside my head. Once the audible shock of it all settled down to a more tolerable level, my eyes reopened, and I glanced around.

Hunched over his keyboard, Glenn hunted and pecked his way toward completing his report.

Was the song xenophobic? Was I racist because my subconscious decided to play it now?

My mind screwed with me occasionally. I knew it was *my* mind because *she* wouldn't send me this song. I was sure of that, like I was sure she hadn't sent the earlier songs at the crime scene. She disliked heavy metal, and she wouldn't make light of a woman's death.

Besides, "Du Hast" was about never wanting to get married. I once looked up the meaning of the lyrics to know what the song was about. Neither of us ever felt that way.

The drums and guitars continued inside my skull. Almost robotically, I wrote my report. Writing against squealing riffs was difficult, but I'd gotten proficient at it over the past half-year. It took intense concentration to ignore not only the music but the discomfort that came with it being so loud.

A hand touched my shoulder, and I started. The cacophony inside my head vanished.

Detective Marci Burkett stood near and studied me. She wore a dark pantsuit and a red blouse. Her recent haircut made her look sort of like Joan Jett. That is, if the leader of the Blackhearts could kick someone's ass without breaking a sweat.

"When's the last time you ate?" she asked.

"What?"

She crossed her arms. "How much weight have you lost?"

Glenn stopped typing and stared straight ahead. It was apparent he heard Marci's question.

Hoping she would drop it, I said, "A few pounds."

"More like twenty. Maybe even more."

"Not that much."

"We're trained observers, Dal. We're going to notice an unhealthy weight loss. Let's get some dinner tonight. I'll buy. Something high in carbs. You can tell me what's going on."

Usually, I appreciated Marci's concern, but calling me out in the middle of the detectives' bullpen was overstepping a boundary.

I turned back to my computer. "I can't."

She leaned in and lowered her voice. "Everyone's talking about how you look. Like something's going on."

Rammstein's pulsating song returned, and I wanted to press a thumb into my eye to help alleviate the pain. I didn't, though. Doing so would show her something was indeed going on.

Instead, I said, "Let 'em talk."

"You're my friend, and I worry about you."

"Don't. The only thing I need is some space."

She put her hand on my shoulder and gently squeezed. Her voice was barely discernable above the music no one else heard. "Space is the last thing you need."

Even though she was my friend, the whole thing pissed me off. She shouldn't pry into my business while we were in public. There wasn't any way to know who was listening.

"Marci, I think the world of you," I shrugged her hand from my shoulder, "but fuck off."

She remained standing there, but I didn't look up. Marci had a well-known temper, but I wasn't worried she would hit me. If she decided to slug me, I deserved it. Besides, a punch would be better than further questioning. No, I didn't want to look at her because I'm sure I hurt her feelings. When she walked away, the music quieted in my head.

"Now, I *know* something is wrong," Glenn said.

I eyed him.

His eyes flicked to the departing Marci before he turned back to his computer. "You clearly have a death wish."

6

After leaving the office, I returned home and dropped into the corner of my couch. It was my familiar hiding spot. My pillow and a blanket were pushed to the opposite end.

One of the sports channels was on the TV, and an announcer droned on. It was the background noise of my home life now. I hoped, if senseless chatter filled the room, that the music in my head would stay at bay. It rarely did, but there was still hope.

My life ended a year ago. Tomorrow would mark one year since my wife died in a single-car collision. Since then, I've plodded through this existence, pretending life matters, nodding at friends and family when they smile, responding carefully to questions those same friends and family ask.

The songs started after her death. At first, they arrived in the morning, popping into my head as my eyes opened. They didn't happen daily, but close enough to cause me to wonder what it all meant. It got so I kept a list of the songs, trying to find a message in them.

For a while, I convinced myself that my subconscious protected me from the hurt of my wife's death. Then I decided she might be sending me messages from the great beyond in the only way she could.

When the songs stopped for a while, it tore me up. I thought something terrible happened to her. She was already dead, and I imagined her dying a second time—or worse.

My brain ran wild with all sorts of childish beliefs. I even wondered if we might have a supernatural relationship like the movie *Ghost*. I read books on spirits and communicating with the afterlife.

Once a song occurred during the day while I was awake—it was a sweet pop song she liked. If my subconscious had initially tried to protect me, what was it doing now? Then it happened a second time. Initially, the songs were peaceful memories of her, wrapping my consciousness like a warm blanket on a fall evening. If that's what they always did, I would be fine. More than that, I would be grateful. I'd happily welcome them like a heroin addict embraces the promise of a high from the prick of a syringe.

But the songs are no longer pleasant—they've turned against me.

The first time it happened was at the scene of an infant's death. Anytime a child dies, homicide detectives must respond.

While on the scene, Anthrax's "Bring the Noise" suddenly boomed between my ears. My knees buckled, and I had to grab the crib to stop from falling to the floor.

It's a ripping song the speed metal band made with the rap group Public Enemy. I had no idea why my subconscious decided to attack me with it. As the music blared inside the walls of my skull, I struggled to understand what was happening.

The officers at the scene had no idea what I experienced. While panic rose in my chest, I gripped the rail of the crib and felt as if I were about to suffer a breakdown. To an outsider, it probably appeared as if I were studying the dead child. To me, it felt as if my entire world were about to be jackhammered apart.

Eventually, I let go of the crib and staggered from the room. The noise faded then.

Instead of sitting on my couch, there were plenty of things I should have been doing around the house. There were dishes in the sink, but they could wait. It hadn't even been a week yet. When I ate, it was usually takeout, and that could be thrown away. No clean-up required.

Dirty clothes were piled in the corner of the living room. They'd need to be washed soon, but it didn't have to be tonight.

Long ago, I migrated from my bedroom down to the couch. That's where I'd slept since February. The trigger for that move wasn't hard to pinpoint. I packed up her clothes one night and planned to carry the cardboard boxes to the basement the next morning. That never happened. The boxes remained where they were. If that night wasn't the last time I slept in the bedroom, it was close.

Those clothes were the last of her. They were stuffed haphazardly into boxes so I could move on with my life. Seeing the tower of cardboard bothered me, so the solution was simple.

I avoided the room.

As the sportscaster droned on, I grabbed my pillow and stuck it underneath my head.

No music played in our home since her death. Over our marriage, we built a substantial collection of CDs—more than a thousand. Now, the thought of even one song playing through the stereo system filled me with dread.

Music was *our* thing, but the silence was mine. Except I couldn't enjoy the silence because it was frequently pierced by songs for one.

My eyelids grew heavy as sleep approached. I checked my watch—almost eight-thirty.

About usual, I thought.

7

I brought her flowers. It wasn't something I usually did. The only other time I did so was on our wedding anniversary. Now, standing at her grave with a bouquet of mixed flowers, I felt stupid.

"I shouldn't have brought these. I'm not celebrating you being gone."

Kneeling near her marble headstone, the wetness of the grass passed through my jeans.

I brushed away some dirt and leaves to clear the inscription of her name—*Roberta "Bobbie" Ann Nash*. Carefully, I placed the flowers on the corner of the marble.

"Is it weird?" I asked. "Still coming here to talk?"

There was no one else in the cemetery.

"I guess I could have these conversations in my head, but there's so much going on in there that I like this better. Seems more normal to talk out loud."

I used to share the songs I heard with her, but I no longer do. Telling her what I'm experiencing now would be admitting I'm cracking up, and she doesn't need to know that.

Why should I make her worry?

"Nothing exciting happened this week. Had a jumper yesterday. Not sure what to make of it. We'll know more on Monday."

I nodded at nothing in particular.

"Dean and Arlene wanted me to come over tonight. They're the only ones who remembered what today was. No one at work did. I'm not sure why I would expect anyone else to remember the importance of it. I've never marked the calendar when anyone else has died, so why would I expect other people to? Did you ever do that? I don't think you did, or you would have told me. Anyway, I told Dean I appreciated the offer, but I wanted to be left alone."

My brother kept tabs on me for most of the year. If I were in his position, I'd do the same. But lately, I haven't wanted to hang out with him any more than anyone else.

I swooned after standing, lightheaded from the rush of blood. I held my arms out until the world stabilized.

"That was fun," I said with a self-conscious chuckle. "Glad no one saw that. Maybe my blood sugar's low. I've lost some weight. Do you know that? Can you tell? Some folks in the department are talking about it. I checked this morning, and I'm down twenty-two pounds. I think. I don't remember the last time I weighed myself, so maybe it's more—maybe it's less. Whatever the number, it doesn't matter. It's no business of anybody else."

A car raced by with its music blaring. I waited until the noise faded, and it was quiet again.

"Funny how people stick their noses in where they don't belong. Like when they ask me how I'm doing because they see I'm skinnier. I tell them I'm fine even though it's your death anniversary and all."

As my mood soured further, I shoved my hands into my jeans.

"Death anniversary. That's morbid, huh?"

She didn't answer. It's been a full year now, and she's never once responded. I guess I should be thankful. If she did answer, I would know for sure I'm crazy. The fact that she hadn't was something I could hold on to.

"I should probably get going even though I don't have much happening. Going to hang out at the house, read a book, take a nap, that sort of thing. Maybe I should eat something."

8

The phone rang, and I bolted upright into a sitting position. The sports channel was on, and an announcer I'd never seen before excitedly broke down a college football game from earlier in the day.

The television's volume was annoyingly loud. I'd fallen asleep to it while a song played earlier in my head. It didn't seem so obnoxious then.

Answering the call, I said, "Nash."

"Dallas—"

Searching for the remote, I patted the blanket over my lap. "Huh?"

"This is Annie in dispatch."

"Hold on."

With growing irritation, I stood from the couch and yanked the blanket away. The television remote flew across the room, clattering onto the hardwood floor.

"Damn."

After collecting it, I pressed *Power*, but the television remained on. Stepping closer to the TV and continuing to mash the button didn't get a better result. Then I tried the volume down button but got the same response—nothing. I pressed it several times, but the sportscaster continued to blather on about the mid-season coach's poll.

I grunted angrily and threw the remote. It bounced across the hardwood floor again. My fingers traveled along the edge of the television, searching for the Power button. Not finding it, I finally reached behind the stand and yanked the power chord.

Silence descended over the house.

I lifted the phone to my ear and said, "Annie?"

"Everything okay?"

"It's fine. What's up?"

"You are. You're next on the rotation."

I clicked my tongue against the roof of my mouth. Glenn caught the lead on the jumper yesterday. Based upon the rotation, that meant there had been three more callouts since yesterday afternoon. "What are we dealing with?" I asked.

"Homicide. Riverside and Helena."

"Suspects?"

"None on the scene."

"I'm on the way," I mumbled. "Gotta get dressed."

I ended the call and checked the time. It was shortly after one.

9

The body lay face down alongside the road—half on the curb, half in the street.

In an area of town known simply as East Sprague, the city aggressively pushed this section as the International District. Everyone else called it Hookerville or Dope Central.

Even though redevelopment occurred along Sprague Avenue, it was the rundown industrial area to the north and the dilapidated residential areas to the south where the illegal commerce continued.

Patrol officers had already cordoned off a block in every direction and were redirecting traffic.

Glenn stood at the closest line of yellow tape, talking with an officer I'd never met. His blue name tag read *Hoffman*, the color of which denoted his rookie status.

"I need to get your name, sir."

"Dallas Nash."

Glenn said, "My partner."

Hoffman nodded.

"Age before beauty." Glenn lifted the yellow caution tape and waved me under.

"How was the body found?"

"A passing taxi driver called it in."

"No one saw it happen?" I turned around and scanned the area.

Several faces watched from the various side streets and hiding spots. This area of town never slept. Someone was always moving.

"Hard to believe," Glenn said.

"Who was the responding officer?"

"That was Hoffman." Glenn motioned toward the rookie. "He confirmed the body, requested fire and a supervisor. Fire arrived and pronounced DOA."

"When was that?"

"Twelve fifty-two."

"And no witnesses. Imagine that."

"It's the life," Glenn said. "Even if there were witnesses, there wouldn't be any witnesses."

We stepped under another line of tape, which marked the inner perimeter. Only investigators were allowed inside this area.

I tugged a pair of latex gloves from the back of my jeans. "Anyone identify him yet?"

"Couple of the guys think he's a local pimp named Everson Wiley."

Mötley Crüe's "Wild Side" ripped into my brain. It was loud and piercing.

Glenn said something I didn't catch. "What?"

"Junior."

"He's a junior?"

"The pimp's moniker."

"Not his real name?"

My partner shrugged and rolled his eyes for added measure.

The Crüe chanted their chorus as I pressed a knuckle against my temple.

"We've got a dead prostitute. Now we have a dead pimp. Think they're connected?"

I frowned.

"Carlotta Winkler," he said.

"We're not sure she was a prostitute."

"We will be when we get her criminal history back from the Polizei."

"*If* she had a history."

From across the street, Geri Utley stepped under the inner perimeter line and approached. A camera hung around her neck, and she carried an evidence kit. She wore a black beanie and a blue winter coat. She'd been part of the forensic unit for years and handled most of the photography duties.

The man on the ground wore a long, black puffy coat, blue jeans, and tan boots. I bent down, started to lift the tail of the coat but stopped. "No exit wounds."

"How do you know he was shot?" Glenn asked. I could barely hear him over the music in my head.

"Playing the odds."

I lifted the back of the coat and checked his pockets. There was a gun tucked into the waistband.

"Never drew it," I said over the music in my head. "Probably didn't fear his killer."

"Why are you talking so loud?" Glenn asked.

Geri bent over and photographed the gun in Wiley's waistband. Then she handed me a paper bag for the weapon. It was a Colt 1911, a .45 caliber automatic. The safety wasn't on, so I pushed it into place before ejecting the full magazine. I carefully removed the round in the chamber, catching it before it could fall to the ground.

After placing all the pieces of the gun into the paper bag, I handed it to Glenn. Then I checked the victim's back pockets. There was no wallet or identification.

"Think he could have been robbed?" Glenn asked.

"They take his wallet, but leave the gun?"

Glenn shrugged. "Unless he handed it to them, which seems as unlikely."

"Ready to roll?" I asked, and both Glenn and Geri nodded.

Carefully, we turned the body over.

He was a black male, late thirties, perhaps early forties. He'd been shot three times in the chest. Blood rings had spread out on his white shirt. The lack of exit wounds in the back surprised me. I opened the coat wider. "Exit wound under his left arm. I don't see any others."

"Round goes in and turns that quick?" Glenn said. "Couldn't have been a large caliber."

I stood and moved out of the way to allow Geri to photograph the body. As I did, a wooziness washed over me. I rocked back and forth several times. Glenn's eyes narrowed. I winked at him.

When Geri stepped back, I knelt again, ignoring my concerns about feeling dizzy.

Inside the right pocket of the victim's jeans was a roll of cash wrapped with a rubber band. I handed it to Glenn, who dropped it into another bag that Geri provided. We would count the money back at the car. From the left pocket, I pulled a flip phone.

None of us commented on how old the phone seemed to be. We knew its use. It wasn't for playing games or sending pictures to loved ones. I tossed it into the same bag as the cash.

Next, I moved to his coat. The right pocket had a set of keys. The left held a vape pen.

I stood as "Wild Side" continued to reach a crescendo, and the wooziness overwhelmed me. Briefly, the entire world tilted, and I struggled to remain calm. Afraid they could sense my fear, my eyes darted to both Glenn and Geri.

However, they continued talking with each other. Geri said something I couldn't hear, to which Glenn nodded. When he turned toward me, he raised his eyebrows. Then he flashed a quizzical look. I responded with another wink, which was stupid because I never winked. My partner jerked his head toward where we both parked.

The lightheadedness passed, and I waved goodbye to Geri. The music faded when we left the crime scene.

As we ducked under the outer perimeter, I stopped near the rookie Hoffman, and pulled out my notebook. I wrote down Everson Wiley's name and a general description of the man. Then I tore off the page and handed it to him. "Know what an AVR is?"

The young officer's brow furrowed for a second. He almost smiled when he answered, "An All Vehicles Registered report?"

"Call dispatch and ask them to run a report on that guy. We found keys in his pocket, but there's no rig around here. If they find one registered to him, ask them to broadcast an ATL."

"Attempt to Locate," Hoffman blurted.

"Now, you're showing off." I patted the rookie's arm.

He grabbed his microphone to call dispatch as we moved on.

At my car, Glenn pulled the roll of cash from the paper bag. He laid the bills on the trunk and began counting. When he was done, he remained silent and slid the bills to me.

I counted them. After I finished, I said, "Fifty-two hundred."

"That's what I got."

"And his killer didn't take it?"

"Maybe they didn't know he had it."

"Maybe killing him was more important."

"Than fifty-two hundred?" Glenn said. "I doubt it in this part of town."

"In any part of town."

Glenn secured the money with a rubber band and tossed it into a paper bag.

I looked back toward the crime scene. "What did Geri say as we were wrapping up?"

"Serious?" He studied me. "You need to clean the wax out of your ears, man."

"I missed it. Sue me."

"She said she'd get us his fingerprints asap."

My partner clucked his tongue, then wandered over to his car to secure the money.

<h1 style="text-align:center">10</h1>

In the morning, the house was quiet—so was my head.

After brewing a pot of coffee, I poured myself a cup. Then I opened the refrigerator and saw two containers of creamer—one for her and one for me. Mine was simple milk and sugar. Hers was peppermint flavored.

She was the one who got me drinking cream with my coffee. Now, I wouldn't think of drinking it without. Since her death, I couldn't bear the idea of seeing the refrigerator without her bottle of creamer sitting in the door. Every two weeks for the past year, I'd buy a new flavor for her, open it, and put it in the door.

I spent a couple of hours puttering around—washing dishes, scrubbing the bathrooms, and doing laundry. When the dryer buzzed, I unloaded my clothes into a basket and set it in the corner of the living room—folding them could wait.

For a few minutes, I fiddled with the TV remote, hoping to fix it. I don't know what I expected. Screwing around with the little device only annoyed me. I grew frustrated to the point of trying to snap the stupid thing in two. Not getting any satisfaction from that, I threw it at the wall.

When it shattered, Ozzy Osbourne's "Crazy Train" blossomed inside my head. Guitars screeched as pieces of the remote fluttered about the living room. A chorus of pain slipped into my brain.

"Shit!" I yelled and kicked the couch, which hurt my foot.

I hollered again and grabbed the nearest thing to throw. My pillow and blanket floated across the room in harmless arcs. The fact that they wouldn't cause further damage angered me.

Ozzy's voice looped inside my head.

My fists balled as rage vibrated through my body. I shouted a string of nonsensical profanities. When I finished, my shoulders slumped, and the music receded. I shuffled about the house and picked up the pieces of the broken remote.

By noon, the house smelled fresh and looked reasonably presentable. There was nothing further to do. I never stepped into our bedroom, though. There was no need.

When Bobbie was alive, there always seemed to be something we needed to do. Usually, it was a chore she created or a house project she wanted to start. Even when there was a break in those types of activities, we did things together. We'd go to the grocery store, the library, or the mall. I hated the mall, but I would give anything now to spend an afternoon walking in circles with her.

The headache from my tantrum settled behind my right eye. I didn't need the music to make me uncomfortable now. I sat at the kitchen table to check emails on my phone. Several had come in throughout the day, but most were informational garbage. A training institute offered a new class on blood spatter. The second email announced the promotional exam dates for the next year. In another, the community policing team wanted volunteers to help with an awareness campaign. I deleted those.

It was the fourth and fifth emails that interested me.

First, both Glenn and I received an email from Ident. The fingerprints had confirmed the dead man as Everson Otis Wiley II, age thirty-seven, with a known moniker of

Junior. They also sent his record from the National Crime Information Center (NCIC). The FBI oversaw this network, and all local agencies connected to it.

His picture was included as part of the record, and I studied it. He had a broad face and deep brown eyes. The booking photo looked as if he were playing poker, not revealing anything.

Wiley's record went back twenty years and was extensive. His earlier crimes were mostly misdemeanor thefts, misdemeanor assaults, and malicious mischief. Then he graduated to more significant crimes—felonious assault and drug possession—for which he was arrested and convicted.

Everson Otis Wiley II was a career criminal. It wouldn't be the first time I investigated the murder of one, and it likely wouldn't be the last.

I moved onto an email from the coroner's office, which stated Wiley's clothes were ready for pick up. As part of processing the body, they would have stripped him and bagged the garments.

Last night, after clearing the crime scene, Glenn and I had logged his gun, money, and car keys onto property. The clothes were the only outstanding items remaining to be placed into evidence.

Since I had nothing else planned for my day, I didn't care if the department paid me overtime or not.

I only wanted a reason to leave my house.

***

Picking up Everson Wiley's clothes from the coroner's office was a simple process. I checked in with the weekend attendant, showed my badge, and provided him the report number. He logged my info into a computer, then disappeared behind a pair of swinging doors to collect Wiley's clothes.

When he returned, the attendant handed me four brown paper bags. Wiley's boots were in one by themselves, as was his coat. The pants and socks had their own. The bloody shirt was by itself.

Before leaving, I recorded the attendant's name and date of birth for my report. This was important for documenting the chain of evidence.

It took me less than ten minutes to drive across town to the property room. There were advantages to working on a Sunday afternoon. On the sidewalk outside the building, my cell phone rang. I answered it after the second buzz. "Nash."

"Detective, this is Juan from dispatch."

"Yeah?"

"Patrol found the Ford registered to Everson Wiley. They located it at Napa and Second."

It surprised me that he registered the vehicle in his name. Many criminals would buy a car but fail to document it with the state properly, thereby keeping their name out of the system. It made it harder for the criminal to recover the vehicle if it was ever towed. Perhaps that's why Wiley registered the Ford. Maybe he liked the car and didn't want to lose it. Or he spent a fair amount of money on it. Either way, he attached his name to it, which meant patrol was able to locate it.

"Thanks for the heads up."

"Some of the guys are like bloodhounds."

"Have it towed for evidence. I'll process it tomorrow."

We ended the call, and I entered the security code for access to the building.

Every piece of evidence is required to be logged and associated with a report number. The city provided a computer to record the entire process. However, I prefer the old-school way and handwrote the entries. A day will come when this is no longer accepted, but it will be after my generation has moved on. Until then, seniority will still have some privileges.

I removed Wiley's boots and examined them. They were tan and made by Timberland. The heels hadn't seen much wear, and there was no visible debris caught within the tread. Also, the toes of the boots were scuff free. They must have been newer, or the guy was a conscientious walker. I placed them back in their paper bag and logged them on the evidence sheet.

There didn't appear to be any blood on the pants. The coat, however, had blood along the zipper, but most of it had dried. There was a small bullet hole in the left side of the coat under the arm. We hadn't noticed it while on the scene. It was still likely he was shot in the chest, but one of the rounds exited through his side. He then fell face down into the street and bled out. I carefully touched the inside of the jacket with my gloved fingers, searching for wet blood. I didn't find any.

I bagged the jeans and the jacket.

The final piece of evidence was the white shirt. It was long-sleeved with the words *King James* down the left arm and a crown in the middle of the chest. I wasn't much of a sports fan, but even I knew who LeBron James was.

Someone had cut along the side away from the exit wound, allowing them to remove it without pulling it over Wiley's head. Three small bullet holes were tightly grouped in the center of the crown. I held it up to see the light come through. The entry wounds were small. I knew better than to surmise what type of bullet had killed him from a hole in a shirt, but since only one round had exited from such an extreme angle, it would likely be a smaller caliber like a .22, perhaps a .25.

The shirt had been soaked with blood and was still moist. I couldn't bag it and put it into evidence where it could mold. Per policy, I needed to dry it out.

I noted the location of the shirt on the form and signed it. I set the bags containing the boots, jeans, and jacket on the processing counter and placed my paper on top.

Then I went inside the drying room.

***

It's the smell that is most disturbing—the sickly aroma that is somehow human, but disturbingly less than the living. The room is used for drying garments and other items contaminated with human material, such as blood, brain matter, and semen.

After the odor, the room's humidity is a close second. There is a drastic uptick in air moisture caused by the drying process of those same materials. The heaviness in the air is a reminder of the pain and death every item contains.

I've been in this room more than a hundred times, and the experience still affects me. No one in the department ever wants to be in the drying room.

Opening the glass double-doors to the drying racks unleashed the full stench of the room. My stomach turned, and AC/DC's "If You Want Blood" blasted inside my head. The world tilted, and I held onto the door handles to steady myself.

Blinking several times, I struggled vainly to fight back the dizziness. I inhaled deeply and wanted to barf as a result.

The chorus careened around my brain.

Bending over with my hands on my knees, I forced my head up and opened my eyes wide. My vision blurred as I struggled to focus on the nearest drying rack. A T-shirt with blood and brain matter was spread over a paper bag. Whoever filled out the evidence card had such poor penmanship I couldn't make out the victim's name.

"If You Want Blood" pounded louder inside my skull. To alleviate the pain, I pressed a knuckle into my eye.

On a small paper bag sat a pair of woman's cotton panties stained red. An evidence card with the name Tanisha Kreshel and a case number was next to them. Bile rose in my throat.

The chorus swung wildly about my head, and the world went with it.

A woman's bloody yellow blouse was carefully arranged on a brown bag. My vision narrowed as I tried to read the victim's name card. Darkness pushed in.

If you want—

***

My eyes opened, and I saw the fluorescent lighting. I'd fainted.

It wasn't the first time I'd passed out, but it was the first time it had occurred at work. The other couple of times happened at home. Rolling over, I pushed myself to my knees. I slowly looked around to ensure I hadn't disturbed anything. My gaze flicked toward the corner of the ceiling, where a camera monitored everything in the room.

I was woozy, but I stood. There was no way to know how long I'd been out. My hands shook, and my tongue felt thick. I struggled to generate enough spit to swallow.

The video log was only for the chain of custody confirmation. No one would review it unless there was a claim of wrongdoing. I certainly wasn't going to report this incident. I had to hope no one ever saw what had occurred.

When my shaking subsided, I set a paper bag on one of the racks then carefully spread out Wiley's bloody shirt. On the small white card next to the shirt, I noted the time I placed it on the shelves. An evidentiary technician would later collect the dry shirt and finish the bagging process.

I closed the doors to the racks, secured the room, and returned to the lobby.

Officer Leya Navarro sat at a long table, filling out a property form. A brown paper bag sat near her elbow. She started when I entered the room.

"Hey," I muttered.

"Were you in the drying room?"

I nodded.

Her eyes surveyed me. "Everything okay?"

"Nothing is okay when you're in there. You just get here?"

"Yeah. How long were you in there?"

"Couple minutes."

She leaned forward. "You're bleeding."

My fingers ran over my forehead, and I felt wet. I pulled them away and saw blood.

"If You Want Blood" started again, but it wasn't overwhelming.

Leya studied my forehead with a suspicious look. I needed to say something—*anything*.

"I hit my head."

"Oh."

"On the table."

"Ouch."

"When I dropped my pen."

"Must have been some whack."

"It was."

My whole speech pattern sounded stupid and mechanical. She slowly returned her attention to her paperwork, but not without a final sideways glance in my direction.

I left without saying goodbye. Once outside, I touched my head again and looked at the red on my fingers.

My consciousness made sure that "If You Want Blood" was loud and clear once again.

I vomited into the landscaping.

MONDAY
NOVEMBER 5th

11

The first thing I did Monday morning was research Everson Otis Wiley II.

On the night of his murder, we hadn't found a decent address for him. The last one on record was a house on Second Avenue the state recently demolished to make way for the new freeway interchange.

We also hadn't found any witnesses. No one stepped out of the shadows to indicate they saw anything.

After we processed the scene, we broke it down and went home. So now, the slow process of discovering the real Everson Wiley would begin.

The man had plenty of arrests dating back to a misspent youth. There was a string of arrests for assaults with some accompanying convictions. Too many appeared to have either been dismissed or withered on the vine. He was once a person of interest in a homicide, but it seemed to go no further than that.

There weren't any Field Interview (FI) reports on him. A man with this level of criminal activity should have had at least a couple of them.

I jotted down the two previous addresses in his history before the demolished house. Maybe someone who lived there would know who he was and where he last lived. Stranger things have happened.

Then I looked for known associates but struck out. I thought there would have been at least a prostitute or two tied to his name.

I considered his namesake and typed in Everson Otis Wiley but left the birth date field blank. Two names populated the screen. I selected the older man and called up his file.

According to his entries, his father had been a career criminal. Drug possession. Robbery. Assaults. An arrest for murder but no conviction. He was a victim of a homicide the year after Junior was born.

The apple hadn't fallen far from the tree.

Glenn wasn't at his desk, so I didn't have anyone to bounce my thoughts off. I pushed away from my desk and headed to Crime Analysis.

***

"Want a donut, Dallas?"

Debbie Wallette held up a box of powdered jellies. Her eyes were as bright as her smile.

"No, thank you."

"You should eat one. Hell, eat two. You look like you could use the calories."

I lifted a hand for her to stop.

"I'm serious. You look like—"

"I appreciate it."

"These are jellies. How can you—"

"*No.*"

She slowly lowered the box, then tossed it on her desk. The brightness in her eyes faded, along with her smile. "What can I help you with?"

"A list of known prostitutes in the East Sprague area."

"How far back?" By her clipped tone, it was apparent I had offended her.

"Let's concentrate on active girls only."

"What's it for?"

"Saturday's homicide was a pimp, but no one came forward either as a witness or as one of his stable."

"His stable?" Debbie's lip curled. "Can you blame them?" She turned to her computer. "I'll email the results."

Debbie was the rarity in Crime Analysis. Most of them were analytic types, more comfortable with their computers and algorithms. But Debbie liked conversing with the officers and detectives. She was a joy to have in the department.

Now, I'd made her mad.

I should have taken the damn donut.

***

Glenn was at his desk when I returned to the detective's bullpen.

"Where you been?"

"Crime Analysis." I settled into my chair. "Working the homicide from the weekend. Pulling prostitutes who might have been associates."

"Got any ideas on who might have done it?"

I shook my head. "At this point, none. Could be anyone, including a random shooting."

"Don't discount it, right?"

"Never."

"Get any downtime yesterday?"

"Some. You?"

My partner leaned back with a mischievous smile. "I went out with this nice girl who—"

"Detective Nash," a male voice interrupted.

I turned to see Lieutenant George Brand, the head of the Major Crimes division. He pushed his round glasses up his nose.

Glenn faced his computer and made an exaggerated show of hunting for letters on his keyboard.

"Sir?"

"My office. *Now*."

He left without another word or acknowledgment of my partner.

Glenn and I both watched him walk away.

"What do you think that's about?" Glenn asked.

"No idea."

***

Lieutenant Brand's office was a model of efficiency. No personal items detracted from his focus. The walls weren't bare, though. Notes made in his distinctive scrawl covered a large dry-erase board. Scribbles filled an annual calendar that hung nearby his desk.

The big man dropped heavily into his chair and removed his glasses. While he spoke, he rubbed the lenses with a cleaning cloth. "We need to get you scheduled with Stephen."

"Excuse me?"

Brand stopped rubbing. "Stephen Yoder, the department's psychiatrist."

I blinked several times.

"At the scene of the jumper. I thought you agreed to see him."

Shit. That's what Captain Ackerman had said and to which I silently agreed.

Brand folded the cleaning cloth before setting it on his desk. Then he carefully put his glasses on. "You look terrible, Detective."

"That's no reason to send me to the shrink."

The lieutenant cocked his head. "That's a perfect reason. Sudden weight loss. Your hair hasn't been cut in months. Your suit is wrinkled. You didn't shave today. This is not the behavior our senior investigator has displayed throughout his career. This is not who you are."

"I'll get a haircut and take my suits to the cleaners."

He was unimpressed with my offer.

"And I'll start eating dessert."

Brand slid a notepad toward himself and lifted a pen. "You know how this works." He wrote while he talked, not making eye contact. "The captain directed me to get you scheduled with Stephen. It's a direct order now. He's worried, which means I'm worried. In other words, the chain of command has taken notice."

"What if I refuse?"

The lieutenant lifted his gaze, and his pen stopped moving. "I'll put you on an involuntary leave of absence until we decide what to do."

"I'll file a grievance."

He carefully laid his pen down. "You, Nash? A union malcontent? Yet another thing to be suspicious of."

Dealing with the union was slightly more appealing than sitting in a small room with the department's psychiatrist, but not by much.

"What if I see the chaplain again?"

The lieutenant shook his head. "We went down that road once before. It didn't work."

"I thought it did."

Brand frowned.

"Shit," I muttered.

"Cursing now?"

"I apologize."

"It doesn't offend me, Nash, but these little things add up. Can't you see? If you do not address them, we need to step in and do it—for the good of the department and, quite frankly, for you."

"Right." I didn't bother to hide my sarcasm.

"This needs to be scheduled by the end of the day."

I stood.

"I can count on you to get it done?"

"Yes."

"If you don't—"

"I *get* it."

12

When I returned to my desk, an email simply titled PROSTITUTES waited in my in-box. It had only taken Debbie a few minutes to run it. Had I not upset her, she could have done it while I waited. There was no reason to have snapped at her, and the confrontation was my fault.

Way to go, Dallas, I thought. Keep kicking your friends until you don't have any.

I only glanced at the email's attached report before printing it. Then I pushed back from my desk and shuffled to the printer, continuing my mental lashing.

Detective Andrew Parker pulled off some papers as my print job started. He eyed me with contempt.

"Looking good, big hitter." His smile was malevolent. "Your iron must have broken today."

When he turned to walk away, I muttered, "Eat some more 'roids, Andy."

As soon as I said it, I regretted it.

Parker spun. "What was that?"

"Nothing," I muttered.

He stepped toward me. Parker was several inches shorter than me but weightlifter thick. His suits always looked as if they were a size too big, and his tie was perennially loosened around his neck. He hated it when anyone shortened his name. Maybe it was a size thing, and he considered it a cheap shot.

"Say it again."

I ground my teeth, knowing better than to open my mouth.

"Unless you're scared."

I leaned down to put my nose near his, but I remained silent.

"Don't be a pussy, old man."

I whispered so no one else in the office would hear. "Eat some more steroids, Andy."

He shoved me, and I stumbled backward. He moved forward and closed the distance.

"Say it again," he taunted.

Mötley Crüe's "Knock 'em Dead, Kid" burst into my head, and I balled my fists. My face flushed, and I wanted to punch him in the face. Instead, I said as calmly as I could, "I hear they make your penis smaller."

He shoved me harder this time, and I bounced into the wall of a cubicle.

"Hey!" Detective Quinn Delaney hollered. His head popped up over his cubicle wall. His anger was apparent.

The Crüe blared between my ears, and adrenaline coursed through my veins.

Marci Burkett stepped around the edge of her workstation, her eyes alert, ready for a donnybrook.

Parker's partner, Jessie Johnson, stepped into the clearing. "The hell is going on?" he yelled.

"This brittle bastard," Parker said, sticking his finger in my face, "wants to square off."

Johnson's eyebrows raised. "I wouldn't advise that, Nash."

"Stay out of it."

"You're getting old," Johnson said. "It won't go as well as you hope."

I glared at him.

He lifted his arms in mock surrender. "Do what you want. It's your funeral." He turned on his heel and went back to his cubicle.

I glanced at Marci. She averted her eyes before disappearing behind her workstation.

The music faded then, but the rushing adrenaline remained in my ears.

Quinn said, "You idiots, knock it off, or take it upstairs to the mat. Some of us are trying to work." He dropped out of sight behind his cubicle wall.

Parker lowered his voice. "Let's go, princess. Me and you."

My face burned, and I was lightheaded. Fainting here would end my career in more ways than one.

He said, "I've been waiting a long time to knock you on your dick."

I tried to move toward the printer, but Parker put his hand on my chest.

"Where are you going, big time? The mat is the other way."

"I don't have time for this." My voice sounded shaky.

"Running scared. Nice."

"I've got a murder to solve."

Parker dropped his hand. "Don't we all, princess? Don't we all?"

He walked away, chuckling to himself.

13

Glenn and I divided the workload for the day. Since he was the lead on the Carlotta Winkler case, he would handle her background. I would chase Everson Wiley's—specifically where he lived and with which prostitutes he affiliated.

Besides, I wanted an excuse to leave the department. The run-in with Parker had set me on edge, and I still felt dizzy.

My first stop was the area where Wiley was murdered. That section of the East Sprague corridor ran several miles long. Even though it experienced recent gentrification, the drug and prostitution trade proved reluctant to abandon that neighborhood. Prostitutes often walked through the area by themselves. Occasionally, a male trailed behind, keeping a watchful eye.

A woman strolled near the corner of Sprague Avenue and Lacey Street, looking over her shoulder, attempting to make eye contact with passing drivers. No one walked behind her.

After stopping her and getting her name, I asked, "You working?"

Shawna Brown wore a white coat with a faux fur fringe. Her flower printed leggings were threadbare and her running shoes dirty. She was slightly built, but her pale stomach peeked out from underneath a T-shirt that read *Property of Lewis & Clark High School Wrestling Team.*

She raised an eyebrow.

"I'm not looking to bust you."

"Nothing to bust me for. I was walking, and you stopped me. Now, we're talking."

"Did you hear about the murder on Saturday night?"

She glanced around and pretended to yawn.

"Was Junior your pimp?"

"You saying I'm a prostitute?"

From my back pocket, I pulled out the list that Debbie from Crime Analysis emailed. I unfolded it and pointed to her name and photograph. "That's you, right there. On a list of *known* prostitutes."

"Whatever."

"So, Junior?"

She turned her hand over and looked at her fingernails. They were chipped and in need of some new polish. "He wasn't mine, no."

"How many pimps are in the game?"

"The game? Listen to you. Acting like you're hard. How would I know how many there are?"

I pointed at the ground. "Let's start with down here. How many work East Sprague?"

Her face flattened. "Two."

"Junior and who?"

She remained quiet.

"I'm going to find out. You can either be my friend or—"

The contempt drained from her eyes. "What does that mean? Be your friend?"

"It means I'll owe you one."

Disappointment registered on her face.

"What did you think it would mean?"

"I thought it would be like what Joey's got."

"Joey?"

"That's right," Shawna said.

"And what does she have?"

"She's got herself a badge daddy."

"A badge daddy?"

"She used to belong to Junior, but her man made sure she could renegade."

I flipped through the names and photographs of known prostitutes. There was only one close to Joey. I stared at the small picture. The woman seemed familiar, but this photograph didn't seem right. "Josephine Greene. That her?"

Shawna shrugged. "The fuck should I know? She's just Joey down here."

I showed her the photograph.

"Yep. That's her."

"Your pimp," I said. "I haven't forgotten. What's his name?"

She looked around, checking for anyone she might know. "You'll owe me?"

"I'll owe you," I said, making a hollow promise.

"Damon."

"That's all?"

Her mouth twisted before saying, "Warfield. Damon Warfield."

I wrote his name next to Shawna's.

"Where can I find him?"

She pressed her lips tightly together.

"Look, lady, I'm trying to solve a murder, not bust a man for promoting prostitution."

Amusement tugged at her expression. "Promoting prostitution sounds so corporate."

I watched her until she grew uncomfortable and whispered, "He holds court in the back booth at Ironsides."

"Was there bad blood between Damon and Junior?"

Shawna laughed. "Down here, bad blood is everywhere. All you got to do is pay attention."

"You think he'd be up for killing Junior? Get his competition out of the way, grow his territory."

Her eyes narrowed before cocking her head. "Not really, no. That's not Damon's style."

"What is his style?"

"Words before action. The man doesn't have to get violent very often."

I showed her my list. "Which girls belong to who?"

Her eyes flicked to the list. "I help you with this, and then you'll owe me two." She held up as many fingers.

"I'll owe you two." This promise was as empty as the first.

"Gimme your business card. I wanna know how to collect on this."

14

"I don't know nothin'," she said.

"Right."

"I'm standin' here, mindin' my own business, and you come round bustin' my balls."

"I only asked if you were working."

The woman was in her late twenties and appeared to be on something. She twitched while she talked. Her faded blue jeans were dirty, and her sweatshirt was too snug. When she moved, it revealed she wasn't wearing a bra.

"Does it look like I'm workin'?" She pointed at the bus stop sign above her. "I'm waitin' for a bus. This is harassment is what this is."

"What's your name?"

"I ain't gotta tell you."

"You're on the stroll. Therefore, I can stop and identify you."

She exhaled forcefully. "Whatever, man. Ain't you got nothin' better to do?"

"No," I said. "Right now, this is the most important thing in the world."

The woman shoved her tongue underneath her upper lip. When it dropped free, she said, "Alexa."

I checked the list of prostitutes and asked, "What's your birthday?"

"January thirteenth."

She checked out, but barely. Compared to her picture, Alexa Pollard was rapidly decaying. The drug she was on, likely meth, was eating her alive.

Alexa stood on her tiptoes and tried to read the list in my hands. "What's that?"

"Who's your pimp?" I asked, already knowing the answer.

She dropped back to her heels and, with a cocky tilt of the head, said, "I ain't got one."

"What about last week?"

"Didn't have one then either."

"Really?" I tapped my list. "Because this 'J' next to your name means you belonged to Junior."

Her face reddened as she again tried to see what I held in my hand.

"You know he's dead. Otherwise, you wouldn't talk so brazenly."

"Who told you I was his?"

"Doesn't matter. What does is you know he's dead."

Alexa smirked. "We all know that. It ain't no secret."

"Why not get out of here?"

"What do you mean?"

"You're not under his thumb anymore. You could leave the life."

"Said the man *not* in the life."

"But he's dead."

"I ain't got no other skills. Can't type. Can't read too good." Alexa jerked twice before continuing. "No man wants a broke-ass woman to take home. I might as well keep trickin'. Only I don't think I'm gonna give my earnings to DeeDee now."

"DeeDee?"

"She was his bottom. Although I don't know if that was going to last."

"What do you mean?"

Alexa glanced around. "From what I heard, DeeDee wasn't takin' orders too good lately. Junior had had about enough of her bullshit. Rumor was he was gonna make a change. Let somebody else be number two."

"You in the running?"

"To be bottom?" She twitched. "I wish. I'm a broken-down mule. I ain't no mare, and I ain't no show pony."

"What's DeeDee?"

"She used to be a show pony. Real pretty like, but she grew herself into a mare. Gotta be careful, or she's gonna be like me."

"I take it you like horses."

"Wanted one ever since I was little." She got a distant look in her eye. "Not ever gonna happen, but that doesn't mean I can't think about them." She twitched, and her focus snapped back to now. "And I know show ponies don't turn into mules, Detective. Don't think I'm dumb. I was making a point."

I scanned the list. The only name that made sense as a DeeDee was Deidra Dobb. Not that nicknames always have to make sense.

When I looked up, there was a woman across the street. Tall and slender, she wore a long tan coat that hung open. Underneath, she wore a knee-length black skirt and a maroon blouse.

"That's Marlene," Alexa said.

"Marlene?"

"She's a do-gooder. Comes down here to get the girls off the street."

"Why won't she come over?"

"She must think I'm talking with a customer."

"I look like a customer?"

"You'd be surprised what my customers look like."

"I probably would. Know anyone who would want to hurt Junior?"

She chuckled. "Hells yeah. All sorts of people. Rivals. Pissed-off johns. Girls who are tired of his shit."

"What about you?"

Her face flattened. "What about me?"

"Are you tired of his shit?"

"I already told you I ain't got nothin' else. I ain't looking to make a break."

"Where were you on Saturday night?"

"Out here."

"I didn't see you."

"If I'm doing my job, you won't."

I studied her.

Her sigh was exaggerated, an effect performed by a bad actress. "I was in some cars, all right? Inna couple hotel rooms, too. Even went to some dude's house before the night was over. I didn't get home until after three."

"That's when you found out about Junior?"

"That's right."

"Where did Junior live?"

"No idea. Never went there. He always came to my place when he wanted to visit. Find DeeDee. I bet she knows."

"How do I find her?"

"She's out here." Alexa's finger circled the area.

"Got a phone number?"

"I only had Junior's."

It was probably a lie, but she'd told me enough. I thanked her for her time, and she moved on.

Across the street, the do-gooder had as well.

15

"Any luck?" Glenn asked.

"Some," I said, dropping into my chair. "You?"

"Definitely. For starters, I confirmed the ex-husband is in Korea. Talked with his first sergeant. Been stationed there for the last eight months and hasn't left the country once."

"Did you talk with him?"

"Briefly. He seemed unaffected by her death."

"How so?"

Glenn cocked his head. "Like it happened to a stranger. He said they hadn't talked since their split."

"Is that normal?"

"They don't have kids. What other reason would they have to communicate? Nostalgia?"

"So, cross him off the list?"

"I'm inclined to do so."

"Anything else?"

"I got her history from the Polizei and spoke with her brother."

"You've been busy. How'd you find him?"

"The Polizei. They were helpful."

"Did she have a criminal history?"

"None."

Glenn handed me a printed email that was attached to Carlotta Winkler's criminal record. It was in German, but the layout was the familiar pattern of most law enforcement agencies. Nothing was listed.

"The brother," I said. "He spoke English?"

"Pretty good, yeah. We had a couple stops and starts, but we got through it."

"What'd he say?"

"That she was a nice girl who fell in love and wanted to go to America. Had ever since she was a little girl. He wasn't a fan of the guy she married."

"So, their divorce wasn't a surprise?"

"He was glad they split up, but he wanted her to come home. She wanted to stay. He knew she was struggling here, but she refused to take help from anyone."

"Did he say why?"

"I think it was more of a pride thing than anything else. I understand, as I've never taken any money from my parents, but it must have been hard for Carlotta. She didn't have any college. Also, it sounds like the family back home didn't have much money to begin with."

"Did you ask if she was depressed?"

"I did," Glenn said, "and he didn't think so. Whenever she called, she sounded happy. He said she'd go on about how much she loved it here, that she hoped to get her citizenship approved soon, and that she was involved with her church."

Something nagged me about my partner's story, and I grabbed my notebook.

"He was broken up," Glenn continued. "Said their parents were going to be devastated by the news."

I flipped through my notebook until I came to my entries on Carlotta Winkler. It was on the second page of my jottings.

"You've got the copy of her employee file?"

He nodded.

"Pull it out and check the emergency contact."

Glenn did as I asked. When he had the paper, he said, "It's blank."

"Her boss said she didn't have any family."

"Maybe she meant local."

"But she has a brother, and her parents are alive. Wouldn't you say you didn't have anyone local instead of saying you didn't have a family?"

Glenn's eyes returned to the paper. "Maybe it was an interpretation thing."

Or maybe it had to do with her divorce. Perhaps she didn't fill it out because she felt abandoned after her husband left, and it was a way to remind herself of the feeling. I hadn't changed any of my emergency contact information in the past year. If something ever happened to me, some administrative type in the city's personnel section was going to reach out to Bobbie with their condolences and instructions on how to activate her benefits. How long would it take for them to know she was dead?

"Too bad she didn't have a record, though," Glenn said. "There goes that theory."

"Huh?"

"That she was a prostitute. Man, are you hard of hearing lately or what?"

"I was thinking."

I turned to my computer and pulled the information on Damon Warfield, the rival pimp to Everson Wiley. He had an extensive drug history, assault, theft, and possession of stolen property. He was not currently wanted.

Then I entered Josephine Greene into the system, the so-called renegade prostitute who had a cop watching over her.

Badge daddy flashed through my mind as I thought about her. I'd never heard the term before. Pimps often require their girls to call them daddy as a weird mental trick to control them. So, badge daddy seemed like a natural growth of slang if a cop was involved.

Joey's last known address was on Sharp Avenue.

She had a history of prostitution and drug possession, but it was the latest entry that caught my attention—a rape report. The date of the entry—only a few months ago—tingled the back of my brain. When I called up the report, everything clicked.

Detective James Morgan transported Josephine Greene to Sacred Heart Hospital. He then requested a corporal to photograph her injuries. Digital pictures were attached to the file, and I clicked them even though I'd seen them once before.

A light-skinned black woman with a short afro, Joey's eyes were swollen, and contusions were around her mouth. Bruising ran up and down her body. Glenn and I were not assigned her case—Johnson and Parker were.

The report indicated she had been held captive in a house on Magnolia Street and repeatedly raped by several unidentified men. At the end of the narrative, there was another report number cross-referenced.

I called it up and saw the county's investigation into Morgan's shooting. This report, I knew better.

His team, the Criminal Task Force, had killed three gang members in a house on Magnolia Street, not the one where Greene had been raped. They had initially responded to that house in response to the rape report. Upon arrival, the CTF discovered the suspects had moved across the street, and that's when the shootout began.

I shadowed this investigation. Any time an officer in our department was involved in a shooting, a sister agency investigates it. We still assign a detective to provide a watchful eye to ensure our officer gets a fair shake. That was my job. I made sure Detective Jim Morgan got a thorough and impartial investigation. Morgan's shooting, along with those of his team, was eventually deemed justified. The final ruling came out a few weeks ago.

Josephine 'Joey' Greene had been the catalyst for it all.

And the streets carried a rumor that a cop protected her. Everything took on a whole new level of suspicion if the rumors on the street were true.

Badge daddy.

I stared at three words from the report—Detective Jim Morgan—and wondered if the badge daddy rumor started before or after the shooting on Magnolia Street.

"You look like you saw a ghost," Glenn said.

I faced my partner.

"You okay?"

Should I tell him? I wondered. Should I keep this quiet until I knew what I was dealing with?

I glanced around before standing. With a jerk of my head, I silently asked him to follow, and we went for a walk.

***

"You can't tell anyone about this," Glenn said. "Not now."

"I know."

"Not until you prove it."

"I know that, too."

We were in the lobby of the Public Safety Building. It was noisy due to people milling about, but it was better than standing inside the quiet bullpen where anyone could overhear us. We sat on a bench near the steps down to the municipal court windows.

Glenn combed his fingers through his hair. "What the hell do you think this means?"

"I don't know."

"If the rumor was true *before* the shooting, was the shooting bad?"

"It was clean," I said. "Morgan and his team did it by the book. County investigated it thoroughly. Besides, the house was full of drugs and guns."

"But how CTF got there," Glenn whispered, "was *that* tainted by Morgan's relationship with this woman? Did he set it up somehow?"

"She was beaten and raped. I can't imagine they would do that for a bust."

"If he *was* her badge daddy, shit, what a concept. Could it have been a revenge shooting? For what those guys did to her? The shooting could still be good, but Morgan could have moved the pieces into place where there was no other result *except* a gunfight."

My eyes drifted down to my hands. I had been wringing them. "Maybe."

"Dallas," Glenn said, hitting me with the back of his hand, "this is bad. This is *really* bad."

I rubbed my face. Glenn was right, but what was I supposed to do? Run to the lieutenant or captain with a rumor? They would flip the hot potato to Internal Affairs and let them deal with it. I wouldn't want anyone to do that to me. Morgan was a turd, but the rest of his team wasn't so bad. They could all get dragged down because of an unsubstantiated rumor. I'd survived more than twenty years in the department with a "live and let live" attitude toward my fellow officers. If I was going to say something, and that was a big *if*, I needed to be sure of it.

Glenn studied my face. "You're not sure Morgan is this badge daddy."

"I'm not."

"And you don't want to stir up a hornet's nest if you don't have to."

"Maybe it's a county deputy or some fed."

My partner's head bounced from side to side as he spoke. "It could even be a railroad cop who flashes his badge whenever he waggles his dick."

"Exactly."

"And you believe that?"

I hesitated to answer, knowing there was no turning back if I peeled the layers on this onion.

Glenn's face paled, and he looked sick. "What are we gonna do?"

"You don't have to be involved with this."

"We're partners, Dallas. I'm with you."

I stood, and Glenn followed suit.

"I'll talk with Morgan. If he sees both of us coming, it'll look like we're bracing him. We don't need him to feel like he's cornered."

"The guy isn't normal."

"It's okay. I got this."

***

I left Glenn and headed to the Monroe Court building where the Criminal Task Force office was located.

The CTF was a specialty unit initially designed to add muscle in the fight against the gang and crack cocaine epidemic of the early nineties. When the department gained traction with that problem, they pointed the CTF in new directions, such as meth and illegal guns. If the city needed swift action, especially something that resembled a hammer-like response, CTF was the blunt tool they pulled from the box.

The second-floor office was almost deserted. Only the team's leader, Sergeant Ken Bynum, remained. He wore a long-sleeve Henley shirt that might have been painted on.

Looking up from some paperwork, he said, "Nash?"

"Hey, Ken. Morgan around?"

The sergeant shook his head. "They had a late one last night, so I let them bounce early."

I nodded.

"Want to leave a message?"

"It'll keep." I left without further discussion. I didn't want Morgan looking for me.

I wanted to be the hunter in this jungle.

16

I lay on the couch and stared at the football images playing on the television. The announcer babbled ineffectually on since his words couldn't reach me. Guns N' Roses' "Welcome to the Jungle" spun inside my head. The song woke me a few minutes before.

Earlier, I fell asleep to the sports channel's feature on the 1960s Green Bay Packers. This week, the channel promised short retrospectives on the greatest football dynasties of each decade. I didn't care much about football. In fact, I didn't care for any sport, but sports reporting is the safest thing to watch when you don't want to be touched by the world. There's no talk of politics, current events are mostly ignored, and death happens only to the elderly.

Hoping for a way to return to sleep, I thought about Bobbie and me in happier times, but the song demanded my attention. The chorus swung wildly through my consciousness.

Rolling over, I shoved my face into the couch and held the pillow over my ears. It was a futile action, as it didn't stop the music from pounding, banging, and circling round and round between my ears.

Sleep altogether eluded me now.

I jerked myself upright and angrily flung the pillow. It hit an illustration of some flowers Bobbie once painted, knocking it to the floor. Even in the low light, it was apparent that the frame had broken.

"Shit," I muttered.

I stood and got dressed.

***

"Welcome to the Jungle" continued to career about my head as I drove through downtown.

Streetlights and neon signs lit up the evening. Bars brimmed with life for a Monday night. Local colleges were in session, so drinking was once again a contact sport.

Several young women ran across the road, and I slammed my brakes to avoid hitting them. Not one paid attention to the traffic. They were focused on where they were headed.

Guitars screeched inside my skull, and I winced.

When I was a patrol officer, I worked downtown for the action. It was humanity at its drunken worst. More than a decade had passed since I last worked a graveyard shift. As a detective, I am often called out at night, but it's a different experience than patrolling through the dark.

In front of a bar, two men shoved each other. They yelled and pointed. Several men I assumed were bouncers stood nearby and watched.

"Welcome to the jungle," I muttered along with the chorus inside my head.

For patrol officers, danger lurks wherever they go. That jeopardy is already gone by the time a detective arrives. Before dispatch ever sends one of us out, patrol officers have done the hazardous work and secured the area. Even though pain and death may await, there is never a need for me to feel anxious or afraid—it's not my pain or my death.

Driving through downtown, a surge of adrenaline kicked in, and wooziness followed closely behind. My knuckles whitened as my hands tightened around the steering wheel. Dispatch didn't know I was out tonight; I had not called to check-in.

I was all alone—except for the music.

***

The small house was on Sharp Avenue near Helena Street. It was dark, and there were no cars in front. A couple of blocks away, the Spokane River flowed—the sound of its rushing waters underscored the neighborhood's silence.

Scanning for threats as I approached the home, my heart pounded wildly. I was more nervous than I should have been. The doorbell dinged a falling warble, but there was no corresponding noise inside. I knocked and listened. There was only silence.

It was after midnight, but I hadn't expected Joey Greene to be there—not with her chosen occupation.

I knocked again—louder this time—and a neighbor's porch light turned on.

When I silently counted to sixty, it was time to go.

***

She was young. Too young to be out after midnight and standing on a street corner.

As I walked toward her, she inhaled on a vape pen, eyed me suspiciously, then blew a large plume into the air. On her top, she wore a heavy winter coat and a red pom-pom hat, while on the bottom, she wore volleyball shorts and ankle-high Converse shoes with no socks. It was the seasonal dissonance prostitutes exemplified in late fall and early spring.

"How old are you?"

She opened her coat to reveal a running bra. "How old do you want me to be?"

"At least eighteen." I showed her my badge.

"Then I'm eighteen." Heavily applied make-up covered her face.

"Let's see some ID."

"It's at home."

"*Right*," I said, filling the word with sarcasm. I reached into my coat for the list of prostitutes and started scanning the small pictures. "What's your name?"

"Tabitha," she muttered. "Listen. I'll leave. I wasn't doing anything, anyway."

When she stepped away, I grabbed her arm and pulled her back. "You'll wait."

"Hey!" someone yelled from down the block.

It was the woman from earlier in the day. She still wore the long tan coat, but now it was cinched around the waist. Anger pinched her face as she hurried toward us. Struggling to recall her name, all that came to mind was *do-gooder*. She yelled, "Let go of her!"

"Yeah," the girl said as she tried to pull free. "Let go."

I tugged the girl's arm and repositioned her so I could deal with the approaching woman.

"Let her go!" the do-gooder hollered unnecessarily. We were only a few feet apart now.

"Get your hands off me!" the girl shouted.

"Give it a rest, kid."

The do-gooder pulled a chain from around her neck and slipped a whistle between her lips. A shrill blast pierced the night, and several people walking the streets stopped to look our way. The woman stuck her finger in my face, clenched the whistle between her teeth as she spoke, and demanded, "Let go!"

The girl struggled to get away, and I tugged her back.

"Lady," I said, "I'm—"

The whistle blasted again.

Amid the commotion, I finally remembered her name. "Marlene."

She froze. Her pointing finger was an inch from my nose, and the whistle remained clamped between her teeth.

I pulled aside my coat to reveal my badge. "Detective Nash, Spokane Police."

"Oh," she said, and the whistle fell from her mouth. Her finger rolled back into her fist, and she slowly lowered her arm. She started to offer her hand, then pulled it back. Then she thrust it out and announced, "Marlene. Marlene Anderson."

We shook hands.

"Are you with an outreach program?"

She nodded. "Her Freedom."

I'd never heard of it, but that didn't mean anything. So many nonprofits tried to save the world that it was hard to keep track of them all. "One of the girls down here said you do good work." That was better than calling her a do-gooder.

Her eyes narrowed. She seemed uncomfortable with the compliment, or maybe she thought there was an underlying sarcasm in my words. Her gaze drifted to the young woman that I still held by the arm.

"Know her?" I asked.

"Chanel? Yes."

I let go of the girl. "So, it's Chanel?"

The girl looked down.

"What name did she give you?" Marlene asked.

"Tabitha."

"She's not Tabitha."

Chanel rolled her eyes.

"And I'm guessing you're not eighteen," I added.

"Eighteen?" Marlene scoffed. "Try sixteen."

The girl lifted her hands in frustration. "Jesus, Marlene! I'll be seventeen next month."

"Are you a runaway?" I asked.

"No." The way she said it was intended to make me feel stupid.

"She's not a runaway," Marlene said. "She lives with her grandmother."

"Where is that?"

The address Chanel gave was about five blocks away. I glanced at Marlene with a questioning look. She nodded in confirmation, then discretely tilted her head, an indication for us to talk away from the girl.

"Sit down," I told Chanel.

"But it's cold," she whined.

"You either sit, or I'll put you in handcuffs and still make you sit."

She slumped her shoulders and sighed.

Marlene said, "Do what he asks."

The girl sat and pulled out her vape pen. We moved a couple of steps away, and Marlene stood near my side so we could both watch her.

"Her mother was in the life. She died four, maybe five years ago, from an overdose. Chanel lives with her grandmother around the way."

"The woman's not upset her sixteen-year-old granddaughter is working the street?"

Marlene's face remained impassive. "She wasn't upset when her own daughter was doing it, so why would she be now? The woman is checked out."

"Drugs?"

"You'd think, but no. It's general laziness, far as I can tell. I think the woman is addicted to doing nothing. Who knows why some people don't care about their kin?"

I studied Marlene then. Her face was almost free of make-up, and she looked to be in her mid-thirties. She watched Chanel with the intensity of a mother protecting a child.

"What's your story?"

Her focus settled on me with something slightly more than disdain. "I need a story to help these women, these *girls*?"

"No."

She remained quiet and her features darkened.

"What's her last name?"

"Nelson."

I reviewed the list once more and confirmed Chanel Nelson wasn't listed. That only meant she hadn't been arrested for prostitution yet.

"What's that?" Marlene asked.

"A list of known prostitutes."

She eyed the papers with interest but didn't say anything. I folded it and stuffed it into my coat.

"I need to run her name."

"Of course, you do." She folded her arms.

I called dispatch. It took them less than a minute to run the girl through the system. When I hung up, I said, "I'm surprised."

"By what?" Marlene's gaze remained on Chanel.

"She didn't pop up with an at-risk-youth status."

"The Becca Bill?" Marlene asked, referencing the state's mandated law for keeping kids in school. "That's going to save her from the streets? What makes you think she's missing school?"

"She's going?"

"If she doesn't, she gets popped under the state's truancy laws, right? She knows how to play the game." She turned to Chanel. "Girl, what's your grade point average?"

"Three point four."

"And she's out here," Marlene said, stepping toward the younger woman.

"You know a lot about this girl."

"I know a lot about many girls." Marlene ran her fingers through Chanel's hair, then moved some errant wisps out of her eyes.

"Who's your pimp?" I asked Chanel.

"I don't have one."

"Was it Junior?"

Marlene glared at me. "Detective—"

"I'm independent," Chanel muttered.

I frowned. "You think this is my first rodeo?"

She shrugged a single shoulder, then inhaled on her vape pen.

"That's not how this game is played. Your pimp is either Damon, or it was Junior."

At the mention of Junior's name, Marlene's face hardened further. She quit playing with Chanel's hair.

"Not a fan of Junior?"

Stepping away from Chanel, she said, "I'm not a fan of any abuser."

"So, who is it, kid?"

Chanel shoved her vape pen into her pocket. "You got everything figured out. You tell me."

"Junior."

"Look at you. Why even ask me?"

"Where were you on Saturday night?"

"Why's it matter?"

"I'm trying to find Junior's killer."

Chanel sighed. "I was working."

"You see anything that might help me?"

"Nope."

"If you did, would you tell me?"

"Maybe. I don't know."

"What happens when another pimp shows up?"

She stood and thrust out her chin. "Maybe he can't have me. I like being my own boss now."

"That's not how it works."

"It does for some girls."

"Not for you," Marlene snapped.

Chanel bowed her head.

I asked, "Were you talking about Joey Greene?"

Marlene stepped between Chanel and me. "Are you taking this girl somewhere, or can I take her home?"

I considered calling for a patrol officer to book Chanel into a mental health and teen addiction center. Pushing the girl there might result in a single night off the street, but she'd be back out tomorrow.

"You'll take responsibility for her tonight?" I asked.

"Of course."

"Got a card?"

From an inner pocket, Marlene handed me a business card for Her Freedom. Underneath the company's logo, it said they were a 501c3 non-profit organization. It listed their address in Spokane Valley.

"Are we free to go, Detective?"

Something had happened. Marlene had turned entirely frosty toward me. I rolled back the conversation in my head. Was it when I asked about Junior, or was it my inquiry into Joey Greene?

"If I have any follow-up questions," I said, "I'll call."

"Whatever." She reached for Chanel. "Let's get you home, kiddo."

The girl grasped her hand, and they walked away like a distraught mother leading a wayward child.

17

I noticed her as I neared my vehicle.

She wore a light blue jean jacket, a hooded sweatshirt, black jeans with torn knees, and Ugg boots. Her dishwater blonde hair needed a cut and rinse.

I diverted my path and wandered over as if I had all the time in the world.

She smiled as I neared. "Hey there, hands—" She abruptly spun around and started walking.

"Stop." I picked up my pace.

She hurried now. "Sorry," she hollered over her shoulder. "Thought you were someone else."

I trotted up to her. "Wait."

"No, thanks," she said and kept walking. "Not interested."

"Police." I grabbed her arm.

She yanked free. "I didn't do nothing, so you got no right to stop me."

"Sure, I do. You're working, and I've got some questions."

Her eyes darted about, looking for either an escape or to make sure no one was watching. When she decided, she leaned back and took me in thoroughly. "You're the detective people are blabbing about—the one trying to find Junior's killer."

"That would be me."

She visibly relaxed. "So, you ain't lookin' to bust me?"

"You going to lie?"

"No, sir."

"Then, we'll be fine."

She smiled and revealed a yellowing tooth.

"What's your name?"

"Scrimmy."

"Is that your real name?"

She shook her head. "Liliya Scrimshaw."

"Mind if I call you Liliya?"

"Whatever," she said with an eye roll and a frustrated sigh. "You're the cops. You call people what you want."

"Scrimmy then."

She nodded once. "Thank you."

I pulled the list of prostitutes from my coat pocket. Next to Liliya's picture was a 'J.' "You were one of Junior's girls."

"*Was*. Yeah."

"Know anyone who would want him dead?"

She looked away.

"Scrimmy?"

When she faced me again, she said, "Everyone *wanted* him dead, but no one had the guts to do it."

"Someone did."

"Not me."

"But no one is talking about it? Making guesses?" I thought back to her earlier word. "Blabbing?"

"Everybody's speculating, sure, but no one has any idea who *actually* did it."

"What about Damon Warfield? You think he could have done this?"

She shrugged. "He could have, but why? They was rivals and all, but they split the field. Know what I mean? They knew there was only so much pie to go around."

I looked at the list and saw Diedre Dobb's picture. I'd made a note—*J2*. She was Junior's second in command—his bottom bitch.

"What about Deidre?"

"DeeDee? Why would she do it?"

"Rumor had it Junior was bouncing her from the bottom."

"You heard that, huh?" Scrimmy rubbed the side of her face. "Well, there's been talk about that, sure, but that's all it was. At least, I think."

"If she was going to get bounced, do you think she could have done it? To get even with him?"

"Who knows? Things get crazy down here."

"Know where she is? I haven't found her."

Scrimmy shrugged. "I keep waiting for her to show up and collect, but she hasn't."

"Why would she collect? Junior's dead."

"It's what we do. If Junior's not around, we go on automatic, which means DeeDee steps up and takes over. I figure that's what's going to happen now."

"So, she'll collect and make sure your apartment gets paid for, you get some cash, that type of thing?"

Scrimmy nodded. "She's sort of a manager. Like a business."

"Got her number?"

"Sure, but it's dead now. Junior got us all burners and added minutes to them each day. But only enough to make sure we could talk with him. Phones are worthless now. I tried to call DeeDee and the message says it's out of commission. Now, my phone isn't working either."

"What's the number, just in case?"

She pulled out her phone, looked it up and gave it to me. I tried to call it and it went directly to an out-of-service message.

"What happens if another pimp shows up?"

"To take over Junior's territory, you mean? Maybe he keeps DeeDee as bottom, maybe not. But no man can have two bottoms. That's science. Someone will have to go. But that's not for me to worry about. All I gotta do is keep earning, and I'll be okay."

Her words sounded forced—the way a person repeats a mantra during hard times.

"What about Joey Greene?"

"Joey?" she blurted.

"Know her?"

Scrimmy stepped back, and her face whitened.

"Talk on the street is she's got a badge daddy."

"I gotta go."

She turned to leave, and I grabbed her arm again. "Who's protecting her?"

Scrimmy's face twisted in anger. "Listen, man. I don't know—"

"It's Detective Morgan, isn't it?"

She stiffened. "That's it. I'm done. If you want to arrest me, then arrest me. If not, then I'm walking."

"Relax, Scrimmy. We're only talking."

"No, we're not. You want me to be a rat, and I don't rat on friends."

TUESDAY
NOVEMBER 6th

18

"I'm tired," I said. "More than normal."

Bobbie's marble headstone remained silent.

"I was out late last night. You probably already know this stuff, right? I figure you can see what I'm doing. Is that wrong?"

I returned home shortly after two. When I finished talking with Liliya Scrimshaw, I drove over to Ironsides, but the bar was closed. Inside, a bartender turned over stools and placed them upside-down on the counter. I hoped to find Damon Warfield, but interviewing the pimp got pushed to a back burner. He would be high on my to-do list for today.

Thinking of the women I interviewed yesterday, I said, "The world's a messed-up place."

"Yes, it is," a feminine voice said.

A chill ran up my back, and my breathing stopped.

I stared at the slab.

Had Bobbie spoken? Had she finally reached out beyond the grave? Was I finally cracking?

There was movement nearby, and I glanced over my shoulder. A woman walked behind me with a cell phone to her ear.

"Exactly," she said. "That's what I've been saying. Pay attention."

My jaw flexed, and my hands balled.

How stupid was I to believe Bobbie was speaking to me? The idea was ridiculous.

I wanted to run after the woman and knock the phone out of her hand. I wanted to yell at her to shut her mouth and have some goddamn decency in a cemetery.

"Get it done," she said. Her voice lessened as she moved further away. "I've gotta go. I'll check in later." She ended her call and continued walking.

I didn't run after her, though. Everything I wanted was in front of me.

For several moments, I stared at Bobbie's marker. Even though it was childish, the idea she had spoken from beyond had given me some hope. When my eyes clouded with tears, there was nothing further to say except, "It's time for work."

19

I tossed Marlene Anderson's business card next to my keyboard and started my computer. Its screen changed to blue as it announced it was installing new updates. Frustration rose in my chest as I stared helplessly at its process counter. "Piece of shit."

Glenn leaned back from his desk. "What's wrong?"

I pointed at my computer but didn't say anything. My shaking head told him enough.

"The geeks were able to pull photos from Carlotta Winkler's phone."

"That's impressive."

"They didn't get anything from the actual device. That's a total loss, but the SD card was still intact. I'm going through the photos now."

"Anything of interest?"

"Mostly selfies. Lots of food pictures, even fast food. Weird. Some pictures of randos."

"What's a rando?"

He leaned toward his screen while he spoke. "Random guys, some girls. Young like her. They appear multiple times, so they're probably friends. They seem happy."

"Too bad they couldn't get her phone directory or text messages."

"She didn't save either of them to the SD card, but the geeks are still working on it. They're working backward to see if she had some sort of cloud-based service. Maybe stuff automatically uploaded to it."

"Need help on anything?"

"Not really." Glenn faced me. "I'll talk with her church today—you know the one we found the schedule for in her apartment?"

I nodded.

"Trying to round out who she was."

"So, you can figure out who *he* is."

"Exactly."

Lieutenant George Brand approached then. Glenn looked up and said, "Lieutenant," before turning back to his computer.

Brand leaned down and whispered into my ear, "Did you do what I asked?"

I could smell coffee on his breath. "Sir?"

"The appointment with Stephen."

"Not yet."

Brand pulled back and studied my face, then leaned down to my ear so he could whisper again. "That was non-negotiable. The captain wanted it done yesterday. I gave you until the end of shift."

I glanced sideways at the man, even though he remained near my ear. At least he was trying to respect my privacy.

"If it's not done by noon today, you will be violating a direct order, and I will place you on involuntary leave until you meet with the counselor. Understand?"

"Yes, sir."

The lieutenant straightened. "I'll wait to update the captain until noon." He walked off toward his office without further comment.

"What was that about?" Glenn asked.

My computer was still updating, so I grabbed Marlene's business card, pushed back from the desk, and walked away.

"Dallas?" Glenn called after me.

***

"You've reached the office of Stephen Yoder. Leave a name and number, and I'll get back to you as soon as possible."

"Stephen, this is Detective Dallas Nash. When you have a moment, please call."

After hanging up, it occurred to me that I hadn't left my cell number. I redialed but hung up before it rang. There was now a message with the therapist proving I called. I had deniability now. Screw the lieutenant.

Maybe Yoder was in a counseling session. If that were the case, it would be some time before he could call me back. I relaxed and dropped the cell phone onto the passenger seat.

Parked on Sharp Avenue, I surveilled Josephine Greene's home. No car was in front. If she worked the East Sprague corridor, this was within walking distance.

Occasionally, a vehicle passed by. The drivers were usually aware that I sat in a police vehicle. They averted their eyes and made sure to have both hands on the wheel. The newer Chevy Impalas like I drove were as easy to spot as the old Ford Crown Victorias the department abandoned years ago. Besides, the license plate ending with a D revealed it was a City of Spokane vehicle. It wouldn't take a rocket scientist to figure out who was behind the wheel.

My cell phone rang as I opened the door. From where it sat on the passenger seat, I could read the number. For a brief second, I considered ignoring the call.

"Nash," I said, after answering.

"Dallas Nash? Hi. This is Stephen Yoder. You left me a message."

"I did. I need to make an appointment."

"Okay," he said, then absently repeated, "okay." He rustled some papers, then tapped a keyboard. "Okay," he muttered a third time before saying, "Let me call up my calendar."

"If I don't meet with you, they'll put me on involuntary leave."

"Okay."

Another okay. What was okay about this moment? Even before calling, I knew I wouldn't like the guy, and it was already proving to be true.

"I can get you in tomorrow morning. I had something personal planned, but I'll reschedule it. I know this is important."

"You don't have to do that."

"It's okay," he said.

How many okays was that? I wondered. Four? Five?

"I don't want you getting jammed up with the department if I can help it. Nine a.m. tomorrow morning. Will that work? Do you know where I'm located?"

"Yeah."

"I'll see you then. Okay?"

"Okay," I said and cringed.

When I hung up, I made another call.

"Lieutenant Brand," he answered.

"This is Nash."

"Nash," he repeated, letting my name alone set the tone for this conversation. Brand often tended to be an impotent leader, lost in his dreams of increased efficiencies, and rigorous adhering to policies and procedures. But in moments like this, when administrative responsibilities were at play, he was a different man. This was his wheelhouse, and he was clearly in control.

"The appointment is scheduled. Tomorrow morning. Nine."

"I'll let the captain know."

"Anything else?"

"No," I said.

It was passive aggressive, but I ended the call without further discussion. I half expected the lieutenant to ring me back and bawl me out for my lack of phone etiquette. When several seconds passed without a call back, I tucked my phone away and got out of the car.

At the door to the small house, I listened for several moments. Black Sabbath's "Paranoid" began playing inside my head.

Leaning into the door, I struggled to hear something, anything, but all I could hear was Sabbath's driving beat.

I spun around and crouched. My gaze swept the neighborhood for anyone watching me. Fear bubbled up as I scanned the windows of the houses across the street.

Inside my head, the drums and bass guitar stuttered out a pounding rhythm.

Nothing and no one seemed to be moving in the neighborhood.

I turned back to Joey Greene's house and loudly banged on the door. From inside, there was a noise. At least, I *thought* there was a noise. I leaned in and knocked louder but could only hear the guitars wailing and the drums thumping inside my head.

An un-mufflered car drove by.

I knocked on the door once more, but still, no answer. Was my mind messing with me? Had I imagined the noise inside the house?

Since there was no fence to stop me, I hurried around to the back, peeking futilely into windows as I went. All the curtains were closed.

"Paranoid" coiled around my brain.

At the rear of the house, I knocked loudly and announced, "Spokane Police. Come to the door."

From the corner of my eye, I caught movement and ducked reflexively. A female neighbor stepped out of her home to see what I was doing. When I turned to her, she disappeared into her house, slamming the door closed.

The song continued at its frenetic pace as I banged on the door again.

Discouraged, I returned to the front of the house, where I knocked and announced once more. "Spokane Police! Come to the door!"

By now, the entire neighborhood had to be standing behind their doors with their eyes glued to their peepholes.

The same guitar riff circled around and around.

I couldn't prove Joey Greene was inside and, even if I did, there was nothing I could do to force her to open her house. There was no reason to detain her beyond a desire to talk.

And that frustrated me.

I hammered the bottom of my fist against the door one more time.

20

Squeezed between a printing company and a small car lot, Ironsides squatted in the shadow of the highway overpass. It seemed out of place for a bar, like it wanted to get near the dirty action of East Sprague, but not too close.

Perhaps that's why this little establishment existed so long while others came and went. It straddled the line between the blue-collar workers and those who moved about the criminal world. The two groups needed each other—one needed money, while the other needed access to illegal dope, guns, or sex.

As the door closed behind me, I nodded once toward the bartender. He stopped working and cautiously eyed me. Thin, slightly slack-jawed with dark bags under his eyes—he resembled a meerkat attempting to sense danger. He swallowed once, flicked his eyes to the man in the rear booth, and turned to the back bar.

The place smelled of stale beer and bleach—the latter, no doubt, the solution used to wipe down the counter surfaces.

Damon Warfield sat quietly in the rear of the establishment. He bowed his head over a newspaper laid out on the table in front of him. He didn't bother to look up as I approached.

On the walls of the establishment hung an eclectic mix of English references. Photos of various royals were intermixed with old concert posters of The Sex Pistols, Yes, and Ringo Starr. The top of the bar sported a line-up of large die-cast models of British cars like an Aston Martin, a Mini, and a Lotus Esprit. There was a red call box at the back wall with an actual working phone, one of the few remaining in the city. At least, it did when I was last in here, but that had been a few years.

Damon turned the page but didn't glance my way. While he read, he sucked on a silver cross attached to the rosary around his neck. He wore a large Dodgers jacket and a white T-shirt. A Dodgers baseball cap lay on the table next to the paper. A holographic sticker from the manufacturer shimmered on the brim. Light-skinned and heavily freckled, he had shaved his head clean.

The Offspring's "Pretty Fly for a White Guy" burst into my head. It was a catchy song about Caucasian guys trying too hard to be cool.

Damon refused to acknowledge me, even though I stood nearby. Besides the bartender, we were the only two in the bar. His gaze remained on the newspaper.

Slowly, I pulled my suit jacket to the side and revealed my badge.

A moment passed before he slowly turned his gaze my way.

"Pretty Fly for a White Guy" continued to play inside my head. He said something I couldn't make out.

"What?"

He raised his voice. "The bouncer job has been filled."

The song in my head faded. "I have some questions for you."

"No introductions?"

"You're Damon Warfield. Pimp."

"Extraordinaire," he said. He rested the back of his head against the booth. "And you?"

"Detective Nash. Spokane Police."

He studied me before speaking. "With the suit, I'd make it Major Crimes. You here to ask about Junior?"

"I am."

"I haven't done anything to necessitate the attention of a homicide detective." His head bounced as he spoke.

The song returned, and I remained silent while it played. Damon Warfield looked like a moron, and my subconscious and consciousness were in firm agreement.

He frowned. "You're not leaving until we chat."

"That's correct."

Damon waved toward the seat opposite him. I sat and pulled out my notebook.

"You already know my name. You require all that other bullshit, too? Birthdate, address, etc."

"Yes."

Damon snapped his fingers. "Always the same," he said and shared his particulars. I jotted them down as he spoke.

When he finished, I asked, "Where were you on Saturday night?"

"Where wasn't I?"

"Shortly after midnight," I said. "When Junior was murdered."

Damon tapped the table. "Here. This table."

"Got an alibi?"

He thumbed toward the bartender. "Him and a room full of jokers. I'm covered, chief. I didn't do Junior—there was no need for it. We had an agreement."

"An agreement?"

Damon lifted his hands then clasped them together. "We were competitors, but that didn't mean we couldn't be friendly about it."

"You were friends?"

"Did I say that? No, I most definitely did not say that. Don't put words in my mouth. I said we were *friendly*. What we were was professionals."

"Professional pimps?"

He inhaled deeply, shaking his head as he did. When he exhaled, he said, "You cops like to think of yourselves as professionals, even though you all bust into the wrong houses on a regular basis."

I tapped my notebook, waiting.

"Don't step on me for thinking I'm one, too. I run my business a certain way with a set of principles."

He was on a roll, so I stayed quiet.

"Junior and me, we learned to co-exist. Our girls worked the same territory and shared the same customers. There are only so many dicks in the sea, but we never went after the other man's girls. That was the agreement. It's called détente."

The use of the diplomacy word surprised me, and my eyes flicked to the newspaper.

"Why would he," I said, pausing to reshape my question, "why would *you* willingly agree to share territory?"

Frustrated, Damon shook his head. "People like to think Spokane is big, but it's not *that* big. There's nowhere any businessman can go without stepping on another man's toes."

"That doesn't answer my question."

"If you're listening, it does."

Trying to control my anger, I glanced down at my notebook.

Damon asked, "Do you know how prostitution works in this town?"

"I think I do but enlighten me."

He closed his newspaper and pushed it to the side. Then he leaned over the table and lowered his voice. "Junior and me, we run the girls down here. East Sprague is an old school stroll. Not the prettiest girls, but they're workers. They put their backs into it if you know what I mean."

If he was hoping for a reaction, it wasn't coming.

"The only other stroll is on the west end. Now, that part of the city is getting pinched by the hipsters moving to those redeveloped projects. It's making the game hard, pushing the girls and customers elsewhere. Most of them head this way."

Known as the West End, it was a ten-block radius that experienced significant gentrification since the Great Recession. It was an island between downtown and Browne's Addition. Once a haven for prostitution, drugs, and gangs, it was now a mecca for redevelopment and community reinvestment.

Damon picked up his hat and put it on, cocking it slightly to the side, then sliding his hand around the brim. He continued, "Besides the strolls, you've got the mamasans and their girls."

My brow furrowed.

"You know, the happy endings?" He mimed shaking some dice.

"The massage parlors? We shut them down."

Damon smirked. "Keep thinking that."

I frowned.

"Relax, man. You're going to pop a blood vessel. Shutting the parlors down is like squeezing water. They move into other neighborhoods not likely to complain. It's sort of behind-the-curtain, wink-wink, nudge-nudge prostitution. Everybody suspects it, but nobody wants to go after it. Gotta hand it to the mama-sans, no pun intended. They've got a racket going."

When I didn't comment, Damon continued his lecture.

"The Russians are the newest players."

"The Russians?"

"Eastern European, if the other term offends."

"What about them?"

"They've got girls working in a couple houses. They're doing specialty flicks mostly, but they still farm them out when they're not rolling tape."

"Where's that?"

Damon's smile faded. "So, you got East Sprague," he said, counting with his fingers as he talked, "the West End, the rub and tugs, the Russian houses, and I almost forgot the Internet escorts who are gobbling up the high rollers."

"The Internet escorts?"

"How out of the loop are you, Detective?"

"Most of the way, it seems like."

"Sex is everywhere. There's probably someone in your neighborhood getting paid for it now. Maybe some bored housewife is picking up a little scratch while her husband is at work. Having online sex with some guy in New Zealand as the old man busts his hump at the ol' nine to five."

"I doubt it."

Damon laughed. "If you say so."

"Back to Junior. Why this lesson in prostitution?"

"If a man like Junior got the unwise decision to start spreading his wings, where do you think he would stick his nose? And I'll give you a hint—he wasn't going to compete with the mama-sans, and he wasn't going head-to-head with the oligarchs."

The oligarchs. I fought the desire to look at the newspaper. His appearance was incongruent with his intelligence.

"Why not go online?"

"Junior and me, we're old school types. Computers are for the eggheads. They got a different type of customer, too. Our clients want to put hands on the product, not hands-on themselves."

The product, I thought—what a way to think about another human being.

"So, Junior pushed into the West End?"

"He tried, and one of his girls got her ass beat for it."

"Who was the girl?" I asked, thinking about the list in my pocket.

He shrugged. "Don't know her name. She was a sweet little ginger who liked the rock, but she was still on the fresh side of ripe. Got herself busted up bad. Never saw her again after that."

"Who did the beating?"

"Tiger's girls. They protected their territory. They know the rules."

"Would your girls do that?"

Damon ran his fingers around his lips. "That's the game."

"If the West End was being squeezed by redevelopment, why would Junior move into that market?"

"When an enemy is weak, you don't let him hold territory to build up an army. You've got to think strategically in these situations."

"You take the fight to him."

"Exactly."

I glanced at the newspaper. Detente. Oligarchs. Strategy. "You put those thoughts into Junior's head, didn't you?"

He said, "I don't know what you're talking about," but there was a glint in his eye.

"You convinced Junior to go after Tiger."

His silence confirmed my suspicions.

"If Junior pushed out Tiger, no harm, no foul. You would still have your piece of the pie. But if Junior pushed and something bad happened—"

"I didn't kill the man."

"Were you working a deal with Tiger? Trying to force out your competition down here?"

"No way." Damon's eyes narrowed. "No one works with Tiger. He's a scary piece."

"What happens to Junior's girls now?"

He inhaled and held it for several seconds before speaking. "They're out of pocket, so my girls are interviewing them. I'll bring them under my wing sooner or later. They're not low-hanging fruit yet, but soon enough, they'll be easy pickings. Junior ran them with a stiff hand." He slapped the back of his right hand into the open palm of his left. "I'm more finesse. But if they don't like my game, that's cool. They can suck dick on the West End. This is my territory now."

"What about the renegade?"

He ran his tongue over his teeth and made a squeaking sound when he opened his mouth. "She's the exception."

"Sounds like everyone knows about her. How's she allowed to do that?"

Damon glanced toward the bar, then back to me but refused to answer.

"I heard she had some protection."

He pursed his lips and moved them from side to side. It was another delay tactic.

"One of the girls called him a badge daddy."

His brow furrowed. "One of my girls? I find out who, I'll smack her for talkin' too much."

"I thought you said you were a finesse player."

He rubbed his hand over his mouth.

"Which cop is it?"

Damon shook his head. "Uh-huh. That's crossing a line."

"What line is that?"

"You sure you're not IA?"

I straightened. "I'm Major Crimes."

"Moonlighting for them, then?"

"I'm no rat."

"Neither am I."

"But if it's a cop—"

"You think I should rat on a cop?" Damon's face reddened. "What do I do when nothing happens to him? He'll come down here and turn my world upside down. No, thank you very much. I wish you the best of luck finding Junior's killer, I really do, but I'm not putting myself in the crosshairs of any law enforcement officer— especially a dirty one."

We stared at each other for several beats. We'd reached the end of the interview.

"There's a sixteen-year-old out there," I said.

"*And?*"

"Keep your hands off."

"You want to be *her* badge daddy?"

My hands balled into fists.

"If you don't want her out here, then get her off the street. I don't want jailbait, anyway. That kind of girl brings the wrong kind of attention—pervs and cops. I don't need it."

"That's decent of you."

"But I can't have her walking around unaccounted for either. It gives the others ideas about going their own way. One is bad enough. I got to work against that bullshit every day."

"You'd bring in the kid to stop her from claiming independence?"

His smirk returned. "No, Detective, I wouldn't bring her in. That's against one of my principles, and believe it or not, I've got them. But I'll make that little bitch's life so damn miserable she'll have no choice but to stay away. Maybe she takes it on the road, but she won't throw pussy in my territory. There are rules to this game."

"Where do I find Tiger?"

He fingered the rosary cross before slipping it into his mouth.

"I can't give you everything," he said through clenched teeth and glanced toward the bartender.

"You better because right now, you stood to gain the most from Junior's death. It doesn't take much to point the finger at you."

He tucked the cross into the corner of his mouth. "I didn't do it."

"Then you'll tell me how to find Tiger."

The cross fell from his mouth, a trail of saliva following it.

"The Hope," he said. "He hangs out at the Hope."

21

Most metropolitan areas are an amalgamation of cities with no discernible break between their borders. Spokane and Spokane Valley were no exception.

I stopped by the office of Her Freedom, a nondescript building on Alki Avenue, just east of Fancher Road, and only a few blocks inside the Spokane Valley city limits. From this location, Her Freedom was a couple of minutes from the East Sprague corridor. It wasn't ground zero, but they were a baseball's throw away.

A wall with a Plexiglas window separated the lobby from the workers. The waiting area was functional but not inviting. Four metal chairs and a little table were the only furniture. Placed on the table were tattered magazines with titles like *Reader's Digest*, *Woman's Day*, and *People*.

A woman behind the clear shield said, "Can I help you?"

"Marlene Anderson, please."

"And who may you be?"

I revealed my badge. "Detective Nash. Spokane Police."

Unfazed by the symbol of authority, she picked up the phone's receiver. She pressed a button and waited. "A Detective Nash is here." Her eyes slid to my badge, then back to the phone. "Uh-huh. He didn't say. Right." After she hung up, the receptionist said, "She'll be out in a moment. She's finishing with a client."

I sat and considered reading one of the old magazines. The newest was a year old, and someone had torn off the mailing labels. I passed on all of them and glanced around the waiting room.

Posters about topics like sex trafficking, domestic violence, prostitution, and rape cluttered the walls. Almost no space was left open. The hangings were all about sending a single, coherent message, and it was a simple one—women need to protect themselves.

Two posters used images of slavery. One had an image of a man's fist next to a young woman's bruised face. The restroom door had a poster of a woman with her mouth covered by red paint and the tagline *She Can't Ask for Help*.

Smaller informational posters about diseases such as gonorrhea, syphilis, and AIDS were interspersed around the room.

Some posters worked to raise awareness of rape. There was one for marital rape, while one focused on college drinking leading to sexual assaults. Near my chair, affixed to the wall, was a black and red sticker that read, *Dead Men Don't Rape*. In the center of the sticker, a cartoon woman stabbed a man in the head.

When I'd had enough of the imagery and its messages, I stared at the worn beige carpet.

The door to the back offices opened, and Marlene appeared. She wore a knee-length brown skirt and a tan blouse. Like the night before, her make-up was lightly applied. However, today she wore large-framed reading glasses.

I stood.

A slender redhead followed Marlene out. She wore an army jacket, jeans, and running shoes. A baseball hat was pulled down to her ears.

The two women hugged.

"Stay safe," Marlene whispered.

"You, too."

When they broke their embrace, the redhead eyed me with something short of suspicion. Fear, perhaps. I cocked my head.

"Detective," Marlene said to catch my attention.

The woman in the green jacket slipped out the front door and didn't look back.

Following the redhead for her brief flash of fear seemed a stupid idea, especially considering the location we were in. The posters on the walls held her truth—she had reason to be afraid of men.

"Who was she?" I asked.

"You know better than that. I won't discuss our clients. Is there a reason for your visit?"

"I'd like to follow up on our conversation."

Her gaze carried the weariness of someone who had seen too much. Officers developed the same stare after years of looking into the worst in humanity. With a sigh of resignation, Marlene held the door to the back open.

Her office was in the rear corner. As we walked through a bullpen area, several middle-aged women watched me with distrustful eyes. They were a pack of lionesses waiting for me to either move threateningly or reveal a weakness. No matter what I did, they would respond accordingly.

When we stepped into Marlene's office, the women returned their collective focus to their work.

"They don't seem to like me much."

"The volunteers?" Marlene asked, as she sat behind her desk. "No, they don't."

I lowered myself into a fabric chair.

"Don't take it personally, Detective. It's not you; it's your profession and your gender. You've already got two strikes against you before you've even opened your mouth. Let's hope you don't make it three."

"I can't do anything about my gender, but why hate the profession? We're on the same side."

She squinted. "You think that?"

"I do."

Marlene removed her glasses and rubbed the bridge of her nose. "You're a detective, which meant you had to be a patrolman before."

"I was."

She resettled her glasses. "As a patrol officer, how many prostitutes did you arrest?"

I couldn't think of a number, but there were quite a few. "Some."

"Ever arrest a john?"

"The department runs stings, and we arrest them. It makes the news it's such a big deal."

A look of satisfaction passed over her face, as if she had put my king in check. "Of course, it's a big deal. Why *is* that?"

Before I could answer, she continued.

"Because it doesn't happen very often, that's why. Also, they use female officers as bait. That's kind of a sexy story, isn't it? A lady cop pretends to be a prostitute. Bait, I remind you. The woman is nothing more than a worm on a hook. The press eats it up. Hollywood loves it. But you, Detective Nash, outside of a sting, did *you* ever arrest a john for soliciting a prostitute?"

"No."

She sucked in her lips while she thought, nodding as she did. When she pushed them out, she said, "What about a pimp?"

"What about them?"

"Ever arrest one?"

"Of course."

She pointed a finger for emphasis. "For promoting prostitution? Not for some other crime, but for actually *promoting* prostitution?"

I wanted to lie, but instead, I said, "No. Never."

"So, Detective Nash, as a man, you never arrested a john or a pimp, but you arrested many prostitutes for their participation in the sex trade."

I stared ahead. This wasn't how I anticipated our conversation going.

"Who has the power in this equation? The pimp, the prostitute, or the customer. Let me give you a hint. It's not the woman." She folded her arms and waited. When I didn't respond, she asked, "Want to know why it's not the woman?"

"I know why," I said, thinking back to Damon Warfield's words. "Because she's the product."

Marlene nodded. "Good answer."

I thumbed toward the outer office. "That's why those women hate the police?"

"That's why they hate *you*, Detective. A white, male cop. You're the stereotypical problem."

"They don't know me."

"They know your type will never help, which you just confirmed. You told me you thought you were helping, but in fact, it's the opposite. You've been hurting them. Therefore, they have every right to be scared of you."

Dokken's "Mr. Scary" burst into my consciousness, and I winced. The blistering instrumental played at full blast.

Marlene leaned forward and said something I couldn't hear. I pressed a thumb against my temple.

"Mr. Scary" clawed deeper into my brain as the fierce guitar lick ran up the pentatonic scale. No song hurt this badly before. Bile rose in my throat. Tears welled in my eyes.

Worry crossed Marlene's face as I reached out to grip the edge of her desk. My fingers hit a wooden picture frame, spinning it around.

The music caused excruciating pain.

In the photograph, Marlene cuddled a small child in her arms. Its mocha skin contrasted with her pale arms. Her eyes beamed at the toddler.

The guitar screamed in "Mr. Scary," and I blinked several times.

Marlene hurried around her desk, put her hand on my shoulder and bent down. Her perfume smelled sweet as her face neared mine. She put her other hand over mine as she continued to speak words I couldn't hear.

"Mr. Scary" shrieked again, and the world went black.

***

I awoke on the floor.

Marlene held my head, and reassuringly said, "Everything is okay."

Several of the women huddled behind her, watching me with concern. Everyone crammed into her office.

"Relax," Marlene said. "You fainted."

With some effort, I sat upright, and a damp washcloth fell from my forehead into my lap.

"Feeling better?" one of the volunteers asked.

"Uh-huh," I muttered.

"Your color is coming back," another woman said.

"Feeling better." I parroted the first woman's words.

"Has this happened before?" Marlene asked.

"No," I said and stood. "I haven't been eating lately."

"We figured it had to do with something like that," Marlene said. "Either that or you were sick."

"Sick?" I handed the washcloth to the nearest volunteer.

"Your clothes are loose."

"Extreme diet, I guess."

"You need to eat," one of the women said, "or this kind of stuff will happen. I've been there."

"Should we call an ambulance?" someone asked.

"No," I blurted.

All of them stepped back—their faces registering different levels of confusion.

Lifting my hands in deference, I said, "I'm sorry. I don't want my boss to know this happened. It's embarrassing."

"Could you get in trouble?" Marlene asked.

It was more than possible; it was guaranteed. An officer fainting while on duty was a risk not only to himself but to others.

When I didn't answer her question, Marlene said, "Let's get you a protein bar. We've got them for the girls who come in. It'll be the first time we ever gave one to a cop."

"Or a man," muttered a volunteer who wandered off.

The rest of the women shuffled out of the office, leaving the two of us alone.

Marlene guided me toward the chair. "That was pretty scary."

I waited for "Mr. Scary" to return, but it didn't. "Yeah."

"Do you want to continue?"

The tables had turned. She was in control of the moment. Maybe I should have gotten up and walked out of there, but I didn't feel strong enough to do so.

"Let's continue."

"So," she said, settling into her chair. "You came to ask questions, and I lectured you."

"It's okay." Okay, I thought and remembered my phone conversation with the therapist. After this fainting spell, talking with him tomorrow might be a good idea.

A volunteer walked into the office and handed me two protein bars and a glass of water. "Eat one now, then eat the second in an hour." She patted my shoulder. "And drink this. You're probably dehydrated." She left without a further word.

"Go ahead," Marlene said with a nod. "Eat it. I don't want you passing out again."

I tucked one of the bars into my coat pocket and opened the other. The first bite was bland and dry, but I forced a grateful smile. "Thank you."

"Ask your questions, Detective Nash."

After swallowing, I said, "I'm following up on the homicide of Everson Wiley. You know him as—"

"*Junior*." She spoke the word as if she'd eaten something spoiled.

"You've had contact with him."

"I know who the pimps are." Her face hardened.

"We can't find where he lived. I've asked around, but no one knows, or they won't say. Can you ask around?"

She briefly lowered her eyes. "The Hilda."

"How'd you know?"

"We hear things."

Mechanically, I bit into the protein bar. "Which apartment?"

"That I wouldn't know."

"You don't like him." I tucked the rest of the bar into my pocket.

"I don't like any of them."

"Where were you on Saturday night?"

"You think I could have killed him? I'm flattered." She didn't smile at her joke. "I was at home."

"Anyone there who can prove it?"

"I was doing an online course for my degree. Not exactly exciting and not something I need an alibi for, but I bet they have my login times and my activity recorded."

It wasn't exactly a strong alibi. Anyone could have been behind the keyboard.

"What degree are you going after?"

"How does this help find Junior's killer?"

I shrugged. "You said you were taking a course for a degree. It lacked details."

"Sociology and it's for my psychology degree." She picked up a notepad. "Now, if there are no further questions, I've got work to do."

Glancing out to the bullpen, "What gets someone like you into this?"

"Someone like me?"

"I mean," I said, turning back to her, "what brought you to this world, to these women?"

Marlene's head dropped while she thought. When she looked up, she asked, "What brought you to law enforcement?"

"I wanted to help people."

Her eyes narrowed. "Save it for the press packet."

I grabbed the glass of water and sipped. Helping people was the answer I gave citizens whenever they asked why I joined. It was the answer everyone wanted to hear. "I thought it would be exciting. Driving fast. Fighting with bad guys. Typical cops and robbers' type of stuff."

"Not me," she said. "I knew I could make a difference here."

She had tightened up, and I was trying to find something to connect with her. My eyes flicked to the picture on the corner of her desk. "Is that your girl?"

Marlene grabbed the frame and turned it toward her.

"Who watches her when you're out at night?"

"I have a babysitter whenever I work late. She was with me on Saturday if you would like to talk with her. Although, we were probably asleep when Junior was—" She considered the girl in the photograph. "Detective, I really do have work to do."

"Do you know anyone who would want to kill Junior?"

"Are you kidding?" A malicious smile formed on her lips. "For starters, everyone in this office. After that, every girl he ever touched. Then some of his competitors. Maybe some johns. The list of people who would want to see that man dead would be pretty long."

From inside my jacket, I pulled out the list of prostitutes and laid it on the desk. She picked it up and scanned it for several moments. When she flipped to the second page, she looked up without a word.

I asked, "Are there—"

"I don't see any pimps or johns listed."

"You've already chastised me for that."

Her eyes narrowed.

"Damon Warfield told me about a pimp named Tiger. Do you know his real name?"

"I don't." Her attention returned to the list. "I only know him as Tiger."

"We should have him in our system," I said, "but if you wouldn't mind asking around."

She didn't acknowledge my request.

"About the johns. Know any that would have it in for Junior?"

Her face pinched. "How would I know that?"

"I thought you could ask around."

Marlene's eyes held mine. "You're asking a lot."

"If you find anyone that I should talk to—"

She tossed the paper onto her desk, and I pointed at it.

"Are there are any names I'm missing?"

"No."

It was too forceful of a denial. The list already did not have the underaged Chanel, so it was likely it could be missing another. From the look on her face, it was apparent Marlene would never provide me with any names to add to it.

A heaviness descended upon the room, and I listened to the whir of the heating unit. The white noise was more enjoyable than any music in my head.

Marlene rested her elbows on the desk. "Junior was a leech. The fact that he's dead should be celebrated. Instead, you're spending a lot of time looking for his killer."

"No one deserves to be gunned down in the street. Saying that makes you sound like a suspect again."

She dismissively flicked a hand. "My saying it shows I have nothing to worry about. I wonder if your department had spent this much time investigating the missing prostitutes in the late nineties if that serial killer would have killed so many women."

I stood and picked up the list from her desk. "Thank you for your time."

"Whoever killed Junior did us all a favor."

There was nothing to say that wouldn't lead to further argument. Sometimes the best decision is to retreat, and that's what I did.

22

The Hilda Apartments occupied half a city block at the corner of Monroe Street and Nebraska Avenue. The three-story brick building specialized in market-rate low-income housing with two floors of apartments above ground-floor retail units. The onsite manager's apartment was near the south entrance.

Faron Beedle wore a dirty winter coat, dirty khakis, and scuffed brown loafers. His yellow stocking cap covered his ears. The weather outside was nippy, but he seemed prepared for a heavy chill. A small set of keys dangled from his waist.

After introducing myself, Faron told me that he owned the building. Once I showed I was duly impressed by that fact, he stepped back and allowed me to enter his combination apartment/office. A desk cluttered with paperwork sat in the middle of the living room. Two metal cabinets stood behind it. A workbench pressed against the far wall.

In the only other room was an unmade bed with no cover. The exposed mattress was gray with age and wear.

The apartment was warm and smelled of a man's funk.

"Junior?" he said in response to my question about Everson Wiley. He put his hands on his hips and thrust his chin out. "Why you looking for him?"

"He's dead. I'm investigating his murder."

Faron's eyes widened. "He's dead? But he didn't pay the rent."

"That's what happens when they're dead."

"Who's going to pay the rent?"

"Not Junior."

Faron turned to a cabinet, yanked open a drawer, and tugged out a thin manila file. He opened it and flipped through several papers. "He doesn't have a security deposit," he groaned in disappointment.

"Is that his rental application?"

The small man's head jerked toward me.

"I'd like to look at it."

Faron clutched the papers to his body.

"Everson Wiley provided that information, correct?"

The manager hurriedly tucked the papers into the folder, put it back into the cabinet, and shoved the drawer closed. He then grabbed the keyring attached to his belt and pulled it from his waist, extending an elastic chord. After selecting the right key, he secured the cabinet. When he finished, he let go, and the entire set snapped back to his waist. Faron turned and defiantly thrust out his chin.

"If you won't let me see it," I said, "I'll get a warrant so I can."

The manager snapped his fingers. "I need to get him out." He spun to a pegboard lined with numbers and keys. "No rent is not good."

"You can't go into the apartment."

His hand hovered above the pegboard.

"Wiley had a lease," I said. "You're required to follow the law to evict him."

His hand lowered, and he looked back over his shoulder. "It's *my* building."

"But it was *his* apartment, and I'll lock it down until I get a warrant to search it. I'll keep it that way until I'm satisfied that I'm not missing anything."

Faron's eyes narrowed. "How much?"

"What?"

"How much for you to go away?"

"Are you bribing me?"

He feigned shock. "No. You're extorting me."

"I'm not going away, Mr. Beedle."

Faron jutted his chin out once again. "The man you want does not live here."

"What?"

"Junior Wiley does not live here. Never has."

"You pulled out a file and said he did."

"I was mistaken."

We stared at each other until I removed my phone from my pocket. I dialed a number I knew by heart.

"Dispatch," the operator said.

"This is Detective Nash. I'm at the Hilda apartments, corner of Nebraska and Monroe, for follow-up on a murder investigation."

Faron's brow furrowed as he listened.

"Got it," the dispatcher said.

"I'm with an uncooperative subject."

Faron's eyes widened. "Now hold on a min—"

"Start a unit."

***

Officer Rodney McCrea arrived in less than five minutes. He parked his patrol car in front of the building and got out. When Faron saw him, he grinned and waved. The officer shook his head, and Faron's smile slowly faded.

The property owner and I waited at the edge of the property. Not allowing Faron to remain in the building by himself, I insisted he join me outside. Based on our earlier interaction, I worried he would either hide or destroy Everson Wiley's rental application or go into the man's apartment.

"Wait over there," McCrea said and pointed near the front of the building.

Faron nodded dejectedly and stepped away.

McCrea was a patrol lifer with a genial disposition. He smiled as we shook hands. "Been a while, Dallas. Nice to see you out among the living."

"Trying to earn my keep."

"You feeling okay?"

"Sure. Why?"

His eyes searched mine. "You've dropped weight."

"I cut back on the carbs."

"Uh-huh."

"And the beer."

"Don't remember you being much of a drinker."

"A little," I said.

A guitar screeched in my head as Motorhead's "Liar" started. The pounding song railed against religious leaders who hid behind falsehoods. As the guttural lyrics blasted inside my head, it didn't take a map to figure out why my subconscious chose this song.

McCrea said something I couldn't hear over the music.

I jerked a thumb toward the building owner and said, "He's skeevy. I don't trust him."

The officer tilted his head but remained silent.

I spoke over the music as it looped inside my head. "He wouldn't let me see the file on my murder victim, and he was going to enter the apartment without proper authority."

McCrea spoke again, but this time concern flooded his eyes.

I feigned understanding by giving a small nod and a half-shrug at the same time. I had no idea what the gesture would mean to him, but McCrea accepted it and walked over to the manager.

As they conversed, I closed my eyes and pressed a thumb into the right socket. The resulting pressure felt good. While the music diminished, I remained that way and watched the light show behind my eyelids.

"Dallas?"

I blinked.

McCrea looked concerned. "You all right?"

"I'm good."

"He'll give you what you need."

"How'd you—"

"Beedle and me—we go back," McCrea said. "You don't work patrol as long as I have and not run into guys like him."

With his hands shoved into his dirty coat, the building owner watched us with disappointment.

McCrea put his hand on my shoulder. "You sure you're okay?"

"Headache." I pulled out the half-eaten protein bar. "This diet is killing me."

The officer watched me take a bite.

"You look like shit. Whatever routine you're on doesn't look healthy."

I stopped chewing and stared at him.

"I'm not trying to get into your mess kit, Dal. You can do whatever you want, but it looks like it's gone too far." McCrea turned to Beedle and waved at him to lead the way into the apartment building.

With their attention diverted, I spat out the protein bar.

***

Everson Wiley's apartment was small and clean—too clean.

Initially, I hadn't intended to search the apartment. I was only going to verify Wiley did indeed live there.

Then I would go back to the department to write a search warrant. But Faron Beedle's actions concerned me enough to want to get eyes on the apartment.

Now, the sparseness of the apartment surprised me.

"You sure he lived here?"

Faron nodded.

"And you didn't make him fill this in completely?" I held up Wiley's sparsely completed application. We got it before coming upstairs. Beyond Junior's given name and cell phone number, no other information was on the form.

The landlord stared sheepishly at me.

"Why not?" I asked.

Faron turned his palms upward. "He paid in cash."

"Of course, he paid in cash. He was a pimp."

The landlord leaned toward the application still in my hand. "It doesn't say that on the application."

McCrea turned to the smaller man. "*Faron.*" He emphasized the man's name with a drop in octave.

"*What?* How was I to know he was a pimp? This is his apartment. I wouldn't lie to you, Mr. McCrea."

"Yes, you would."

"Okay, maybe sometimes." Faron chuckled and jerked his head about. "But not today. I'm not lying about this."

I stepped into the studio apartment and looked around. Some crumpled covers were on a mattress that lay directly on the floor, but that was it. There was nothing anywhere else. The kitchen counter was bare. I pulled open several drawers—empty.

"He didn't live here," I said.

Faron pointed at the floor. "This was *his* apartment. I'm telling the truth."

"Where's his stuff?"

The landlord shrugged.

"If he moved out, would you have seen him?"

"Yes, of course."

I stood there with my hands on my hips, confused by the empty apartment. I glanced back. "How long has he had this apartment?"

"Two years," Faron said.

"Were you ever in here with him?" McCrea asked.

The landlord shook his head.

I frowned. "Did you see him move in?"

"No."

If this was all he kept in the apartment, why have it? Did he use it as a hideaway? If so, that would mean he had an apartment somewhere else.

But Marlene knew about this apartment. How was that?

Or did Wiley use this location as a smokescreen? Is this where he told everyone he lived yet kept a separate apartment elsewhere?

I glanced at McCrea, who shrugged in return.

"Weird," he said.

It didn't make sense to lock down the apartment and search it again. Wiley wasn't killed here, and there wasn't much in evidentiary value.

I pulled out my phone and photographed the apartment and rental application.

23

I changed my clothes in the living room and tossed my suit over the armchair.

On the sports channel, the announcer prattled about the upcoming Thursday night football game between the Patriots and the Jets—something about divisional rankings and playoff implications added importance to the match-up.

I turned off the sound, then dropped into my usual corner of the couch to let my mind drift through the day and the Wiley case.

I went back to the first night and thought about the crime scene, how his body was positioned, and how we didn't find any identification on him. That might be more of a lifestyle choice than a robbery. We'd found money on him, so theft was likely out. I believed in our early theory that it was either execution or self-defense.

We hadn't found his car at the scene. His car, I thought. *Damn.*

It had been towed and secured by patrol, but I forgot to process it. I would do that in the morning. How could I have forgotten that? There were a lot of things I missed lately.

The channel featured another dynasty tonight—the 1970s Pittsburgh Steelers. Players moved about the screen as their names and positions appeared below them. With the television silenced, they ran and caught passes, made tackles, and intercepted the ball.

My thoughts drifted to Marlene and our interaction. It shouldn't have been as contentious as it was. Her description of cops, prostitutes, pimps, and johns held some truth. It clarified some of her resentment toward me and my profession, but it didn't explain the intensity of it.

I didn't know much about her, and I tried to remember what her background check showed, but I couldn't remember for the life of me. Hadn't I run her? If I didn't, it was yet another thing I intended to do, but failed to accomplish. The list was growing.

Hunger nagged, so I grabbed the other protein bar from my suit jacket. This one was as bland as the first, but it wouldn't require me to make anything or go anywhere. As soon as I was finished eating, I could go to sleep.

My watch showed a quarter to eight.

I should stay awake for at least another fifteen minutes.

WEDNESDAY
NOVEMBER 7th

24

When I arrived at the department, Glenn was at his desk.

He glanced over and said, "Morning." Then he turned his attention to his computer.

Before I could say anything, his head snapped back.

"What?" I asked.

"You look good." He sounded surprised.

"Thanks."

"Got court?"

"No," I dropped into my chair.

He observed me a little longer, then turned back to his computer. "Well, whatever it is, it's good to have you back."

That morning, I spent extra time and energy getting ready. My appointment with the psychiatrist was at nine, and the last thing I wanted to do was look like a ragbag. My hair was combed and gelled. Lieutenant Brand was right—I needed a haircut.

My face was stubble free. I took extra care in shaving, ensuring no spots were missed.

I wore my cleanest suit and pressed a white shirt. I even shined my shoes. It was the most care I'd put into my appearance in a year.

After powering on my computer, I typed the search warrant for Everson Wiley's vehicle. I expected it to be a standard warrant and to go smoothly. Detectives use boilerplates, which meant the only details needed were the elements of the crime, the location of the search to take place, and what items were being sought. If I couldn't get the warrant completed before I met with the counselor, I would finish it after.

An email popped up, letting me know Everson Wiley's autopsy was scheduled for tomorrow morning at seven. That early in the morning meant it would be the first of the day.

Glenn leaned back in his chair. "Did I tell you the latest about Carlotta Winkler?"

"No." I said as I continued to type.

"I went to her church and her pastor talked with me."

"And?"

Glenn said, "Sounds like she was a wonderful woman. He seemed truly devastated at the news of her death."

Not bothering to look his way, I said, "Huh."

"She volunteered at the church."

I glanced at my partner, but my fingers didn't stop working.

"Supposedly, she was the model parishioner."

"So, nothing new."

"On my way out, the receptionist pulled me aside to ask if she was really dead. She burst into tears when I confirmed it."

My fingers hovered over the keyboard. "Tears?"

"That's what I'm saying. Everyone loved her. She volunteered on various committees. She was one of their most loyal members. Went every Sunday and on

Wednesdays, too. I showed her the pictures I printed from Carlotta's phone. She said the others were part of the church's singles group. They met every week for their own ministry. The girl went to church a lot."

I stopped typing and faced Glenn. "She had a support network that loved her."

"Seems that way."

"A church girl was entertaining a man at her apartment." I used two fingers on each hand to air-quote entertaining. "Maybe we misunderstood what she was doing."

"The neighbor said it was a transaction. Hard to misinterpret that."

"Is her apartment still secured?"

"It is."

"Let's take another look."

"Now?"

I checked my watch. "I have something to do. Give me an hour and a half, and then I'll meet you back here."

Glenn eyed me, obviously wanting to ask the question, but keeping it to himself. He turned back to his computer. "Do your thing. Let me know when you're ready."

25

"We've never talked before."

"No," I said.

Stephen Yoder's office was on Broadway Avenue and walking distance from the Public Safety Building. Its location was supposed to be convenient for officers in the event they ever wanted, or needed, to chat with a mental health specialist.

Unfortunately, its proximity was the opposite of convenience. It meant it was always under the watchful and suspicious eyes of the department.

An officer visiting another tenant inside the same building could start a rumor of mental instability. Several members of the department had voluntarily chosen to speak with Stephen, and those actions forever pigeonholed them as weak, unstable, or unreliable.

In a world of evil, officers could never show weakness. Admitting a physical ailment was bad. Disclosing a mental ailment was tantamount to career suicide.

"The administration is worried about you," Stephen said.

"I've heard."

He sat in a maroon wingback chair. A spiral notepad was on a small round table next to him. Bookshelves lined the far wall.

Tucked tightly against the left armrest, I rested on a spongy-like couch.

"Why do you think they worry?" he asked.

"They don't like the diet I'm on."

Stephen appraised me. "How much weight have you lost?"

"About twenty."

"About?"

"Twenty-two," I said.

Stephen wore a white shirt and a brown sweater vest. His short beard was more gray than dark. "How are you losing it?"

"Counting calories mostly. No bread. No potatoes. That sort of thing."

He rubbed the underside of his beard with the back of his fingers. "How long has it taken to lose the weight?"

"Since February."

His eyes went up as he thought, then they flicked to the notepad. His thought must not have been worthy of recording because his gaze returned to me. "Doesn't seem so bad. Ten months. Two pounds a month. Give or take."

"That's what I think."

"You look fairly normal."

"Fairly?"

His smile was kind. "For a man with a recent weight loss. Your shirt collar is too big, and the shoulders are baggy. Planning to buy a new wardrobe?"

"I'm not much of a shopper."

"Did your wife do that? Buy your clothes?"

I didn't answer.

"They told me that, too." His words were gentle, and his face showed he was doing his best to be empathetic. "It's been a year now. This week, I believe."

I kept my face impassive, but frustration built inside my chest. He'd gotten a fair amount of information from the department.

"How did you handle her death?"

I opened my mouth to speak but slowly closed it. I wasn't sure how I wanted to proceed. Keeping quiet still seemed my best plan.

"You don't want to talk about it?"

My gaze drifted about his office. There were line drawings of various Spokane landmarks, but no photographs. I searched for his degree, but there was none displayed. Several moments passed before I realized he'd stopped talking, too.

We stared at each other for several moments until he asked, "When did you meet?"

It was a safe enough question. "High school."

"High school sweethearts?"

I nodded.

"Ever date another girl?"

"Not after her."

Stephen watched me and let the silence work. I knew what was occurring as I had used it for years. Stop talking and let the suspects walk themselves into their own confessions.

"I handled it fine." I couldn't believe I was the one to crack.

"Following her death, the department asked that you meet with the chaplain."

My eyes narrowed.

"It was after an incident with a public defender, correct? That doesn't sound like you handled things fine."

"You talked with the chaplain?"

"Of course not. That was between you and him. Whatever is said in this room stays between you and me."

"But you know we talked." I folded my arms, and my gaze went to a line drawing of the Monroe Street Bridge.

"Just so we're clear—" He waited until my attention returned to him. He frowned now. "I am the gatekeeper." His voice was harder than before, and its edge was sharp.

"Excuse me?"

"I'm supposed to assess you, Dallas. That's why you're here. I can recommend a return to work or some length of leave. Indefinite, if need be. Continued counseling is also an option or some combination of all those things. Make no mistake, I must give a recommendation. Whatever you do, whether you participate in our discussion or whether you choose not to, will have a bearing on that recommendation."

A song came alive inside my head. It wasn't overly loud, but it was there, making its presence known.

"If you won't talk, then we won't. I can't force you, but that will leave me with nothing to report but an uncooperative subject."

"I said I was fine."

"Which, according to the department, you are clearly not."

I clicked my teeth together.

"If you don't give me something, that's your choice. It's your job, your life, not mine."

The song looped, and I pressed a knuckle into my eye, hoping the pressure would stop the music. I was thankful it wasn't blaring. It was only circling its chorus over and over.

"Headache?" Stephen asked.

I shook my head.

He waited.

I'd been battling the music for months. No, it had now been a year. It was affecting my sleep, my days, and my work. I'd fainted more than a few times recently. Maybe that wasn't related to the songs, but how was I to know?

The weight loss wasn't normal. The agitation I constantly felt wasn't who I usually was.

The song looped again. "After she died…" I said, dropping my hand into my lap.

He uncrossed his legs and cocked his head.

"I heard music."

"What kind of music?"

"When it started, I heard all kinds. Some stuff I liked, some she liked, some I hated. I even heard the theme to *Cheers*. Know that one?" He nodded. "And the Coca-Cola song. The one about buying the world one to keep company."

Stephen leaned forward and put his elbows on his knees. "Are they full songs?"

"Snippets, mostly," I said. "Like a verse or the chorus. Maybe a guitar riff or a piano melody. Other times, it's more, but never a full song and they loop over and over."

"When do you hear these?"

"At first, I only heard them when I woke up. They'd be there, inside my head."

He gnawed on his lip before speaking. "Sort of like a dream hangover?"

I shook my head. "No. They were never from a dream. They were just… there."

"Do you think they mean anything?"

I wanted to tell him that I thought they did, *at first*. That I believed Bobbie was sending me the songs, especially when one of them helped me solve a murder. But I kept those thoughts to myself. "No. I don't think so."

"And these songs, they're still coming?"

"Yes."

"Does that worry you?"

I met his gaze. "They don't come in the morning anymore."

His brow furrowed. "When do they come?"

"Anytime. Day or night."

"In stressful situations?"

"Sometimes. Mostly, they show up for no reason."

"Are they still random?"

"Not really."

"Then how are they triggered?"

"Somebody says something, a word or a phrase, and a song plays in my head."

"You don't think about a particular song. Instead, it appears."

I nodded. "Imagine a stereo inside your head that you can't control. Occasionally, someone turns it on—really loud."

"What kind of music do you hear?"

"Mostly heavy metal and hard rock."

Stephen's face scrunched. "That's the kind of music you like?"

"I do. I *did*. Now, it bugs me."

He studied me before asking. "Is there music playing now?"

"There is."

"What song?"

"You know hard rock?"

"We're roughly the same age, Dallas. I may not enjoy that type of music, but it was tough to ignore when we were kids."

"'Alive.'"

"I don't know that one. Whose it by?"

"Pearl Jam."

He shook his head. "Is there some significance to it?"

I looked at my hands. "The song is about a boy learning that his father, his real father, the one he never met, is dead. It's about living after the dead have gone. And, yeah, I know that's survivor's guilt."

We sat quietly for a few minutes and listened to the hands on the clock tick their way around. Finally, Stephen asked, "Do you feel life is passing you by?"

"It stopped a year ago."

Stephen rubbed his beard again. "When you hear these songs, does it affect your job in any way?"

"No," I lied.

He crossed his legs, putting his left leg over his right knee. His fingers quietly drummed on the side of his shoe. "Before the music showed up, did you notice any hearing loss?"

"Not really."

"Any ringing in your ears?"

I shook my head.

"When's the last time you had your hearing tested?"

"I don't know. When I came on the department, maybe. I think they did that."

"Twenty years or so?"

"Or so."

He looked up at the ceiling as he thought. When his gaze returned, his fingers stopped dancing on his shoe. "Would you say you're depressed?"

"Huh?"

His eyebrows raised. "Do you need a definition of depression?"

"I know what depression is."

"Would you say you are?"

"No."

"Do you spend much time with family and friends?"

I shrugged.

"Got any hobbies?"

My eyes drifted to the line drawings. "No."

"What time do you normally go to bed?"

"What's normal?"

Stephen cocked his head, refusing to provide me with an answer so I could dance around the initial question.

"Ten to eleven," I lied. "Somewhere in there."

"No insomnia?"

"None."

"Would you say you have a healthy sleep pattern?"

"Except for those nights when I get called out."

Stephen's smile was soft as he nodded. "Except for those nights, yes."

He grabbed his notebook and made some notes. I remained silent while he wrote. It was only a couple of minutes, but it gave me a perspective of what suspects must feel in the interview room when we do the same thing. However, I stayed calm and watched, searching for any tells that might hint to what he was thinking. When he finished, he closed his notebook and set it aside.

"I've read about this but have never seen it," Stephen said. "You're experiencing auditory hallucinations. To put it another way, musical hallucinations."

I didn't like how it sounded either way. "Hallucinations?"

"Your mind is presenting you with a reality—the music—which isn't true. Therefore, the hallucination. You're not seeing things, are you?"

"Definitely not."

"Okay then." It was the first okay he'd spoken since our phone call. "I'm going to recommend two courses of action. First, I want you to go in for a hearing test. In a number of these cases, there is an associated loss of hearing or tinnitus."

That didn't sound so bad, I thought.

"The other course of action is continued sessions."

And there it was.

"I think there are things you're not telling me."

"I've told you everything."

"If you have, then I'll make the recommendation to the department to place you on immediate leave pending a more thorough evaluation. Or you can stay in your position, and we can meet once a week, every Wednesday let's say, as a continued check-up. Your choice."

It was a clever technique, one that we deployed with criminals all the time. Give them two choices, neither of which were good. Allow them to pick as if they had some control in the manner. The reality was they didn't. Neither did I.

"I think you're depressed, Dallas, and you're not admitting it. Until you do, we can't move forward. *You* can't move forward."

Reluctantly, I said, "I'll see you next week."

"I'll let the department know."

When he stood, we shook hands.

"If you need anything, Dallas. Please call."

26

"What was the thing?"

"Huh?"

"The thing you had to do," Glenn called out.

We were in Carlotta Winkler's apartment to take another look at the woman's home life. I was in the living room. He was in the bedroom.

I hesitated before answering. "I had to speak to Stephen."

Glenn's head appeared in the doorway. "The headshrinker?"

"The department insisted."

"*Who* insisted?"

"Ackerman."

"Of course." Glenn disappeared into the bedroom. "Then it rolled downhill from there."

"Yeah," I muttered and pulled back the couch to look behind it. We had done this previously, but I was doing it again to retrace our steps.

"You know Ackerman didn't come up with that idea on his own," Glenn said. "Someone must have put the idea there."

"I probably did."

His head reappeared in the doorway. "What?"

I shoved the couch back against the wall. "Last year, I got in trouble, and they gave me a choice to talk with Stephen or the chaplain."

"And you chose to speak to the hand of God?"

"It seemed less offensive."

He returned to the bedroom. "Didn't take you to be a religious man."

"I'm not, but I didn't want people knowing I spoke with Stephen."

"Why not?"

I sat on the couch and studied the two papers on the coffee table. "Because they'll think I'm mental. That I can't carry my water."

"No one will think that."

"I would if I knew someone was talking with him. You totally would."

He leaned out of the doorway. "I would not."

"You called him the headshrinker. You don't respect what he does any more than I do."

Glenn glanced away briefly before saying, "But I would support you."

"I'm talking with him because I have to, otherwise they'll put me on indefinite leave."

"For real? Any chance for a grievance?"

"You think I want to drag my dirty laundry through the union? Then everyone will know what's going on in my life. Better to comply with their demands, meet with the counselor, and move on with my life."

Glenn stepped fully into the living room and thumbed to the bedroom. "We didn't miss anything in there."

I nodded and continued to study the paperwork on the coffee table. There were only two items—the church sermon and the denial for citizenship from U.S. Customs and Immigration Services.

"Think it will help?"

"What?"

"Talking with the shrink— I mean, Stephen."

Secretly, I hoped so, but I said, "I doubt it."

Glenn nodded and started opening cupboards in the kitchen. He noisily moved items around.

I pulled the government document closer and stared at the signature block. "We should talk with Lynn Slater."

"The woman that denied her application?"

I picked up the document and walked over to my partner. I handed him the piece of paper.

"You watch football, right?"

Glenn patted his chest. "Is the Pope Catholic?"

"Who's the greatest wide receiver to ever play for the Pittsburgh Steelers?"

"Lynn Swann," he said, then his eyes went to the paper. "Huh."

"That's what I thought."

"Maybe we should ask him why he denied her."

"Ask him why," I said. "It's the only thing that even comes close."

When we returned to the department, Glenn set about getting us a meeting with Lynn Slater, and I called up the file on Everson Wiley. I wanted to type up my notes from Marlene Anderson's interview.

As the report came up, I flashed back to my fainting spell in her office. I didn't tell anyone in command about it, and I hadn't told Stephen about the recent rash of them. They were dangerous episodes which would certainly get me sent for a medical evaluation at minimum and could get me relegated to some sort of light duty away from Major Crimes. I didn't want that.

After Bobbie's death, I avoided coming back to the job. Now, it was something to hold on to. Giving it up seemed unthinkable.

The fainting spells might be attributable to my diet, or lack thereof. I needed to force myself to eat, to get back on a regular schedule of consumption. Whether I cared for food right now didn't matter. If I wanted to work, I needed fuel. I made a mental note to get another protein bar.

Thinking of that food item reminded me Marlene and her co-workers saw me pass out. I hoped there was no reason they'd want to notify the department about the incident.

My fingers hovered over the keyboard. I switched applications on my computer and called up the NCIC search engine. I didn't have much to go on except her first and last name and a general age—late thirties.

Several Marlene Andersons popped up in our area, but only one matched the general description, and her background was alarming. When I called up a booking photo, it left no doubt it was the woman I'd met.

Marlene Priscilla Anderson had multiple arrests and convictions for prostitution. I leaned back and crossed my arms. That's why she was drawn to those women.

She was one of them. Well, *had* been.

I scrolled through her record. There were multiple arrests for drugs with some resulting convictions. She had a single driving with a suspended license arrest and conviction. There was also a single public nudity arrest with no conviction. A handful of contacts had been recorded as Field Interviews reports.

A couple of the FIs were available digitally, so I called them up one at a time. Each report identified Marlene as a "known prostitute" working in the East Sprague area. Both FIs indicated the officers did not have anything to arrest her on, hence the informational report. They were written about six months apart about six years ago.

I went back to the NCIC screen. Marlene's record was clean within the last six years. No more arrests, no more contacts.

But there were all those previous arrests that I was curious about.

I printed the screen and pushed away from my desk.

"Hey," Glenn said, covering his phone's receiver.

"Huh?"

"Lynn's voice mail. It's a woman's voice. Maybe we got it wrong."

"Or maybe it's his assistant."

Glenn turned to the phone and said, "Hi, this is Detective Higgins with the Spokane Police Department. This message is for Lynn Slater."

***

The county records department had changed drastically since I started. Previously, it was a paper behemoth. It had to be as they handled reports from both Spokane PD and Spokane County Sheriff's Office, the two largest departments in the region, as well as several smaller jurisdictions within the county. Records received, entered, and stored all the reports.

As each organization went digital, the need for paper records declined, but the demand for an efficient records department remained. They were slowly archiving all the old reports to a digital filing system, but that was a slower process than most had predicted. In the Spokane Police Department alone, each year generated almost three hundred thousand reports.

Helen Dorval met me at the counter. Her smile was bright. "Dallas Nash. Long time, no talk."

I handed her the screen print-out. "Can you pull these?"

Her smile faded as she slipped the paper from my hands. "Been ages, but straight to business, huh?"

"Sorry," I said. "Just busy."

Helen's gaze fell to the paper. She started to say something, but I cut her off.

"How quickly can I get this?"

"We'll get on it, but you still need to fill out a request." She dropped the paper on the counter and reached for a blank document in a stack marked *File Requests*. "You on a diet or something?"

"Or something."

"What are you doing? I'm doing the Weight Watchers thing and I'm only down eleven pounds."

I didn't reply. Helen stood nearby for a few moments as I started ticking off boxes on the document. When I completed the form, I looked up and she was gone. I left the form in the request bin and went back to my desk.

Before arriving at the property room's vehicle warehouse, I got the search warrant signed and checked out the keys from evidence storage.

Corporal Mark Tripp met me inside, ready to take part in the evidentiary search. Part of a corporal's duties were to photograph crime scenes or potential ones like this. We both wore blue latex gloves, and a camera hung around Tripp's neck.

It was a late model Ford Expedition that was extremely clean on the outside. There was no damage, not a ding on it.

The key fob unlocked the doors. I opened the driver's door and Mark moved to the rear passenger side.

"All seats are down," Tripp said.

"Sort of funky in here. Like body odor and—"

"Too much cologne."

I scanned the driver's seat and floorboard before grabbing the steering wheel to pull myself in.

"I think there's blood back here."

I stopped before getting completely into the vehicle. I moved to the rear passenger door and opened it. From the opposite side of the vehicle, Tripp pointed to an area near the middle of where the third-row seats lay down.

It was all black fabric, and I struggled to see what he saw. I moved my head slightly and saw a darkened pattern. "You sure that's blood?"

"Looks like it. Not a lot, but I'll verify."

He stepped away from the SUV and went to his evidence kit. A moment later, he returned with a small bottle of Luminol and a portable black light. He sprayed a bit onto the area he suspected, and it illuminated a bright blue.

Tripp continued to spray the back of the trunk with the Luminol, but the blood seemed to be contained to a limited area. When he finished, he asked, "What do you think?"

"Maybe he was shot here and dumped on the street."

"Doesn't look like enough blood for that."

"Yeah," I agreed. I scanned the interior walls of the vehicle.

"And I haven't found any casings. Maybe the killer was meticulous and picked them up."

"Maybe."

"Or maybe it was a revolver."

I checked the back of the seats. They looked perfectly normal. "I don't see any damage in here from the round that exited his body."

Tripp scanned the interior now and confirmed my suspicions. "So, it's unlikely he was shot inside the vehicle."

The blood spot was in the middle of the floorboard. "Maybe it was from sex, and she was menstruating."

"That's a lot of blood from menstruation. Think it was rape?"

"Who knows?" I said and flashed back to the *Dead Men Don't Rape* sticker hanging in the Her Freedom waiting room. "Just in case, cut that fabric out and test it."

He nodded.

I returned to the front of the vehicle and continued the search. There was the normal detritus people leave in their cars. Napkins, gum wrappers, and receipts from stores. I also found several empty condom wrappers, a marijuana pipe, and a bottle of unidentified pills.

After stepping back out of the vehicle, I said, "Nothing else."

"I'll fingerprint it, then cut the carpet."

I handed him the bottle of pills. "Would you identify these and put them on property when you log the carpet and blood?"

"Not a problem."

29

In the department's parking lot, I leaned into the backseat of my car to grab a box of macaroons. I had stopped by a specialty bakery around the corner from the property room.

A male voice said, "You're a hard man to find."

I righted myself and left the confections in the car.

Detective James Morgan leaned against the trunk. He wore a brown leather jacket, blue jeans, and scuffed leather boots. He was a thick-chested man with an angular face. It was the type of face made for fighting and intimidation.

"Excuse me?"

"Heard you were asking around about me, so I made it a point to find you. But you're never around. Out screwing off?"

"I'm not like you."

Morgan's lip twitched. "What do you want, Nash?"

"Let's talk inside."

"No," he said, "we'll talk here."

I folded my arms, but a flash of officer safety concerns zipped through my brain. I'd never been anxious around another officer before. I lowered my hands and held them at the ready.

Morgan noticed my change in body position and a smile creased his lips.

"Joey Greene," I said.

Something I couldn't read flashed in his eyes.

"There's a rumor going around a cop is protecting her."

"Don't believe everything you hear on the street."

"When several people say she's got a badge daddy, I start to listen."

"Badge daddy?"

"It's cute, don't you think?"

"Those people talking—they actually say my name?"

"They're too scared to say."

Morgan smirked. "So, my name wasn't mentioned."

"No."

"Then why are you asking around about me?"

"Because you rescued her, took her to Sacred Heart. Her accusation led to your team killing three men. We never heard the rumors of a badge daddy during the investigation. I wonder if things would have turned out the same way if we had. Does your team know?"

Morgan pushed off the trunk, straightened, and squared his shoulders. It wasn't a big signal, but it was enough. The man was ready to fight. "It's not what you think."

"You have a relationship with a prostitute."

"She's a snitch."

"She's registered as a CI, then?"

Morgan frowned. "It's an informal thing."

"Then what's the deal with the badge daddy rumor?"

"She had a pimp. He was smacking her around. I made him stop."

"Allowing her to run renegade."

"What business is it of yours?"

"She's the only independent down there. That gets a lot of attention."

"And she gives me a lot of information."

"Is that the only thing she's giving you?"

He stepped toward me, his voice low and threatening. "Watch your accusations, cake-eater. You're not looking so good."

Accept's "Balls to the Wall" blasted in my head. I did my best to give Morgan a hard look, but the screeching guitars in my head caused me to wince.

His eyes narrowed, and his head cocked as if he heard the same music.

My heart pounded and my mouth turned dry. My fingers tingled and I felt woozy.

When he raised his eyebrows in a questioning manner, I said, "What?"

"Are you threatening me, Nash?" I barely heard him over the music.

He was so close I could smell his breath.

"You need to be brought down a peg, Nash." His lips pulled back like a snarling dog.

The world tilted, and I put a hand on my car as nonchalantly as I could. The music continued to blare inside my skull.

"I'm not accusing you of anything."

"Sure as hell sounds like it." I could barely hear him.

"I'm trying to understand things."

My fingers tried to tighten around the car's curved roof. Fear of fainting gripped me. The thudding rhythm in my head sounded like it was coming from the bottom of a well.

"Skells talk shit," Morgan growled. "If you were any kind of detective, you would know that."

I focused on my breathing, deep inhalations now, desperately trying to settle the spinning world.

"You going to puke, Nash? Can't hold your mud?"

"Food poisoning," I muttered.

He stepped back.

My eyes locked onto his as my world remained unsettled. "There's a lot of talk."

"Doesn't mean you should believe any of it."

I wanted to turn and run away but doing so wasn't an option. Not as a cop. Not ever in front of Jim Morgan.

"What are you gonna do about this?" he asked.

"The pimp she had?" My voice sounded fragile. "The one you made go away? He's dead."

Morgan inhaled then and shoved his hands into the pockets of his jacket. "That's what this is about? You're on the hunt and you got my scent in your nostrils? You think maybe I did him?"

"I'm trying to find a killer." I sounded weak. He had to have heard it.

"I didn't do your guy."

The music faded and the world calmed. I let go of the car and straightened. "What about Joey?"

"She didn't kill him either."

"I want to talk with her."

Morgan checked his watch. "I'll make sure she finds you."

"That's convenient."

"I'm a team player." Morgan didn't bother to dampen his sarcasm.

"Did you know about the homicide?"

"Sure, but he was a pimp. He never provided any intel. As far as I was concerned, he served no purpose in my life. His death neither helped nor hurt the balance of power."

"What about Damon Warfield?"

"The Great White Hope?" Morgan chuckled. "The only reason he had any success down there was Junior let him stay. He'll try to assume the turf, but it's Tiger's for the taking. Damon's days are numbered."

"You know Tiger?"

Morgan nodded. "Raekwon Gaskin. He's a climber. He'll easily suck up East Sprague. Junior was the only thing that kept him at bay."

"I want to talk with him."

"Get that on your own, Nash, unless you want to do it my way. Fair warning, he doesn't like me. We have history."

"Who don't you have a history with?"

Morgan shrugged.

"Get me a sit down with Joey. That's all I need from you."

I reached into my car then and grabbed the box of macaroons.

"Sweet tooth?" Morgan asked.

"They're for Debbie in Crime Analysis."

Morgan's grin was malicious. "Making a move on the number cruncher. I would never have expected that from you, Nash. She's a little loose in the caboose, but nice work nonetheless."

"It's not like that."

"It never is until it is." He walked away, chuckling. He said it again, "It never is until it is."

I stared at the box of multicolored sweets in my hands. They weren't for anything more than to apologize about the misunderstanding over the donut. But I didn't want to send the wrong signal. Hell, I didn't want to send any signal.

I tossed the box of sweets back in and slammed the car door.

***

When I walked into the department, Detectives Delaney and Burkett were walking out.

"Quinn. Marci," I said, with a nod.

"Hey," Quinn responded with a polite smile.

Marci, however, ignored me and continued out the door.

Her partner turned back and shrugged. "Sorry, man."

Maybe I should have given her the box of cookies.

I was about to sit at my desk when Glenn returned to his cubicle.

He pulled his coat from the back of his chair and slipped it on. "I've got a meeting set with Lynn Slater tomorrow morning at nine, if you want to go. Set it up with his assistant."

"I'll join you."

"How'd the search of the pimp's truck go?"

"Found some blood in the back compartment."

With his coat on and open, Glenn put his hands on his hips. "Think it might have something to do with the shooting?"

"Maybe it's got nothing to do with nothing. These guys, they live a violent life. Blood seems to follow them around."

Glenn shook his head. "There's a thought to end my day on."

As he walked by, he patted the back of my neck. "Get some sleep, Dal. We've got another big day tomorrow."

Before leaving, I ran the name of Raekwon Gaskin. In a moment, my screen was filled with his history. He was thirty-five, black, six foot two, and weighed two hundred pounds.

His criminal history was impressive in a weird sort of way. The charges went back to his childhood. Vehicle theft, possession of stolen property, malicious mischief, and various levels of assault. A suspect in a homicide. Yet, there were no charges related to promoting prostitution.

Marlene's words about the difference in enforcement rang true.

I printed his history, added it to my file, then headed home.

30

The sports channel showed the football dynasty of the 1980s—the San Francisco 49ers. I stared at the television, watching the famous plays of Joe Montana, Dwight Clark, and Ronnie Lott. I had silenced the commentators since my thoughts were elsewhere. They were on my meeting with Stephen Yoder and his question, "Do you feel life is passing you by."

I had answered truthfully when I said, "It stopped a year ago."

It seemed silly to say she was my everything but, by the crater her loss left in my world, there was no other way to describe it.

Life *had* left me behind. Every day, I mourned—lamenting the absence of her, grieving the loss of our time together. I had not moved forward since that day. I stayed stuck in the same spot where I had been the moment I learned of her death.

What good is living without her if this was how it was going to be?

A melodic guitar riff began. Fates Warning's "Life in Still Water" played loudly in my head. I closed my eyes and listened to the few words looping in my head.

It's a song about being stuck, afraid to make a change and move forward.

Did I fear moving ahead and losing her memory? Or was I afraid of forever living in the purgatory of aloneness?

I sat upright as the music continued to loop.

On the television, the 49ers celebrated yet another Super Bowl win. I stood, felt along the screen's edge until I found the button, and shut it off. The house was suddenly dark.

I turned on a lamp and went to my CD collection. Since our collection was alphabetized, it took only a moment to find the album, *Parallels*. I turned on the stereo, dropped the disc into the player, and clicked to the second song.

With a spin of the dial, the volume was cranked. The opening guitar riff struggled to overwhelm the music in my head. I turned it off.

I stood in the middle of the living room with my eyes closed, listening to the music in the lyrics playing for an audience of one.

Was this the life I longed for—stuck in limbo and suffering alone? Of course not.

I put on my shoes and coat and headed for the door.

***

My flashlight illuminated her headstone.

Even though the cemetery had been closed for many hours, that didn't stop me. I climbed over the fence. I probably could have found her blindfolded.

"When you died, I died." It was a redundant statement. I had told her this many times over the past year.

Several cars raced by the cemetery with their horns blaring. They faded into the distance before I continued.

"I went back to work because I thought the department needed me. It gave me a reason to be, but you know what? They don't need me. I pretend I make a difference, that my work makes a difference, but it doesn't. I could leave tomorrow, and they'll replace me. The world will go on. I wasn't the first detective, and I won't be the last.

Bad guys will continue to do bad things and someone else will be there to track them down. I'm only one spin in the cycle."

Tears welled in my eyes.

"And if I'm not that special, then why do I hang around here?"

Another car drove by.

"Without you—" The words caught in my throat. I started a new thought. "Life was special with you. It's not like that anymore."

I shoved my free hand into my pocket. The flashlight dangled loosely in the other as I slowly traced her name with the beam of light.

"So, this is what I'm thinking—either I start living again or I join you, but I can't be in the middle. It's killing me. Things are happening—"

The marble slab stared silently up.

"I don't want you to worry, but the music has gotten worse—so bad it hurts. I've fainted—a few times now."

A plane flew overhead.

"I know what I'm saying, and I know you would disapprove, but you're not here. You're not the one left behind. I hope you'll forgive me whichever way I choose."

Outside the cemetery, a car pulled up. A door opened, but it never closed. A radio squawked, but it was quickly silenced. I turned off my flashlight and tucked it into my back pocket.

It took a couple of minutes for him to find me. He illuminated me with his flashlight.

"Excuse me, sir? The cemetery is closed."

I faced him and lifted my hands.

He briefly lifted his flashlight to my face. "Detective Nash?" It was the rookie, Hoffman. We'd met at Everson Wiley's crime scene. "What are you doing here, sir?"

"Paying respects."

He moved his flashlight to the marker. It lingered there a moment.

"I was having a bad night."

"I'm sorry, sir." Hoffman tucked his flashlight into his armpit and let his hands hang together in front of him. "I'll let radio know I didn't find anyone."

"No," I said. "I'm trespassing. I shouldn't be here."

He stared in the awkward way rookies watch senior officers and detectives.

"I should go," I said.

"I can give you a few more—"

"Now is fine."

Hoffman turned and waited for me to join him. As we walked, we remained silent.

Near the road, the man-gate was open. He must have gotten the code from dispatch. Hoffman locked it behind us, and we shook hands.

"I'd appreciate it if we kept this between us," I said.

The rookie nodded. "I understand."

THURSDAY
NOVEMBER 8th

31

The medical examiner, Rima Sepulveda, leaned over the body of Everson Wiley and announced, "Three entry wounds. One exit."

Sepulveda was in her late forties. A dash of gray highlighted her dark hair. She wore blue scrubs and a pair of clear goggles. A paper mask hung loosely around her neck.

Wiley lay naked on the stainless-steel gurney, his body brightly illuminated not only by the suspended lamp, but by the autopsy room lights.

Standing ten feet away, dressed in scrubs, I was there to witness the autopsy. It wasn't necessary to make a case, but it was something I tried to do whenever I was the lead investigator.

She glanced in my direction. "You look tired."

"Late night."

"And you've lost more weight."

"Yeah, but I'm done. I've gone too far."

"You're on the unhealthy side of skinny now."

"That's your professional diagnosis, Doctor?"

"Hey, my patients are all dead people. Think about that when I call you unhealthy looking."

"I'll eat a cheeseburger at lunch."

"Don't do that. Your heart will thank you."

Rima's attention returned to Wiley as she moved around the gurney, continuing her visual inspection.

The clock on the wall showed a couple of minutes after seven. It took willpower to drag myself down there that early. I would have preferred to stay on the couch.

"You didn't come for the woman who jumped," Rima said. When I didn't answer, she cast a sideways glance.

"When was that?"

"Yesterday. What a mess. Not the worst I've ever seen, but close."

"You've seen worse?"

She lifted an eyebrow.

"Of course you have."

Rima continued circling Wiley.

"What did you find on the girl?"

"Nothing."

"Nothing?"

"And you checked for pregnancy? STDs?"

She smirked.

"Right. Sorry."

The room tilted, and a wooziness overwhelmed me. I tasted bile.

"You okay, Dallas? You're looking sort of green."

"I'm *good*," I said. "It's this place." I made a circling motion with my hand.

"I forget sometimes everyone isn't as oblivious to it like me."

The room leveled, and the wooziness faded. "Back to the woman," I said. "Nothing?"

"That's what I said. Except for the incredible number of broken bones, but you'd expect that from the height she fell."

Inside my head, a stuttering rhythm started, and a voice yelled. It was the opening for Alice in Chain's "Them Bones," a song about us all ending up in the grave someday. The room tilted again, and I reached out for a nearby counter to steady myself.

Rima walked over. "You don't look good."

"Under the weather."

She stepped back and lifted the mask over her face. "Stay away. I've got tickets to the symphony this weekend. I don't want to get sick."

"I promise not to get too close."

"You can take off."

"I'm good." I said, my voice developing an edge as "Them Bones" looped inside my skull.

"All right, relax. I was only worried about you."

Rima returned to the body and flashed me a disapproving look. Her foot pressed the floor pedal below the gurney to begin the audio recording. She lifted a file from a nearby stand and read, "Everson Otis Wiley, the second. Gunshot victim. Today is November eighth."

She grabbed a scalpel, leaned over his chest, and inserted it into his skin.

"Them Bones" exploded inside my brain. I reached out and grabbed the counter.

Rima turned to me, but I couldn't hear her. My stomach flipped upside down as the music wailed inside my head. Bile rose in my throat and panic constricted my chest.

I spun and bolted, slamming into the double doors of the autopsy room, throwing them open. The song reached a crescendo as I sprinted down the hall. I covered my mouth and held back what wanted to escape. Lowering my shoulder, I banged into the restroom door, thrusting it open. In the middle of the room, I stopped and vomited.

The world seesawed, and I stumbled into a stall, slamming the door closed behind me. I bent over the toilet and retched again.

***

An hour later, Rima walked out of the autopsy room. Her mask hung loosely around her neck.

Seated on a bench in the hallway, my head rested against the wall. After cleaning up my spew from the restroom floor, I removed my scrubs.

"You okay, Dallas?"

I nodded. "Probably sick." I was embarrassed I ran from the autopsy room.

She put her hand on my shoulder, no longer worried about catching an illness. "A lot of guys get affected at one time or other. Even those who have seen it before."

"I'm sorry I snapped at you."

"It happens. I'm a bear when I don't feel well."

"Regardless, I'm still sorry."

She patted my shoulder a couple of times then stepped back.

"What did you learn?" I asked.

"I removed two rounds." Rima handed me a small plastic bag with as many bullets.

The bag was sealed and labeled with her signature. I held the baggie up to the hallway's fluorescent lights. The small rounds were likely from a .22 caliber gun. Maybe a .25. Ballistics would confirm it, but the smaller bullets were one of the few I felt comfortable assuming, even if it might make an ass out of me.

"Based upon their location," she continued, "and their clustering, they destroyed his heart. One severed his aorta, another got stuck inside there. The third detoured out his left armpit. All three chewed the heart up so bad he was probably dead before he hit the ground."

I stood and shoved the baggie into my pocket.

"Thanks, Rima."

"Go home, Dallas. Eat some soup. Take a nap."

"I'll do that."

"Sure, you will," she said. "More than likely you'll put that on property and go back to the department."

"What can I say?"

She patted my arm once more, then headed off down the hallway.

32

The Thomas S. Foley Federal Building stands at the corner of Monroe Street and Riverside Avenue. An eclectic mix of services resided on its ten floors. The U.S. District Court and the local office of the Department of Justice are located there. The Internal Revenue Service is on the fourth floor while the U.S. Marshals are on the second. The Citizenship and Immigration Services Field Offices are on the sixth.

Before we made it through the lobby's walk-through scanner, a security guard waved Glenn and me to the side. He stepped away from his counterpart and smiled.

Ian Deaton retired from SPD several years ago. He had been a Property Crimes detective who hit his twenty-year mark and left. Today, he wore a blue blazer and tan slacks. There was a bulge under his left arm. He was grayer and heavier than I remembered, but he also looked happier and more relaxed.

After the three of us shook hands, Glenn asked, "How you been, buddy?"

Ian and my partner had been friends through the years. Not that Ian was a bad guy, but his personality aligned more with my partner's than mine.

"Good," Ian said. "Real good."

"Like the security gig?"

Ian glanced around, making sure his counterpart couldn't hear him. "It's mind numbing, but it pays the bills until I can start collecting full retirement. Plus, I can get a second retirement through the government."

"Double dipping," Glenn said and stuck out his fist.

Ian bumped it with his own. "Who are you guys here to see?"

"Lynn Slater."

"Oh." Ian frowned.

"What's up?"

"Guy's a douche. He in trouble for something?"

"We're following up on an investigation. We want to know why he denied a woman citizenship."

"Did you schedule an appointment?"

"We did," my partner said, checking his watch. "And we're going to be late if we don't get a move on."

Ian pointed at both of our waists. "You guys carrying?"

We nodded.

"Can't let you in with them."

"Serious?" Glenn asked.

"No one comes in with them. You need to leave them in your car. Come back and I'll send you up."

"Not sure I like doing my job without a gun," Glenn said.

I put my hand on my partner's shoulder. "If no one has a gun in the building, we've got nothing to worry about."

Glenn clucked his tongue. "We'll see about that."

***

After securing our weapons in the trunk of our car, we returned to the Federal Building's lobby. Ian Deaton waved us to the front of the waiting line. We passed through the metal detectors without incident.

Glenn got Ian's phone number, and we shook hands with him a final time before the elevator took us to the sixth floor.

As we entered the Citizenship and Immigration Services Field Office, a receptionist greeted us. She had light brown skin, a purple blouse, and bored eyes. She blinked a couple of times, waiting for us to reveal our reason for the visit.

"Detectives Higgins and Nash," my partner said, "to see Lynn Slater."

The receptionist checked something on her computer before lifting the phone. When she hung up, she said, "He'll be with you in a moment."

The lobby was shallow, leaving us near the elevators and not allowing us to see behind the receptionist. The walls were shiny dark wood with the doors cut in the same material, attempting to make them disappear completely.

A loud click sounded, likely a magnetic lock releasing, and the door to the left of the receptionist opened.

A man in his mid-fifties stood in the entryway. He wore blue jeans and brown shoes. His plaid shirt was tight around his belly and his belt buckle pointed toward the ground. His hair was unnaturally dark. He seemed underdressed as a representative for the U.S. government.

"Detectives?"

"Mr. Slater?" Glenn said.

"Come on back," he said with an exaggerated wave.

When we were in the rear offices, he let the heavy door swing closed. It clicked into place behind us.

The Federal Building was constructed in the late sixties, but the office of Citizenship and Immigration Services looked as if it had been remodeled only a few years ago. Everything seemed new.

Offices lined the outer ring, and the interior appeared to be where the assistants or junior investigators sat. Each computer on every desk had two large monitors attached to it. Inside the glass-walled conference room, a large-screen television hung prominently.

Through the windows, the view of Spokane's north side was spectacular. The southern view was over the rest of downtown. It wasn't as majestic, but it would have still been a great sight to see every day.

Slater had one of the southern offices. He led us into his office, then closed the door.

The chairs for Glenn and me were new and comfortable. Slater's was a high-back leather affair. Everything in the office exuded the idea that no expense had been spared.

Slater pushed away a stray hair from his forehead. "Any trouble in finding the building?"

Glenn and I looked at each other.

The immigration officer chuckled. "Of course not. You're cops. You should be able to find anything in town. Am I right?"

"Mr. Slater," Glenn said.

"Call me Lynn," he said with a smile full of incredibly white teeth. His eyes jumped from my partner to me, then back to Glenn.

"Lynn, we'd like to ask you a few questions about—"

"Carlotta Winkler. That's why you called my assistant and set up this appointment."

"That's correct."

My gaze drifted around the office as Glenn engaged him. On Slater's wall were photos of him with a black Labrador. The photos had been taken through the years as the dog had grown bigger and thicker. Slater was seen in various hunting vests and proudly displaying a shotgun and some type of pheasant.

"How can I help?"

"Ms. Winkler is dead."

The color drained from his face. "Dead?"

"That's right," Glenn said.

"What's that got to do with me?" There was an odd waver in his voice.

I glanced at Glenn, but his attention was fully on Slater.

"She fell to her death."

"Was it… suspicious or something?"

"We're investigating it as a homicide."

Slater pulled back slightly. "A homicide?"

"That's right."

"Where did this occur?"

"At the Western Bank Building."

He blinked multiple times. "The woman who jumped on Friday?"

"*Fell*," Glenn corrected. "She was the woman who fell. We don't know if she jumped."

Slater must have realized what Glenn was intimating. "She might have been pushed?"

"That's what we're trying to determine."

"You don't think—"

"Think what?" I said, jumping into the conversation. Something about Slater bothered me. We never play good cop, bad cop. We did, however, use different tones. Glenn had been respectful so far, which meant I should be blunt.

Slater swallowed before responding. "You don't think I could have had something to do with it?"

"Did you?" I asked.

My partner leaned in and studied Slater's reaction.

"No." Slater's voice was soft now. Then he repeated with emphasis, "No! I most certainly did not. I resent—"

Cutting him off, I said, "Duly noted." I returned my attention to the pictures on the walls.

Glenn took over the interview again. "You rejected her citizenship request."

"I— I don't see how that is relevant."

"We don't know if it is," Glenn said. "Mr. Slater— Lynn, we're trying to understand why a woman would possibly want to harm herself. She had a support network. Many people loved her. And from the people we've talked with, she seemed like a nice person who was building a better life for herself."

"I don't know about that."

I turned around to see Slater's face harden and his normal color return.

"How's that?" Glenn asked.

"She lied on her application."

"How did she do that?"

He crossed his arms. "That's privileged information."

"She's dead," I said. "It's classified a homicide."

His eyes lifted to mine. "Still."

"*Still?*" I repeated.

Glenn raised a hand, calling Slater's attention to him. "You won't tell us how she lied on her application?"

"She lied, and I rejected her. I don't answer to you."

"Perhaps," Glenn said, "she killed herself because of that denial and revocation of her work permit."

Slater sniffed dismissively. "If she did, she did it on her own. I didn't have a hand in her jumping— or falling, as you put it."

Glenn cocked his head. "Her record back home was clean, and her employer said she was doing fine work. I'm trying to understand what you saw that would cause her to be denied—"

"We're done." Slater stood and moved to his office door.

Glenn's eyes shifted to me, and he raised an eyebrow.

I shrugged.

My partner turned back to Slater and said, "Thank you for your time, sir. We'll be in touch."

***

Neither of us said anything until we recovered our weapons from the trunk of Glenn's car.

"What do you think?" my partner asked.

I looked up at the building, counted windows, and imagined where Slater's office might be. I thought someone was watching us, but it was only my imagination. There was no way to see that clearly. It was a trick of light and shadows.

"He's hiding something," I said and climbed into the car.

33

Raekwon Gaskin's last known address was on the fourth floor of the Hope Apartments in the west end of downtown. The Hope had originally been built as a single-room-occupancy hotel and decades ago was converted to apartments. It was one of the few places still available for low-income, market-rate housing.

Tiger's photograph was in the folder I carried. While I searched for Gaskin, Glenn returned to the station to assemble a profile on Lynn Slater.

There was no security at the front desk of the Hope, only an on-duty manager behind a Plexiglas window. I didn't bother stopping in to announce my presence. Instead, I walked through the lobby, avoided the elevator, and ascended the stairs.

Cinderella's "Still Climbing" burst to life inside my head. The military style snare drum riff was instantly recognizable. My shoulders slumped and my feet slowed.

It disappointed me that the music continued. I had hoped my discussion with Bobbie about getting involved in life would have made the songs stop. After a couple of more steps, it occurred to me that I hadn't done anything yet—I only proclaimed I wanted things to change. A transformation needed to occur, only I didn't know what that looked like.

An overweight man who doesn't change his diet and won't exercise is going to remain fat. He has no one to blame but himself.

"Still Climbing" looped mockingly around as I ascended step after step. Each footfall brought a slight increase in volume until my entire world was this song.

On the third-floor landing, the world rolled. I grasped the banister, kicked my head back, and inhaled deeply. It didn't help. It made things worse.

The world tilted in the opposite direction, and I dropped to a knee. I exhaled forcefully and almost vomited. Releasing the banister, I collapsed to the floor. Carefully, I dragged myself to the wall and sat with my back against it. Bending over with my head between my knees, I struggled to get any air.

The staccato snare drum rhythm continued as guitars squealed over them.

A woman came up the stairs. As she passed, she hesitated, as if considering the idea of rendering help. She didn't, though, and kept walking.

When the song faded, so did the wooziness. I stood and warily took another stair. No music accompanied it.

On the fourth floor, I banged on the door, the sharp raps echoing in the wide hallway. A chain slid behind the door and the dented knob turned.

A mid-twenties woman with acne scars stood in the doorway. She wore a tank top with no bra and light-green pajama bottoms. Over her left breast, a tattoo of a sunflower poked out from underneath her shirt.

She leaned out to survey the hallway. Satisfied there was no one watching, she straightened and ran her fingers through her wet hair.

"Detective Nash," I said. "Spokane Police Department."

Her eyebrows lifted briefly before settling back into place.

"And you are?"

She pursed her lips as if to twist them into a lock to maintain her silence.

"Is Raekwon Gaskin home?"

The woman rested against the door frame and crossed her arms, which pushed her breasts up. It seemed a deliberate act, but I didn't break eye contact. She glanced slowly down at herself, then remade eye contact.

"Know where he's at?"

The woman's head moved slightly, as if she was dancing to an unheard rhythm. "Don't know the man," she said.

With that, she stepped back and swung the door, but I stopped it from closing. Her eyes snapped to my hand.

"Let's try this again," I said.

She opened her mouth slightly and shoved her tongue under her lower lip. It moved its way slowly around. My eyes remained on hers as she performed this clumsy routine. When she finished, she asked, "Got a card?"

I looked past her into the small apartment. It was sparsely decorated with mostly feminine touches.

"He live here?"

"Want to come in, maybe sit for a while?"

"What's your name?"

She gnawed on the inside of her lip before saying, "Ashlee."

I pulled the list of prostitutes from my pocket, ran my finger down page one, then flipped to the second.

"What's that?" she asked.

When I found her picture, I said, "Pulver." With satisfaction, I folded the list. "Ashlee Pulver."

Her brow furrowed.

"How often does he come around?"

She frowned.

"Who?"

"Maybe we should have this conversation down at the station."

"We can have it inside. I'll make you comfortable."

"I only want to talk with the man."

"Is he in trouble?"

"No more than you."

That brought a smile to her face.

"How often does he—"

"Daily."

"To collect?"

Her eyes rolled to the ceiling as she thought. When they dropped back into place, she said, "I don't know what you're talking about."

"Where's he live?"

She shrugged. "He comes here when he wants. He goes when he wants. That's what I know."

"It's important he and I talk. Where do I find him?"

"Go toward the light."

"What?"

She pointed downstairs. "The Lamplighter."

***

I yanked open the door and sunlight flooded the establishment. Several loud groans emanated from inside. As I crossed the threshold, someone yelled, "Shut da door!"

An aroma of stale beer and cigarette smoke hung in the air. The cigarette smell surprised me, since smoking inside an establishment had been illegal for nearly twenty years. It was probably baked into the walls, furniture, and gold shag carpet.

The floor covering was threadbare in the heavily trafficked areas. Why anyone ever put carpet in bars was a mystery, but I'd seen it more than once.

The clientele of the Lamplighter was eclectic. Some white, some black. Mostly old, a few young. More men than women. For the noon hour, the dingy dive was nearly full.

Nearby, a tall, thin bartender watched me intently. His ashy gray skin made it hard to determine his age. He was dressed nicely although his clothes were many years out of style.

I consulted the photograph in my folder and scanned the room again.

Raekwon Gaskin, the man known as Tiger, sat at one of the low tables with short vinyl chairs. He wore a white sweatshirt with the hoodie dangling from the rear of his head. He had a glass of brown liquor in his hand.

A woman in her early thirties sat near him. Her dark skin shone under the light hanging directly above her. She leaned into Tiger, whispering intently into his ear. Her heavy coat was draped over a nearby chair. She wore a shimmering green blouse.

He nodded as she spoke, a small grin hinting at the edges of his lips.

An early seventies funk song played. It was something I'd heard before but couldn't place.

Gaskin's eyes locked onto me as I closed the folder in my hands. He put his drink on the table and his other hand dropped under the table. I hesitated, switched the folder to my left hand, and pushed my coat away from my gun. Tiger whispered something to the woman, and she faced me.

"Get you something?" the bartender asked.

"No."

My eyes stayed locked on Gaskin.

"Don't want any trouble," the bartender said. "This is a nice place."

As I approached, the woman pushed back from the table and stood. She smoothed her blouse and stepped directly in front of me. She looked familiar.

"Hey, baby."

I tried to step around her, but she lightly put a hand on my chest.

"Where you goin' in such a hurry?"

"Get out of my way."

"Buy me a drink. Let's get to know each other."

Snatching her arm, I said, "Lady, I'm a cop."

I pulled her to the side and stepped toward Gaskin.

Something caught my foot, and I fell. I grabbed a chair to stabilize myself, but it slipped out from underneath me. I landed on the floor.

Gaskin sprinted toward the door. I reached for his foot, but he jumped over my outstretched hand and was outside.

As I stood, the woman reached down, entangling me with her arms. "What happened, baby? Are you okay?"

"You tripped me."

She held a hand to her chest. "I din't do that. You fell all by yourself."

I pointed at her and was about to say something when the bartender interrupted.

"Sir, I think you tripped yourself. The lady didn't have anything to do with it."

Through clenched teeth, I asked, "What's your name?"

"Am I in trouble?"

I pulled back my coat to reveal my badge.

She glanced toward the bartender before saying, "Carol Hurley."

I removed the list of prostitutes from my pocket and consulted it. She was huddled with Gaskin when I walked in, and she pushed up on me when I approached. She knew the game.

The woman glanced at the bartender questioningly. He moved to the end of the bar, where he wiped away something imaginary with a cleaning rag.

Her picture was there on the front page, which was why she looked familiar. "Deidre—"

She shoved me backward onto a nearby table. She then ran toward the rear of the establishment. As she sprinted by her table, she scooped up her purse, slinging it over her shoulder.

"Is there another way out?" I asked the bartender.

He lowered his eyes and shook his head. He muttered, "All she did was corner herself."

I stood and waited for her to come running back out. After a minute, I moved toward the bar. "She been here before?"

"Never seen her."

"What about Tiger?"

The bartender nodded. "Man's in here all the time. First time with that one, though."

I sat on the stool, leaned an elbow on the counter and watched the hallway to the restrooms. "Got any coffee?"

The older man set a small brown mug near my arm. "Tastes like dirt, but it'll keep you awake."

The coffee was burnt. Regardless, I mumbled my thanks and kept my attention on the back hallway.

After I checked my watch for the umpteenth time and emptied the mug, I asked, "You sure there's no other way out?"

"Positive. She's prolly sitting on the john counting the minutes until she thinks you've gotten tired of waiting."

As if he were a prophet, she strolled out of the hallway like she owned the joint. Then she caught sight of me. I lifted the coffee mug in mock salute.

She froze. Then she turned around but didn't go anywhere. Her shoulders rolled forward and her head shook. Slowly, she faced me.

I waved her over.

Her walk was despondent, like a dog that had peed on the carpet and knew it was in trouble.

She halted in front of me.

"You assaulted an officer," I said flatly.

The woman looked confused. "I didn't hit you."

"Assault is legally defined as any unwanted touching."

She tried to give me the prostitute's version of puppy dog eyes. "Then I've been assaulted my whole life."

I didn't doubt it, but I wasn't a sucker, either. "Deidre Dobb," I said. "Or should I call you DeeDee?"

Her eyes narrowed. "How'd you…"

"You were Junior's bottom."

She nodded and sorrow replaced the puppy dog eyes. "It's a shame what happened to him."

"Yet, here you are, talking to the competition."

"Tiger?" she said with an embarrassed smile. "He wasn't after my man's territory. That would be Damon. You should be talking to him about Junior's murder. I think he's the man who done it."

"I did talk to him."

"You did?"

"And he said the same things others were saying."

"What others?"

"That Tiger is the man to be feared."

DeeDee shrugged. "I wouldn't know."

"Word is Junior sent some girls down here to push into Tiger's territory. That one of them got beat for it."

She stared ahead.

"It's true?"

"Junior tried to grow. Tiger taught him a lesson."

"What happened to the girl who took the beating?"

"She quit and went home. Bitch had no heart."

"Where's home for her?"

"Wyoming, or one of them cowboy states. Good riddance is what I say. She was too fragile for the life."

"Who was she?"

DeeDee clicked her teeth together several times before she said, "Nessa."

"Nessa?"

"Nessa Bolkan."

I slid the list from my coat. There was a Bolkan listed—Vanessa Bolkan. Age twenty-eight. The redheaded woman staring back at me seemed familiar. Was it because I had seen this picture before? I'd looked at this list so many times over the past few days that I lost count. "And Nessa left the game?"

"Girl lost her will. Quit and went home."

I folded the list and put it away. "How long have you and Tiger been talking?"

"Ain't no *how* long. We only just met. Right before you came in. First time."

"We're getting off to a bad start with all your lying."

She feigned being hurt. "It ain't a lie, Detective."

"You practically had your tongue in his ear."

"I was making friendly."

"DeeDee, stop working me. I'm not a customer."

Her face slackened. "Cops are gonna believe what cops wanna believe."

"Then this is what I believe—Tiger and you made a plan to take Junior out."

She inhaled sharply. "We didn't."

"Word on the street was Junior was unhappy with *you*."

"That ain't true."

"He was getting ready to replace you. That's why you aligned with Tiger—to take him out."

"Bullshit!" she hollered.

"Hey!" the bartender yelled. "Watch your mouth, woman."

She lifted a hand in his direction but didn't look at him. "Junior wouldn't bump me for *no one*. I did him right."

"Word was you were talking back, making it difficult."

Her upper lip curled. "Who said that?"

"Maybe he'd put Scrimmy in your place?"

"That skank couldn't bottom if her life depended on it. Half the time she's high as a kite. The other times she's looking for ways to get high. She's a jitterbug."

"Why were you talking back?"

She looked away.

"Better give me a reason—a real reason—to believe you."

DeeDee faced me. "Because the man's thinking was clouded."

"Clouded by what?"

She lowered her eyes. "Pills."

I thought about the bottle of bills I found in Junior's vehicle. "What kind?" I asked.

"Oxy. They messed with his head. He wasn't making smart choices."

"Yeah? Tell me about those choices."

She remade eye contact. "Moving into Tiger's territory, for one. That was plain dumb. Lost a good worker 'cause of it."

"You said she was fragile."

"She was young and pale, the way you white boys like them. Her shelf life might have been short, but those girls get premium attention. Junior should have taken that into consideration."

"That's why you two were on the outs?"

"Not just that."

"What else?"

"After the beat down, he should have walked away. Learnt his lesson and been happy with what he had. Instead, he wanted to war with Tiger, fight the man for his turf, but Junior didn't have an army. He only had his girls."

"So, what should he have done? Wait for Tiger to invade his territory?"

"Huh?"

"Redevelopment is squeezing the game out of the West End. From what I hear, they're even redeveloping the Hope soon. Won't be much left down here but citizens."

She snickered. "Who do you think we trick for, Detective? Broke motherfuckers don't pay the rent."

"Everything you're saying makes me think Tiger had the most to gain with Junior out of the way. He gets an enemy off his back and takes over his land."

"I don't see it."

"You don't *want* to see it. Where were you Saturday night?"

"Working."

"Gonna need something better than that."

"Doing a bachelor party."

"A what?"

"Junior had me at a house party on the prairie. He dropped me off, took their money. Said he would pick me up in the morning."

"What were you doing there?"

Her eyes deadened. "What do you think? Don't look so disgusted, preacher man. It puts food on the table."

"You remember the address?"

She walked to her purse, grabbed her phone, and opened the gallery. She showed me two photos—one of the house and one of the house numbers. "I texted those to a friend."

"You do that often? Text photos of the places you go?"

"I didn't do it ever before, but a friend was raped in a house by some guys. You can't be too careful nowadays."

"This friend—would that be Joey Greene?"

"Why's it matter?"

I shrugged. "I hear she used to be one of Junior's girls until she got herself a badge daddy."

DeeDee's smile was sorrowful. "That shit didn't go over too well with the man. He was gonna kill the cop. Threatened as much."

"What did the cop do?"

"He didn't take the threats lightly."

"Did he confront Junior about them?"

"Of course he did. Junior backed down like a schoolyard bitch. Didn't sit too good with the man. Or us, quite frankly."

"There was bad blood there."

"Some of the worst. You looking to bust him?"

"Morgan?"

Her eyebrows lifted.

"I know he's protecting Joey."

She sighed. "I'd love to see him go down."

"For the beef with Junior?"

"For anything. He never helped any of us like he did Joey. Figure fair is fair."

"Why *did* he help Joey?"

"Why do you think?"

"If you knew she was talking to him, why would you remain friends?"

"Girl wasn't giving him anything he could use. Besides, what kind of shit would a woman like her know, anyway?"

"I thought that's why he looked out for her."

DeeDee laughed. "He looked out for her because he liked what she gave him, and it wasn't information. Know what I'm saying?"

I knew what she was saying, but it didn't square with the Morgan I thought I knew. "How often do you talk with Joey?"

"Any time I want."

I handed her my business card.

"Let her know I'm looking for her. Same goes for Tiger. Why'd he run?"

"Because you're the law."

"Well, now he's suspect number one. Every patrol officer is going to come down here and look for him. They're going to crawl up in his business, your business, just so I can talk with him. If he didn't do anything, he's got nothing to worry about. I'm looking for a killer, not a pimp."

She stared at my business card.

"When I find him," I said, "what's Tiger going to say about why you two were talking?"

She licked her lips.

"The truth, DeeDee."

"I told him I could deliver Junior's girls."

"And what do you get out of it?"

"A better place to stay. Maybe a better rung on the pecking order. He's already got a bottom. I ain't knocking her out. At least, not today."

"What if some of the girls defect to Damon?"

DeeDee shrugged. "Then they defect, but I ain't working for no white boy. No offense."

"None taken. I've met him."

She fought back a smile.

"Where did Junior live?"

"He bounced from place to place."

"Come on."

"He had a pad at the Hilda, but he barely spent any time there." Melancholy filled her eyes. "He spent his life bouncing from bed to bed, girl to girl."

"Did you love him?"

"He didn't love no one but himself, so how could I love him?"

I pointed at the business card. "If you think of anything, call me."

"You're not going to arrest me?"

"Consider it me paying it forward."

Her fingers rubbed the card.

I moved toward the door, then stopped and turned back to her. "Chanel," I said, thinking about the young girl I'd met with Marlene.

"The young buck?"

"Leave her alone. Don't bring her to Tiger. Understand?"

DeeDee's eyes narrowed. "Got a thing for the little ones?"

"She's sixteen," I said, my voice hardening.

The prostitute lifted her hands in surrender. "Whatever. Just trying to understand the rules. But I think you're too late."

"What do you mean?"

"She's already making plays for a new daddy."

34

As I drove east, I contacted dispatch and placed an Attempt to Locate on Raekwon Gaskin. Afterward, I called Glenn to check in.

"Higgins," he answered.

"It's Dallas. How are things?"

"I went back to the neighbor and showed her Lynn Slater's picture."

"And?"

"He's the man Carlotta entertained. He was there several times."

"How many is several?"

"At least three. That's what she said."

"Did you ask what time of day?"

"Of course."

"And?"

"He came by at night—each time."

"That seems inappropriate for a citizenship officer."

"My thinking exactly."

"Want to approach him again?"

"I do," Glenn said, "but not at his office. He's got too much authority there. I want to snatch him up elsewhere."

"Tonight?"

"Not yet. I'm still working on his background. Either tomorrow night, or we grab him on the weekend. You up for that?"

"Anytime," I said. "You name it."

"What are you doing?"

"Follow-up interviews on Everson Wiley."

"Getting anywhere?"

"I think so."

"All right. Call if you need anything."

***

When I stepped into the office of Her Freedom, the receptionist picked up the telephone. By the time I got to the counter, she hung up and said, "She'll be with you in a moment."

The side door opened, and Marlene appeared. "Detective Nash. Looking better."

"Feeling better. Can we talk?"

"Of course." Her smile was soft. She still didn't have on any make-up, but she had styled her hair differently. She wore a knee-length skirt and a button-up sweater over a turtleneck.

The women in the back still watched with the eyes of predators, but I don't think they worried about me as much now. My moment of weakness had shown them something unexpected— vulnerability. After walking into her office, I closed the door.

"What can I help you with today?" she asked as she headed for her desk.

"Why didn't you tell me you worked for Junior?"

She stopped midway to her chair, and the smile on her face vanished. "Why would I ever admit that to anyone?"

"I'm investigating his murder."

"I don't care."

The soft appearance she had shared with me a moment before was gone. Now, she was as hard and cold as marble. She dropped into her chair.

"You do social work in the area where he was murdered. You have a history with the man, along with an obvious hatred for who he was and what he did."

"I didn't kill him." She set her jaw and folded her arms across her chest. "My joy in his demise does not make me guilty."

I rubbed my temple as I thought.

"You look at me differently now."

"What?"

"The first time we met you treated me like an equal. Now that you know my history, you see the real me." She tapped her sternum. Marlene continued speaking, but the rest of what she said was lost. I held up my hand for her to wait.

WASP's cover of "The Real Me" blasted inside my head. This song is about how the people around us are unable to see us as we really are. She squinted as she studied me. The song's chorus, along with its blaring guitars, looped several times before it faded.

When I lowered my hand, she asked, "Are you okay?"

"I'm fine."

"It doesn't look it."

"I checked your background. I had to. I needed to know who you were."

She shook her head. "I was a prostitute, Detective Nash. *Was*. I had sex for money. I lowered myself to support a drug habit that almost killed me. You will never understand what it means to carry that around in your heart, your soul, your head for the rest of your life. I can never escape it."

I understood some of it.

"Then you walk in here with that judgment in your eyes—"

"I'm not judging you."

She paused. The red in her cheeks had fully bloomed. "Then what are you doing?"

"Wondering why you lied."

"I didn't lie."

"You hid the truth."

"It wasn't a truth you needed."

"How can you determine that?"

"Because I didn't kill him—that's why—and only I can determine if my truth should be shared."

We sat quietly for a few minutes.

"You help these women because you were them."

Her shrug was barely perceptible.

"When did you stop?"

"A while ago."

"You stopped showing up in criminal records about six years ago."

"And?"

I pointed to the back of the frame that sat on the edge of her desk. "I can't help but notice the age of your daughter."

Her eyes flicked to the picture, then slowly drifted back. She would have made a great poker player.

"Is she his?" When she didn't respond, I asked, "Did he know?"

"He suspected."

"Did he want custody?"

She frowned. "And have legal responsibility? You still don't know the man you're so desperately trying to avenge."

"I'm not avenging him."

"Then what are you trying to do, Detective?"

"Bring a killer to justice."

"Why?"

"Because it's right."

"Someone removed an evil from the world. They should be rewarded, not vilified."

"I need to verify you were at home on Saturday night."

She inhaled deeply before answering. "Then come over and meet my daughter, but she isn't going to make the most reliable witness."

"Children don't. I'd like the name and number of the online course you're taking. I'll call them and verify the course activity that night."

She turned to her computer and spent a few minutes clicking. When she found what she wanted, she jotted something on a piece of paper before sliding it across the desk. "That's the name of the school, the course, and my instructor. That's also my address in case you want to stop by and see what my home life looks like. You'll see I'm not a killer."

I folded the paper and tucked it into my pocket.

"Do you have a way to get a hold of Chanel?"

"What about her?"

"Deidre Dobb said she tried to contact Tiger."

"Are you serious?"

"That's what she said. I don't know what Chanel is up to, but if she keeps looking for trouble, she's going to find it."

"I'll find out what she's up to."

When I stood, Marlene did as well.

"I'm sorry for getting defensive," she said. "This is my problem, not yours."

"I understand."

She studied my eyes. "I think you do. You're hiding something as well, aren't you?"

As I left, "The Real Me" played inside my head again.

35

The sound remained off while grainy images of football players moved about the television screen. Tonight, the sports channel highlighted the team of the nineties—The Dallas Cowboys. Various plays by Troy Aikman, Michael Irvin, and Emmitt Smith were shown.

I unenthusiastically ate a protein bar I purchased from a gas station on the way home. Diana Krall's *Stepping Out* played on the stereo while I floated away not only on the jazz music, but the memories associated with the album. It came out shortly after I graduated from college. Bobbie and I were newlyweds, and we lived in a rental house in Greenacres, a locale since gobbled up by the incorporations of both Spokane Valley and Liberty Lake.

We didn't have a TV back then, so we listened mostly to music. That was our thing and remained so throughout our marriage. On most nights, we traded picking music back and forth. I'd choose an album then she'd pick one. Or if we were enjoying some wine on a Friday night, we'd go song for song. Music was integral to our lives.

Krall was a favorite of Bobbie's, and I chose it to remember my wife. Cutting music from my life this past year had not only been a form of sacrifice, it had been a punishment—a way of flogging myself.

My cell phone rang. It was a number I had dialed numerous times recently. I muted the stereo and answered the phone.

"Nash?"

"I heard you're looking for me," the woman said. They were the same words James Morgan had spoken. "If you want to meet, I'm open for the next hour. After that, I'm busy."

"Come into the department tomorrow and we'll—"

"No. I'm not going to allow myself to be videotaped or watched by other officers."

Maybe Joey Greene had been in one of our interview rooms before, or perhaps Morgan had coached her. If, after talking with her, I suspected her of being involved in Everson Wiley's death, I could always change the dynamic by detaining her. But right now, I didn't have anything more than a desire to speak with her.

I sat upright. "All right." The protein bar wasn't doing it for me, anyway. "Where?"

***

She stood in the parking lot of the Hi-Lo Convenience Store on East Sprague Avenue. Her hands were thrust into a dark coat with a hood hanging behind. She wore black leggings and black boots with scuffed gray toes. A pink *Carhart* beanie cap was pulled down over her ears.

"Joey?"

"You got ten minutes."

"We'll need more than—"

"That's all you get." She pulled her hand from a pocket and checked a large silver watch—a man's watch—that hung loosely around her wrist. "And the clock is ticking."

"Why is Detective Morgan protecting you?"

She shoved her hand back into the coat pocket. "He's not. Whoever said that is lying."

"He didn't save you from Junior?"

"No, he didn't."

"What did he do?"

Joey started to speak but paused. She cocked her head slightly, as if thinking. "He told Junior to back off. That's a big difference from saving."

"Right," I said. "Big difference, but people call him your badge daddy."

"You made that up, Detective."

"Ask your friends down here."

She rolled her eyes. "I don't have any friends. Is this really what you wanted to talk about? If so—"

"Why did Morgan save you from Junior?"

"Like I said—"

"Fine. He didn't save you, but what was Junior doing that motivated Morgan to step in?"

She twisted her lips before answering. "He smacked me around."

"Lots of girls get smacked around."

Her face went flat.

"In your line of work, that's the cost of doing business. You better give me something better than that."

"He hit me," she said, defiantly, "in the face with his fists. I thought he was going to kill me."

"Why?"

"The man said I wasn't working hard enough."

"From what I heard, Junior was a professional." It felt dirty to parrot Damon Warfield's words. "He might have smacked you around, but I doubt it was in the face with his fists. How could he get top dollar if your face was messed up?"

Joey's gaze drifted away, and her hand lifted toward her right ear. She stopped as if she'd been shocked by electricity, and her eyes locked onto mine. She shoved her hand back into her pocket.

I grabbed her by the coat and jerked her so I could look at her ear. She turned her face away.

"Get off me!" she hollered.

"He's listening!"

"Who?"

"Where is he?"

She struggled to get away, but I held onto her. She continued to keep the right side of her face turned away.

"Let me see your ear."

Joey hit my chest. "We're done!" she yelled. "We're done!"

I scanned the area for any vehicles that seemed out of place. Joey slapped my face and screamed, "Help!"

"Where's he at?"

"Let me go!"

"Where's Morgan?"

She slapped me a second time.

"Stop it," I said. "I'm taking you—"

"You don't have probable cause!"

"What?"

Her hand froze in place, ready for another slap. "You don't have probable cause to detain me." A strange calmness seemed to come over her. She lowered her hand. "This was a voluntary contact and I'm exercising my right to leave."

The words were legal and valid, but they were all wrong in this moment—for her, this place, this time. They were Detective Jim Morgan's, and he fed them directly into her ear. That didn't make them any less right.

I didn't have probable cause to arrest her for Everson Wiley's death. I didn't have any reason to detain her for questioning. I could arrest her for assaulting an officer, but the charge would be tenuous at best, and it would never stick. I released my grip, and she stepped quickly away.

"Saturday night," I said. "Where were you—"

She smoothed her coat. "Working."

"Got an alibi?"

"Some random johns."

"That it's?"

She held her palms up in a plaintive position. "What do you want, Detective? I didn't kill him. I didn't have a reason. I can't give you anything more than that."

"Tell Morgan," I said, pointing at her, "to be in my office at nine a.m. tomorrow morning or I'm going to the captain."

Joey Greene's lips tightened, and her eyes narrowed.

"I'm serious."

She stood still with her hands balled defiantly into fists.

I waved her off and went back to my car.

36

The meeting with Joey Greene put me in a foul mood, and I couldn't sleep most of the night. When I needed the depression to work its magic, it failed and turned into insomnia.

I got to sleep around three in the morning and at six I burst back into consciousness with Vinnie Vincent Invasion's "Love Kills" blaring inside my head.

Sitting up, I leaned forward and put my head in my hands. The chorus looped over and over.

Frustrated by the song circling in my brain, I stood and stumbled to my CD collection. I hadn't expected to find the album. With the collection I have, I tend to forget the one-off purchase I might have made twenty or more years ago. No luck.

The chorus continued to circle around my consciousness.

Randomly, I picked a different album and put it into the CD player. I worried the neighbors would hear the music inside my house. It was six in the morning, so the worst I'd be doing was waking them for work.

"Love Kills" now played louder inside my skull and drowned out the song coming from the stereo. I angrily flicked off the stereo and sat on the edge of the couch.

Maybe this wasn't my subconscious messing with me. Maybe it was Bobbie—

I cut that thought off.

The song was not from her. It came from my subconscious. Entertaining any thoughts of supernatural communication was detrimental to my mental health.

Yet, if my subconscious was sending a message to my conscious self, then what was "Love Kills" supposed to tell me?

I remained on the couch for some time. When I eventually decided it all meant nothing, it stopped—the song simply vanished.

Slowly, I showered and got dressed for work. After brewing a small pot of coffee, I grabbed my creamer from the refrigerator. I briefly eyed Bobbie's unused creamer—my same morning ritual—then closed the door.

On the drive into the department, that morning's song bothered me. I hadn't woken to one in months. What was different? Had something changed? Was it an anomaly?

After starting my computer, I checked my email. The only one of interest was an email that had come in late yesterday afternoon from Corporal Mark Tripp. He'd confirmed the bottle of pills in Everson Wiley's vehicle were Oxycontin. Deidre Dobb said Junior was using the drug, and it affected his decision making.

Next, I called up the Hot Sheet via the department's Intranet. The Hot Sheet was the daily briefing the data crunchers in Crime Analysis put together. They review the previous day's reports and cull the most useful information. Armed with that info, they develop a trend analysis for certain types of crimes. The CA team shares that information with the rest of the department.

It only took a few minutes to get through the bulletin. As I finished, though, it occurred to me that I hadn't read the previous day's wrap-up. I called up Thursday's Hot Sheet.

I wondered what had caused me to miss yesterday morning's briefing. It took a moment to recall going to Everson Wiley's autopsy, a quick stop at the property room to put the two rounds on evidence, and then the interview with Lynn Slater. My morning routine had been thrown off.

That got me thinking about the rest of the week—Monday through Wednesday. I called the Hot Sheets up for those days. I hadn't read any of them. I'd been distracted each morning, and my daily routine had fallen to the wayside.

Patrol officers are taught to read the Hot Sheet before their shift. Detectives usually did it whenever they had a free moment. If I didn't set time aside for it, they would get pushed to a back burner and often forgotten—just like what had occurred.

I read them backwards, Wednesday, then Tuesday, before finishing on Monday.

The only case that seemed odd was the report of a stranger-on-stranger rape Andrew Parker was investigating. The woman had been found in Liberty Park by a Good Samaritan who transported her to the hospital. When the responding officer arrived, the thirty-year-old victim was uncooperative. She'd been beaten by a white male of average height and weight. Not many of those in a city with a population of eighty-five percent Caucasian.

I yawned. I hadn't had a cup of coffee yet. I hurried through her criminal history, which was extensive with misdemeanor assaults and thefts, along with a list of known aliases she used. Then I closed the Hot Sheet and pushed back from my desk to get a cup of coffee.

I stood to leave but stopped and slowly lowered myself back into my chair.

Calling up the Hot Sheet again, I went back to Parker's rape case. The victim's name was Tanisha Kreshel. I'd seen her bloody panties in the drying room right before I'd fainted.

But that's not what gave me pause.

Below her name on the Hot Sheet was a list of aliases she'd used.

Krishawna Tanisha.

Tanisha Kreshner.

Tanisha Gaskin.

***

Andrew Parker came in shortly after eight. His red face glistened as if he had recently finished a workout. I intercepted him as he walked toward his cubicle.

"Parker."

He glanced back. "Nash," he said, almost spitting the word.

His collar was unbuttoned, and his tie loosened.

"Got a minute?"

He dropped his backpack near his desk. "For?"

"Questions about a case."

Suspicion grew in his eyes. "Mine or yours?"

"Yours."

"Which one?"

"Kreshel. The rape from Friday night."

"Saturday morning."

"Right," I said, "Saturday morning. What can you tell me?"

His eyes narrowed further. "Why are you asking?"

"She's got an alias that pinged my radar."

"Which one?"

I hesitated.

Parker leaned against his desk and crossed his arms. "Don't want to play nice, but you want me to spill? Is that the big dog way?"

"I'm not the big dog."

"You're the senior investigator in this department, Nash. Everyone thinks you walk on goddamn water."

"No, they don't."

Parker snickered. "That's right. Johnson and I think you're full of shit."

"I'm sure plenty of others do, too."

Agreeing with him seemed to throw him off balance. His brow furrowed. "Which alias?"

"Gaskin."

He moved his head as if trying to pop a crick in his neck. "What bell did that ring?"

"My homicide victim from Saturday night has a rival named Gaskin."

"Think there's a connection to my victim?"

I shrugged. "That's why I'm asking. The Hot Sheet described her as uncooperative."

"She initially refused to submit to a rape kit, but she came around. It took a little talking."

"She was found in Liberty Park?"

"Couple high school kids who were there to hook-up stumbled on her. They took her up to the hospital, which is where the first officer contacted her. She told the kids she was raped, but she wouldn't say squat to us at first. One of the hospital workers called a counselor who got her to open up to us. She was a big help."

"Who was the counselor?"

"Some gal from Her Freedom." He reached inside his suit jacket and pulled out his notebook.

"Marlene Anderson?" I asked.

"That's her." He tossed the notebook on his desk.

"And she said what?"

"That a white male raped her."

"With average height and weight."

"That's right."

"You believe her?"

"That she was raped? Yeah. Girl was beat to fuck. Do I believe it was some average white dude? Not a chance. She knew the guy, and she kept her mouth shut."

"Why do you think she did that? Fear?"

"Of what? That if she talked, he'd come back and hurt her worse? She was already with us. No, she didn't talk, but it was for some other reason."

"If you had to guess—"

"She hadn't made up her mind."

"On what?"

"On how to handle it."

"Like maybe revenge."

"Maybe."

"Got an address for her?"

He picked up his notebook again. "What are you thinking?"

"My homicide victim had blood in the back of his SUV. She's got an alias matching his rival's last name. Is it too far-fetched to think my guy raped your girl and they're somehow connected?"

"And the rival shoots your guy in retaliation?"

"The rival ran when I tried to contact him."

Parker eyed me and his lips twisted as he thought. "I've worked with less," he said grudgingly. Parker flipped through his notebook until he found the address of the girl. "Need a back-up?"

"I'll take Higgins, but if we get anything more on the rape, we'll let you know."

***

When I returned to my desk, Glenn was at his computer. "You look worse for wear."

"Lousy night of sleep."

"Let's make a run at the Immigration Officer later today."

"Sounds good. I've got some follow-up on the dead pimp to do. Want to run with me on that?"

Glenn pushed back from his desk. "Let's go."

I checked my watch. There was no way I'd make it back before nine, which is when I told Joey to have Morgan be at my desk. Did I really expect him to show?

"Got a hot date?" Glenn asked.

"Just checking the time."

On the way out of the department, Lieutenant Brand was coming in. He caught my eye and waved me over.

"Gimme a second."

"I'll meet you at the car." Glenn nodded at the lieutenant as they passed each other.

"Stephen called," Brand said.

My heart jumped even though I had expected the phone call. Having a therapist update the department was unsettling.

"He said you made your meeting, participated willingly, and that you two have a plan for going forward."

I did my best to keep a poker face, but my cheeks warmed.

Brand's eyes narrowed.

"Did he say anything else?" I asked.

"He said you should be fine to continue working."

"Should be?"

"You know how things work, Nash. Everyone needs wiggle room, legally speaking, in case you end up *not* being fine."

My heart rate slowed. "I'll be fine."
Brand nodded several times. "Okay, Nash. Okay."
Now, he was doing the okays.

37

The door opened a crack, revealing a brass chain. Half her face remained hidden. Only a brown eye surrounded by dark bruising peeked out.

"Spokane Police," I said. "I'm Detective Nash. With me is Detective Higgins. We'd like to talk with you about Saturday morning."

Tanisha Kreshel said, "I already talked to the cops."

"Yes, ma'am. We're here to follow up."

Glenn stepped closer to the door. "We're the senior detectives in the office, ma'am. We're sent out on important cases."

She looked down with the single, exposed eye. Then she gloomily said, "Hold on" and shut the door.

Alone in the hallway, I glanced at Glenn. "Senior detectives?"

"Let's use age to our advantage."

The chain slid noisily, and the door reopened, this time fully. Tanisha stepped back, allowing us to enter.

She wore a blue sweater, faded jeans, and socks. Her hair was cut short. She wore no jewelry or earrings, and her face was free of make-up. There was bruising around the left side of her mouth. Her right eye was mark free.

She turned and led us into the living room.

It was a small one-bedroom apartment. The kitchen and living room were essentially one room, with the bedroom and bathroom a few steps away.

Glenn and I sat on a well-worn couch. Tanisha perched on a bonded leather recliner with cracks on its arms. Her legs were tucked under herself.

"Ms. Kreshel," I said, "I'd like to go back over your statement from that night."

Her eyes narrowed.

"You told the officer you were assaulted in a van, correct?"

"I was raped," she said, her lip curling.

"Raped," I repeated. "But it occurred in a van."

"That's correct."

"How did you know it was a van?"

"I know what a van is."

"Could you have been mistaken?"

"I told the other detective this. Wasn't it in his report?"

"I'm sorry to go over this again, Ms. Kreshel. I'm trying to get a deeper understanding."

Tanisha looked at Glenn again, who nodded in return. She refocused her attention on me.

"Ms. Kreshel, where were you when you were grabbed?"

Her lips pursed, then she forced them to the side. "You're not here for follow-up."

"Ma'am?"

"You're trying to poke holes."

I held her gaze.

"You think I'm lying?"

"That's not true. I believe you."

Tears welled in her eyes. We sat quietly until she composed herself.

I asked, "Why weren't you cooperative after the incident occurred?"

Her lips tightened and trembled. "I'm right. You want to poke holes."

"Maybe you were in shock," Glenn said.

She nodded slightly. "Maybe."

My partner leaned forward. "That could explain some of the uncooperative behavior. Yeah?"

Tanisha rubbed her hands together and nodded again.

"Ms. Kreshel," I said, "can I ask you about the trouble you've been in?"

She stood. "Is that why you don't believe me?"

Glenn stood as well, but I remained seated. It was clear he had the better rapport with her. Sometimes that occurs in interviews, and it must run its course.

"Please, Ms. Kreshel," Glenn said. "Tanisha. We're here for follow up. We're not here to make things more difficult."

Tanisha glared at me.

"I believe you," I said. My voice remained calm.

"Then why bring up my past? It's got nothing to do with what happened."

"Gaskin," I said.

"What?"

"You used that alias before. Tanisha Gaskin. It was during a shoplifting arrest when you were eighteen. Why?"

"Why what?"

"Why that last name?"

She slowly sat. "I don't know. I didn't want them to find out who I was. Didn't matter any. When the cops showed, they still got my name."

"But Gaskin. Why that name?"

"People normally use something close to them," Glenn suggested. "Like a friend's name, boyfriend's name, that sort of thing."

"I don't remember," Tanisha said.

"Eighteen wasn't that long ago," Glenn continued. "Did you have a friend named Gaskin in school?"

"I dunno. Maybe."

"What about a relative?"

She shrugged. "There was a kid in school with that last name."

"What school did you go to?" I asked.

"Huh?"

"What school?"

Tanisha glanced away as she mumbled, "Rogers." When she turned back, she confidently said, "I didn't know her too much."

"Remember her first name?" my partner asked.

I glanced at Glenn, but his eyes remained locked on Tanisha.

"Not really. Wanda, I think."

Her eyes flicked to my notepad. I jotted the name down and was about to line through it, but hesitated. The explanation for the surname wasn't reasonable. The rest of it sounded like a lie, but in every good lie, there should be an element of truth.

Tanisha's gaze returned to my partner, who gave her a safe harbor in this interview.

It was time to ask her a more pointed question. I leaned forward. "Ever hear of a man named Everson Wiley?"

Her brow furrowed and her lips tightened. After a moment, she asked, "Who's he? What's he—"

"Junior," I said. "Everson Wiley is also known as Junior."

Her eyes locked onto mine and a fire of hatred burned behind them. I wasn't sure if the hatred was for my question or if it was for Wiley.

"He's a pimp," I said.

Tanisha's face hardened further as she forced an exaggerated frown. "Never heard of him."

"What about Raekwon Gaskin?"

Her face relaxed, and she shrugged. She'd been prepared for that one with the question about the alibi. She had to have known it was coming.

"You don't know him either?" I asked.

"Who's he?"

"A suspect in Junior's murder."

She swallowed with difficulty. "A murder? That's why you're asking about that name I used one time a long time ago. Never heard of him. Must be one of those coincidences."

"Yeah," I said. "A coincidence."

But I didn't believe in coincidence. No cop did.

Now, we were at a point of no return. She was lying about knowing Gaskin and Wiley and I wanted to pursue that questioning further. However, she *was* a rape victim—I believed that.

The damage on her face and the evidence Parker had collected confirmed it. Even if she was holding back information, I had to take the latter into consideration.

My eyes met Glenn's, and he nodded. He must have been thinking the same thing. We both stood.

"Ms. Kreshel, thank you for your time."

"I hope you catch who did this," she said. It was an insincere statement.

***

On the way back to the station, dispatch called out, "Ida twenty-five, are you on the air?"

I grabbed the microphone. "Ida twenty-five."

"Patrol units are out with your Attempt to Locate, Raekwon Gaskin, at the corner of Pittsburgh and Sprague."

"Pittsburgh and Sprague," I repeated. "We're on the way. I'm with Ida twenty-four."

38

Raekwon Gaskin stood defiantly on the corner. Officers Leya Navarro and Rodney McCrea stood nearby and alert. Gaskin was not handcuffed. The officers could have chosen to do so for officer safety. Whatever their reasons, they hadn't found him threatening enough to do so.

As we approached, Navarro stepped away and intercepted us.

"We patted him down," she said. "He let us search his pockets, too. Only some cash and car keys."

"What was he doing when you contacted him?"

"Talking to a known prostitute."

"Which one?"

"Liliya Scrimshaw."

"Where's she at?"

"She disappeared while we were detaining Gaskin."

Several onlookers gathered across the street. Within the crowd were a couple of prostitutes, but Scrimmy wasn't one of them.

"Good work," I said.

The three of us headed toward the corner where Gaskin stood with Officer McCrea.

"You the one who ordered me detained?" Gaskin asked. "Better be a damned good reason for holding me or I'm calling my lawyer."

"You've got a lawyer?"

His laugh was sharp. "You know I do."

"What's his name?"

"*Her* name. I like women protecting me."

"Fine. What's her name?"

"Wanda Acosta." The way he said it was supposed to make me afraid.

"Don't start off lying."

He puffed his chest. "That's straight truth."

"No," I said, "it's not."

His lip curled.

"You see, Wanda has a personal code. She doesn't handle wife abusers or rapists. Generally, anyone who hurts women. You fall into that category."

Wanda was one of the toughest defense attorneys in the city. The last time I encountered her, I overstepped my boundaries and ended up with a verbal reprimand from the chief. I doubted she had the code I described, but my gut said Gaskin only knew her street reputation as a cop-eater and had never talked with the woman.

His lip uncurled as I continued.

"Maybe you got her number in your pocket, thinking it might be a Get-Out-of-Jail-Free card, but I know what she'll tell you if she learns you put women on the stroll."

"She's my lawyer." It didn't sound any more convincing.

"Then call her. We'll give you time."

He surveyed the onlookers. "Nah. Not yet."

"You sure? I don't want you to think I didn't give you a chance."

He gestured for me to continue. "Say what you gotta say."

"Where were you Saturday night?"

"Home."

"Where's that?"

He smiled. "You were already there. Met my girl. My alibi."

"Is that your home address?"

"As far as you—the government—is concerned, that's where I lay my head."

"What are you doing down here?"

He glanced at the building next to us. "Shopping."

"For what? Antique furniture?"

"Can't a man build a collection?"

"Of what?" Glenn asked. "Wicker end-tables?"

"Maybe."

Behind him, both Officers Navarro and McCrea rolled their eyes.

"What are you driving?" I asked.

He pointed to a Cadillac Escalade. Arguably, it would be able to carry a large piece of furniture.

"Heard you were talking to Scrimmy," I said.

"The lady I asked directions from?"

"Directions to where?"

"Starbucks." Gaskin grinned. "I like a latte every now and then. What can I say?"

"The woman you were talking with is a known prostitute."

"I would never have guessed."

"We can arrest you for promoting prostitution."

His smile faded, and he shrugged. "Go ahead, but it won't stick."

"Soliciting would."

"Arrest me for whatever. It's not my first rodeo."

We stared at each other for a few moments.

"How was your relationship with Everson Wiley?"

"Who?"

"Junior."

Gaskin nodded. "*That* motherfucker."

"You didn't like him."

"Does Coke like Pepsi?"

I glanced at my partner.

"Does Drake like Pusha T?"

"I don't know what that means."

"It means a man doesn't like his competitor."

"That's all he was? A competitor."

"Sure."

"So, if he stayed on his side of the tracks, you would have stayed on yours?"

"That's the rules we lived by."

"But he didn't live by those rules. Rumor is he tried to sneak into your territory."

His face soured. "Wasn't no rumor."

"What did he do?" I asked, already knowing the story.

"He sent one of his girls down. My girls politely asked her to leave."

"That's how you politely ask?"

"It's business. You don't half-step when someone is trying to take market share."

"Did Junior take the hint?"

Gaskin shrugged. "Took some convincing."

"What kind of convincing?"

"We had a parlay."

"And?"

"And nothing. The man agreed to stay on his side of the tracks."

"Then he messed with your sister."

He rubbed his lower lip with his thumb. "He didn't know my sister."

"Your daughter, perhaps. But you'd have had to have been young—"

"My daughter? Ain't got no daughter."

"Who is Tanisha Kreshel to you?"

Tiger put his hands in his pockets.

"Take your hands out of your pockets," Glenn said.

Gaskin glanced to the sky before pulling his hands free.

"Tanisha Kreshel," I repeated.

"Don't know the bitch."

"She knows you."

"No, she doesn't."

"She used Gaskin as an alias."

He shrugged. "So? If she used Peter Pan as an alias, would you be talking to Captain Hook?"

I smiled.

"You think that's funny?" Gaskin asked.

"I do," I said and glanced at my partner. "You?"

Glenn's face remained solemn. "No."

"I don't think my partner likes you."

Gaskin's lip curled. "Then we're even."

"You get his info?" I asked Navarro and McCrea.

"I did," the female officer said.

My gaze returned to Gaskin. "You're free to go."

"Damn right, I'm free to go." He stepped to the corner and raised his arms in victory to the crowd across the street. "Free at last, free at last!"

They cheered in response.

"If we could only get the blood results from the SUV," I said.

Glenn shook his head. "You know the drill. Even with a rush, we'll be lucky to get them in less than three months. I think only Oklahoma is worse on turnaround times."

"And the rape kit could take as long as a year to process."

"That's the pace of the state's technology. We play the cards we're dealt."

I smacked my hand against the steering wheel. We were driving back toward the station.

"Am I thinking it wrong?" I asked.

"What's that?"

"Kreshel's rape and how it ties into Wiley's murder. Maybe she really was raped by an average height and weight white male."

"Maybe she was," Glenn offered, "but let's run it down. First, stranger-to-stranger rapes are the rarest, right?"

"Yeah."

"Second, she said she was grabbed and pulled into what she described as a van. That's the most basic description of a vehicle she could give—a van. No color. No make. No nothing."

"And she had no physical evidence under her fingernails."

"Maybe her attacker had on a large coat, like Wiley did. So she couldn't scratch him."

"Yeah, but the attacker left no semen. And no pubic hairs were recovered."

"Maybe he manscaped. Do you remember seeing anything down there during the autopsy?"

"I didn't pay attention."

Glenn glanced at me.

"But we can call Rima and ask her if she did."

"You'll do that?"

"When we get back. Right now, the only connection between the rape to our case is the Gaskin alias. So, let's check the high school. If we find a Gaskin there, we'll know the truth."

***

Several years ago, Rogers High School underwent a multi-million-dollar renovation. The facility is now state of the art. Glenn and I walked into the administrative office. Both of us had been in the school while we were patrol officers. The updates were startling. For years, the school had been run-down, the laughingstock of locals. Now, it was cutting edge. The new students would never know how lucky they were.

A rail thin woman with curly blond hair stood behind the waist-high counter. She greeted us with a bright smile. "How may I help you?"

"Detectives Nash and Higgins," I said. Both of us showed our badges and identification cards.

Her face blanched as she stepped back. "Is everything okay?" Her eyes darted around.

"Yes, ma'am. Everything is fine." The fears of a school shooting never entered my mind but had obviously invaded hers. "We're following up on a case."

"Oh."

"We'd like to know if a certain person ever attended this school."

She breathed a sigh of relief and moved closer to the counter. "I'm sorry. Worst fears and all that."

"We understand."

"You want to know what now?"

"If a certain person ever attended this school."

Concern passed over her face. "I'm not sure if I can share that."

Glenn lightly touched my arm as he stepped forward. He leaned an elbow on the counter. The grin he affected was not one he ever shared with me. It was disarming and sweet, and the assistant grew a small, slightly embarrassed smile in return.

"We're not asking that you do anything inappropriate," Glenn said. "Unless, of course…" His eyes flared with a bit of mischievousness and the woman blushed. "We have a suspect who said she went to high school here with a friend. We only want to confirm this person actually went here. We won't need printouts or schedules. A simple yes will do—even a nod of the head. Will that work?"

Her eyes remained locked on Glenn as he spoke. She nodded in response to his question.

"Tanisha Kreshel," Glenn said, his voice low and smooth.

The assistant turned to her computer and began typing. The woman glanced several times at Glenn. His smile never faded.

"She was here," the woman said. "But never finished."

"Dropped out?"

"Uh-huh."

"What about a Wanda Gaskin?" Glenn asked, his voice slow and smooth.

Her fingers danced across the keyboard. "There was a Gaskin. A Simone Gaskin. Same grade as Ms. Kreshel. She didn't finish either."

A little too excitedly, I asked, "How about Raekwon Gaskin?"

The woman's fingers lifted from the keyboard. "I don't know about this."

Glenn reached out and lightly tapped the counter. "We're almost there. Just a little more."

Her eyes returned to Glenn.

"We're homicide detectives," he said. "This is follow-up to a murder investigation."

"A murder?"

"Uh-huh. That's right."

The assistant put her hands on the keyboard and focused her attention on the monitor. "He was here. A few years ahead of the girls. He finished his schooling."

"One more question," I asked.

"I can't," she said, regretfully shaking her head. "I've already done too much. If you want more, I think you should come back with the appropriate paperwork."

Glenn straightened and whispered into my ear, "Wait in the car."

"Huh?"

"Wait outside."

Without another word, I left the office.

***

Ten minutes later, Glenn dropped into the passenger seat. "Let's go."

"What was that about?"

He glanced at me.

"You asked me to wait in the car."

"I wanted to ask her out."

"Serious?"

He nodded. "We're going out tonight."

I slipped the car into gear, and it lurched from our spot along the curb. "I thought you were getting my question answered."

"I got that, too."

My eyes snapped to my partner.

"Raekwon Gaskin and Simone Gaskin are siblings. They had the same address."

"Another string to pull," I said.

"Another string," Glenn said.

Pulling into traffic, I asked, "So the question is, are Tanisha Kreshel and Raekwon Gaskin still connected today?"

40

We planned to confront Lynn Slater away from his office that night. Glenn called Ian Deaton, the security guard at the Public Safety Building, and asked for a heads-up if Slater left early. Deaton was more than happy to provide that information.

This meant we had a few hours still to work. We headed back to the department. I dropped Glenn off near the front doors, then headed into the parking lot. After climbing out, a Dodge Charger pulled up. Its passenger window rolled down and Detective James Morgan leaned over.

"Get in."

"I've got to—"

"Get in," he repeated, "unless you want everyone to know about your mental problems."

I stiffened and glanced around the parking lot.

Morgan gunned the engine when we drove off.

***

"You get what you needed from Joey?"

"Why ask me? You heard the whole conversation."

We turned westbound on Boone Avenue, blowing through a stop sign.

"Why do you think that?" A hint of a smile played across his lips. I couldn't see his gaze due to the baseball cap that was pulled low—the rolled brim hid his eyes.

"Don't bullshit me, Morgan. You were in her ear, coaching her on what to say."

The engine whined as he accelerated through a yellow light at the intersection of Boone and Monroe to turn northbound.

"Where are you taking me?"

"Nowhere," Morgan said. "We're driving and talking."

"We could do this at the station."

"There are too many eyes and ears."

"Ask your questions then. I've got work to do."

"This is work, cake-eater. Did you clear Joey yet?"

"I don't know."

His head jerked in my direction before returning to the road. "How do you not know?"

"I mean, I don't know."

"She didn't kill Junior. She had no need to."

"Because she had you."

"That's right."

"So maybe you *did* kill him."

Morgan sneered. "Are you fucking retarded, Nash?"

Metallica's "For Whom the Bell Tolls" blasted into my consciousness. The music felt like a knife slicing into my brain. I pressed a thumb into my eye to push the pain away, but it didn't work.

I opened a single eye as Morgan continued to speak. His words fell harmlessly against the circling lyrics and the hammering rhythm. As the guitars crunched and the drums pounded, my stomach turned, and I wanted to vomit.

Morgan shoved me. "Why would I do that?"

"Do what?"

"Are you retarded *and* deaf? Why would I kill Junior?"

"So he'd leave her alone."

"He was already doing that."

Metallica thundered inside my head. I removed the thumb from my eye and blinked it open. "Junior wanted to kill you. He even threatened to do so."

"That's old news—a couple years ago. Not last week."

"Ever tell the department about it?"

Morgan raced through the intersection at Monroe and Indiana, turning westbound. "What is it with you, Nash?"

"What do you mean?"

"You and your holier than thou act."

"I'm not holier than anybody."

"That's the first honest thing you've said."

"But I'm not in love with a prostitute."

He stuck a finger in my face but kept his eyes on the road. "Don't spread that shit. She's an informant."

"Then why doesn't she have a CI flag?"

He slammed on the brakes, cranked the wheel, and pulled into a parking lot. A car behind us blared its horn. "What is it with you?"

Metallica continued to play for only me. "Huh?"

"You think that's necessary?"

"What?" I asked, barely hearing the detective.

"To flag someone every time we make them a goddamned informant?"

"Yeah. I do. Otherwise, it's hinky."

"Hinky? The last guy I tagged as a CI ended up dead. Maybe I don't trust this department enough to do that anymore."

I turned in my seat to fully face him. "If your girl—"

"She's not my girl," he interrupted.

"—has any information on who killed Everson Wiley—"

"Stop making him sound like a goddamned citizen."

"—maybe that would change my mind about what kind of relationship you have with her."

"I don't have a relationship with her," he said. "Get that through your fucking skull."

"You seem awfully concerned about protecting her."

"She's a source, Nash. If you actually worked the street, you'd know how valuable they are."

"If she's so damn resourceful, why doesn't she have any info on Wiley's shooter?"

"She doesn't know who did him."

"Well," I said, tossing my hands in the air, "there you go."

Morgan shoved my shoulder. "The fuck does that mean?"

"It means I should go to Ackerman."

"Do what you want."

"I will."

He glared at me before he softly said something I could only make out from reading his lips.

The music faded, and I said, "Say it again."

"You heard me."

"Pretend I didn't."

"Go to Ackerman and I'll burn down Major Crimes."

"You wish."

"Try me."

I remained silent.

"How do you think I knew about you spilling your guts to Sigmund Freud? I got eyes and ears everywhere."

"A lot of people talk with a therapist."

I mentally chastised myself. *You stupid bastard. You knew this would happen.*

He held up his thumb. "I've got dirt on the glory hounds."

"Who?"

"You know who."

I did. More than one group had derogatorily referred to Delaney and Burkett as that. I could never imagine them being dirty.

Now Morgan's index finger popped out, along with his thumb. "I've got dirt on the hot heads, too."

While I imagined Parker and Johnson occasionally cutting a corner, I wouldn't consider them dirty.

Next, his middle finger extended. "I've even got your partner. Loverboy has more dirt than you can imagine."

"Stop it."

"Everybody's got dirt. Real dirt. Except you, cake-eater. No dirt on you, right?"

"Give it a rest."

"Nice and respectable, Dallas Nash. Like a bowl of warm vanilla ice cream."

I punched him as hard as I could. It was a terrible shot with my weak hand from a seated position. It clipped his mouth as it traveled past his nose and knocked his baseball hat cockeyed.

Morgan smiled as blood covered his teeth. He resettled his baseball cap.

"Attaboy, killer," he said. "Now, get the fuck outta my car."

41

"Where the hell you been?"

It took twenty-five minutes to walk back to the department.

"Talking to Morgan."

Glenn glanced around before asking in a low voice, "About what?"

"What do you think?"

He stood and moved near me. "Is he protecting the prostitute?"

"She doesn't need protection. She's not involved."

"Then he's meddling."

I nodded.

"You have enough to talk with the chain of command. Go to the captain. Ackerman has a hard-on for him. He'd bite on anything, even if it was circumstantial."

"He threatened to burn down Major Crimes if I said anything."

"Burn down?"

"He's got dirt on everyone."

"What kind of dirt?"

"I don't know, but the guy's a dirt collector."

Glenn's eyes narrowed. "I haven't done anything."

I whispered, "He says he's got stuff on Quinn and Marci."

My partner leaned in, "You don't think they're—"

"Even if they are, it's none of our business. This is what Morgan does. He threatens and intimidates. He may have something, he may not, but it's the fear of having something that keeps everyone in line."

Glenn moved back to his chair and dropped into it. "Did he say he had stuff on you?"

"He has it on everyone."

"Oh, man. I'm sorry."

I shrugged and dropped into my chair. "It is what it is."

"I looked up Simone Gaskin."

I turned to Glenn. "And what did you find?"

"She's dead. About a decade ago. Drug-related overdose."

"This day keeps getting better."

"Yeah, but we have a chance to turn around."

"How so?"

"The immigration agent." Glenn smiled. "We're still planning on talking with him later, right?"

***

"Ian texted he drives a blue Ford Fusion."

"Think that's a government car?"

Glenn's thumbs danced over his phone's keyboard. In a moment, he said, "His own."

It was almost five, and we were parked on Lincoln Street near the corner of Main Avenue. We couldn't see the front of the Federal Building, but rather the parking garage, which only allowed cars to exit our direction.

"Ian says he's a creature of habit. Out the door a few minutes before five every day—even Fridays."

"How does Ian know? He's in the lobby."

"He used to work the garage."

We sat quietly and watched the vehicles passing in two directions—southbound on Lincoln and eastbound on Main.

By a searching Department of Licensing and then city property records, we knew Lynn Slater lived on the South Hill. Our expectations were for him to exit the parking garage and continue eastbound on Main Street toward his home.

A blue Ford Fusion pulled to the light. "Car," Glenn announced and lifted his chin.

"I see it." I leaned forward. "Female driver."

"You sure?"

"Long hair, so I'm assuming." I fell back into my seat.

When the light changed, the Fusion passed through the intersection. It was indeed a woman behind the wheel.

Glenn yawned before asking, "You really think Morgan has dirt on everyone?"

"No. Some people maybe, but not everyone."

"Me, neither."

"But I wouldn't put it past him to make up a rumor to sully somebody's reputation."

"How's a guy like that stay on the department?"

"I'd like to blame civil service and the union."

"But?"

"The man gets results."

"And the chief loves him."

"There's that."

Another blue Ford pulled up to the intersection.

We both leaned forward this time, straining for a better look.

"It's a guy," Glenn said.

The light changed, and the Fusion moved through the intersection. As it passed, my partner averted his gaze. "It's him."

We stayed a couple of lengths behind as we drove through downtown. At the Main and Washington intersection, Slater failed to signal his turn southbound.

I wanted to swing out into traffic and catch up to him, but I was boxed in. Several seconds passed before the light changed and we were able to move. I activated my emergency lights to get cars out of my way. As we raced southbound, the engine of my Chevy Impala protested.

"See him?" I asked.

Glenn's head swiveled about. "Far left lane. Almost a block ahead."

After a check of my mirrors, I crossed several lanes and sped ahead. Cars moved out of the way. When I pulled behind Slater's car, he turned onto First Avenue and pulled over.

I grabbed the microphone. "Ida twenty-five, a traffic stop."

"Twenty-five," the dispatcher called back.

"Out with a blue Ford Fusion." I phonetically read the license plate. "Ida twenty-four is with me. Code four."

"Copy, code-four."

We both exited the car and approached Slater's vehicle. Glenn did so on the passenger side. Slater repeatedly checked his side and rearview mirrors.

I bent toward the open driver's window. "Mr. Slater."

"*You?*"

"Do you know why we stopped you today?"

"What did I do?"

"You failed to signal a right turn back there."

"I signaled."

"No, sir, you did not. License, registration, and proof of insurance, please."

"This isn't right. You're harassing me."

"License, registration, and proof of insurance, please."

"I'm not giving that to you. This is harassment."

I stood and looked over the hood of the car to Glenn. "Call for a supervisor."

Glenn headed toward the car.

When I leaned back down, I said, "A supervisor is on the way."

"What for?"

"You're required to provide the information I requested. When you refused, that became an arrestable offense."

"But I didn't do anything."

"It's usually a cite and release arrest, but still it's a misdemeanor."

"I think we've gotten off on the wrong foot." Slated reached for his wallet. "Gimme a second, and I'll get you what you need."

He hurriedly pulled out his driver's license, then found his insurance card and registration in the glove box. "Here you go."

When Glenn appeared at my shoulder, "A sergeant is on the way."

Slater blanched. "I'm cooperating. Tell him he doesn't need to come anymore."

"Step out of the car," I said. "My partner would like to talk with you."

* * *

"We've already been over this." Slater leaned his butt against the trunk of his car.

"I know," Glenn said, "but I have some more questions."

The federal agent's chin dropped to his chest.

"You went to Carlotta Winkler's apartment."

Slater lifted his head and crossed his arms. "So? That's what I'm supposed to do. I'm *supposed* to see where they live."

"Three times? Maybe more. It took you three times to see where and how she lived?"

"So."

"At night?"

"I never went there at night."

I glanced at Glenn. By the way his eyes narrowed, I knew he'd caught the lie.

"Mr. Slater, we know you were there after normal business hours."

"No, I wasn't." He set his jaw. "Never."

Glenn cocked his head. "Why did you go to her apartment multiple times?"

"I had follow-up questions."

My partner had said Slater visited her house three times twice now, and the man did not correct him. Glenn had walked him halfway to where we needed him to be. Could he get him the rest of the way?

"When you visited her apartment, what kind of questions were you following up on?"

"That's confidential."

Glenn's brow furrowed. "You had confidential questions?"

Slater's tongue peeked out to wet his lips. "Not for her, but the process is confidential."

"A witness said it looked more friendly than follow-up."

"A witness?" Slater said. "What witness?" He straightened, dropped his arms, and stepped away from the car. "You got no—"

"Put your butt back against the car."

Slater considered Glenn's order, then did what was asked.

It was a subtle win for my partner but getting compliance would help him continue to move the interview along. If an interviewee thought they got the upper hand and refused to follow directions, they were less likely to share info later.

Glenn asked, "Were you there for personal reasons?"

"I was doing my job."

"What about her?" My partner rubbed his chin. "Do you think she could have seen it a different way?"

"I doubt it."

"Maybe she thought there was something between you two."

Slater's eyes drifted down. "I don't know. I didn't try to lead her on."

"Of course, you didn't try, but could she have thought differently? You made repeated visits to her home, some of which were after hours. Could that have confused her?"

The immigration officer looked up. "I guess."

Slater now confirmed he visited Carlotta after hours. He missed it because Glenn offered him an excuse for why she might have seen their visits for something other than official.

"So," Glenn continued, "looking at it in a different light, when Carlotta dressed up and made herself look pretty, maybe she thought you two had something going."

The immigration officer licked his lips again. "I didn't see it before, but yeah, now that you're saying it that way, maybe she did."

"She was pretty, wasn't she?"

Slater shrugged.

"You weren't attracted to her?"

He shook his head. "No."

"I would have been."

"I was doing my job."

"But you had to have at least responded, subconsciously speaking, right? You're a man and I'm a man. If a girl were making herself available, I would have spotted it—especially a pretty thing like her. You had to."

Slater's face hardened. "I didn't. I had no idea what she felt." He must have seen where Glenn was leading him.

"We've requested her phone records," I said.

Slater's eyes locked onto mine.

"Will it show any phone calls from you?"

His brow corrugated. "Of course. That's standard for the process."

"What about text messages?" Glenn asked.

Slater's eyes snapped to my partner.

"We can request a transcript of those text messages. What will they say?"

The immigration officer's jaw flexed. "Nothing. They won't say anything."

"Really?"

"I only asked her to meet. That's all."

"What for?"

"The follow-up questions."

"That's it?"

"And what were those questions?" my partner asked.

"As I said before, that's confidential."

Glenn glanced at me, and I rolled my eyes.

Slater moved away from the trunk. "I don't know why you two are harassing me, but unless you're writing me a ticket, I'm leaving."

"You're free to go," Glenn said.

"I'm reviewing this with my supervisor." Slater pointed at us both. "I'm sure he'll be in contact with yours."

"We look forward to it," Glenn said.

When Slater drove away, I asked, "Do we have enough to get him in the box?"

"He admitted to after-hour visits, that she was pretty, that he sent text messages, and that she might have gotten the wrong idea."

"Not enough."

"But we're getting closer," Glenn said.

"He was worried about the text messages."

My partner nodded. "I know. Now, we know what we need to track down."

42

I'd fallen asleep sometime during the sports channel's ode to the team of the aughts—the New England Patriots. When my cell phone rang, I jolted awake.

The television's sound was still on, and the sports channel was re-running an earlier program. I ignored the announcer's chatter and answered the phone. "Nash."

"It's Parker."

I held the phone away from my face to see the time of the call. It was shortly after midnight. "What's going on?"

"Gaskin, right?"

"Huh?"

"Get up to speed, Nash. Raekwon Gaskin. That name mean anything?"

I rubbed my face. "Yeah."

"I'm out with him now."

Swinging my feet off the couch, I sat upright. "What'd he do?"

"He died."

"What?"

"He was murdered."

"How?"

"Three shots to the chest."

I stood, suddenly awake. "Where did you find him?"

"Riverside and Hogan."

"That's a block away from my victim. The M.O. is the same."

"We'll be out here for a while, in case you want to stop by, maybe take a look."

"Let me get dressed."

"All right, man."

"Hey, Parker."

"Yeah?"

"Thanks for the call."

"See you in a bit," he said and hung up.

***

On the way to the Gaskin crime scene, there was a nagging in the rear of my brain. It became louder until I headed toward the freeway. The small piece of paper with her home address was still in my notebook.

She lived in the valley on Liberty Avenue in a neighborhood known as Millwood. The houses were mostly built post World War II, and the cars that lined the streets were older sedans. To the east of her house was a small park. Nothing moved at that time of night.

I parked a couple of houses away and grabbed the radio microphone. "Ida twenty-five."

"Twenty-five," a female dispatcher responded.

"Log me on. Out for follow up." Then I gave the East Liberty address.

"Copy twenty-five."

After exiting my car, I quietly closed my door.

The porch light brightly burned. I unscrewed the bulb until it darkened, then rang the doorbell. For several minutes, there was no activity from inside the house. I rang the bell again before loudly knocking.

Several lights flicked on inside and there was a noise from behind the door. It opened a crack and Marlene Anderson peered out. Her eyes were closed slightly, and her hair was mussed.

"Detective?" she whispered. Her voice was hoarse from sleep. "What's going on?"

"Can I come in?"

She blinked a couple times, holding the last one longer than normal. "It's a little late."

"Raekwon Gaskin was murdered tonight."

She shushed me. "Lower your voice. My daughter is asleep."

"I'd like to talk with you about it."

"Why?"

"I want to make sure you're not involved."

Her face scrunched with anger. "I didn't kill him any more than I killed Junior."

"Then let's talk."

Marlene stepped back and opened the door. She wore a baggy sweatshirt. Her long legs were bare. "Let me put some pants on."

I averted my eyes when she walked away. After stepping into the house, I closed the door.

A moment later she returned, buttoning a pair of Levi 501s. She now wore a pair of glasses. "Ask your questions, then go. Or if you want to talk more, we can do it tomorrow."

"Where were you tonight?"

She opened her hands. "Are you kidding?"

"Is there anyone that can provide an alibi?"

"My six-year-old and my pillow."

"No adult?"

"No one is sharing my bed, if that's what you're asking." The defiance in her voice was clear.

"I wasn't asking that."

She ran her fingers through her long hair. "Then why come to my house?"

"To rule you out."

"I hoped I would have proved my innocence by now."

"I would have thought that, too, but your name keeps coming up."

"How so?"

"Tanisha Kreshel."

"What about her?"

"You responded to her rape. Why were you there?"

"The hospital called. What was I supposed to do?"

"When did you become a rape advocate? That's not what your agency does, is it?"

"We're there for *any* woman. Our mission is empowerment. When a woman has been raped, her power has been stolen. We want to get it back as quickly as possible."

I remembered the posters and especially the sticker that clung to the waiting room wall—*Dead Men Don't Rape.*

"Why did the hospital call *you*? The city has its own rape advocates."

"And they do a fine job," she said. "We're another resource. The hospital must have given her an option. I'm one of the counselors at our agency."

"But you don't have a degree."

Her face flattened. "I have life experience. That's a little more insightful than a degree."

"Did she tell you she's close to Raekwon Gaskin?"

"Why would she?"

"She went to school with him and his sister. She used Gaskin as an alibi once. That's how we connected her to Tiger."

"What's that got to do with me?"

"Her rape—we believe Junior did it."

Marlene's jaw flexed before she answered. "She didn't tell me that."

"If she had, would you have told me?"

"Maybe."

"Would you have told her to tell the cops?"

"That's a stupid question."

"Is it? Dead men don't rape."

"What?"

"The sticker in your office."

"What sticker?"

"There's one in your lobby."

"I didn't put it there," she said.

"If Junior raped her, he'll never do it again."

"That's for sure." Her eyes narrowed. "But she didn't tell me who raped her."

"You sure you didn't want to get even with Junior?"

"Watch yourself, Detective."

"For all those years of being turned out."

Even though I saw it coming, I stayed put. She slapped my face. Had I expected remorse, I would have been disappointed.

"You want to arrest me for assault, do it. But I didn't kill Junior, and I didn't kill Tiger."

Neither of us noticed her until she said, "Mommy?"

Marlene's eyes widened, and she hurried over to the little girl. With a deft swoop, she lifted the child. "I'm sorry, Sadie. Were we talking too loud?"

The girl nodded.

"This is mommy's friend, Dallas." She pointed at me. "You don't have to be scared. He's a nice man."

I held out my hand. Sadie shook it twice, then buried her head in her mother's neck.

"I was here all night," Marlene said, her voice soft.

"Can we talk tomorrow?"

"Yes, Detect—" She eyed her daughter. "Dallas. Tomorrow would be fine."

I waved goodbye to Sadie before heading to my car.

***

Raekwon Gaskin lay on the sidewalk. He was on his back, staring up into the night sky.

"Did he have a gun?" I asked.

"In his waistband," Andrew Parker said. "Guy never pulled it."

Nearby, Jessie Johnson, Parker's partner, talked with the forensic team.

I knelt next to the body. "Three shots at close range—never expected it."

"Knew his attacker, right?"

"Or didn't fear them."

"Probably both."

When I stood, the world swayed. I bent over and put my hands on my knees.

"You okay?" Parker asked.

I took a deep breath. "Just lightheaded."

"You're not eating right."

While my world stabilized, I surveyed the area.

It was eerily similar to the Everson Wiley crime scene. Several faces peered out from the crowd. Patrol had interviewed some of them, but no one had reported seeing or hearing anything. A couple of prostitutes huddled together, watching us. I knew them by name now—Shawna Brown and Alexa Pollard.

Nearby, a woman with a baseball hat pulled down stood alone. Her hands were shoved into her army jacket. With her intense gaze and ginger hair, she looked familiar. I struggled to place her.

Bile rose in my throat, and I struggled to hold it back. I closed my eyes and forced it down. Her Freedom, I thought. The woman with the baseball hat had met with Marlene. When I opened my eyes, the woman was gone.

"What took you so long to get down here?"

"Didn't realize it was a long time," I muttered, searching the crowd for the woman in the baseball hat.

"Whatever."

He was irritated with me, but I didn't want to tell him about Marlene. If I told Parker about her, he'd work it backwards until he discovered why. Then there would be one more person who knew about her life as a prostitute. She didn't need that.

I asked, "You going to talk with Tanisha Kreshel again?"

"You think she's involved with this?"

I replayed my conversation with her.

Parker pursed his lips and stared at the body. "I'll talk with her."

"When?"

"After I break from here, I'll see if she's home."

"Mind if I join you?"

"Me and you?"

I nodded.

"All right, Nash. We'll talk with her together."

43

The morning sun hung low on the eastern horizon.

"I'm going on a follow-up interview with Andrew Parker today." With my hands in my pockets, I tugged my coat tighter and stared at her marker. "I know. Weird, huh?"

I nodded at nothing in particular.

"We tried last night, but the woman wasn't home. We agreed to make another run at it today."

I looked up. There weren't any clouds in the sky.

"Playing nice with Parker. I guess I'm trying something new. Maybe it'll make you proud."

My gaze returned to her headstone. "I'm sorry about the other night—for being so weird. I was having a bad night and…" I looked away. "I shouldn't have brought it here. I'm sorry."

I bent and brushed some dirt away from the marble. The letters of her name were rough under my fingers.

"I haven't said it in a while, but I want you to know I still love you. I've never stopped. Even when I'm sad, it's not because of you, it's because—"

Tears formed in my eyes.

"Well, you know why. I guess I don't have much more to say than that."

***

Andrew Parker knocked on the door, then studied me. "You get any sleep?"

"Some. You?"

He shrugged. It was shortly after ten and we were in the hallway of Tanisha Kreshel's apartment building. Parker wore a light jacket and a hooded sweatshirt underneath. The relaxed outfit was a far cry from the ill-fitting suits he wore during the week.

The door cracked slightly, and the bruised eye appeared again.

"Detective Parker. Remember me?" His voice had raised an octave and softened considerably. Concern washed over his face.

"From the night," Tanisha said.

"That's right."

"Can we come in?"

Her eye moved to me and narrowed. "I guess." The door closed.

Parker considered me. "She doesn't like you."

I shrugged.

"Way to go, Big Time."

Before I could respond, the door opened, and Tanisha stepped back. She wore a tan sweater, white jeans, and tan boots.

Parker followed her inside the apartment, and I closed the door behind us. She climbed into the leather recliner, pushed off her boots, and tucked her feet under herself. Parker and I took up positions on the couch.

"Ms. Kreshel—" Parker began.

"Tanisha," she said.

"Tanisha." His voice was still soft and an octave higher than normal. "I'm sorry to bother you." A transformation had taken place in Parker. Gone was the collected anger that always rode face forward. Instead, his expression was open and caring. I'd never seen the man this way.

"Officers were here yesterday." She glanced at me.

"Yes, ma'am, I know." Parker didn't look in my direction. Instead, he concentrated solely on her. "That's why I'm here."

"I don't understand?"

"Raekwon Gaskin."

She remained stone-faced. "What about him?"

"Detective Nash," Parker said, "seems to think you know him."

"I told him I didn't. I knew a Gaskin in high school, but that's about it."

Parker rubbed his cheek. "Well… that's good."

Tanisha looked between Parker and me. "Why do you say that?"

"Last night, Raekwon was murdered."

She lifted her hand to her mouth.

"Shot three times in the chest, like—" Parker turned to me. "What's his name?"

"Everson Wiley," I said. "Junior."

Tears welled in Tanisha's eyes, and she shook her head.

Parker leaned forward. "Raekwon was murdered in the same manner as this other man."

The tears streaked down her face now. Parker stood and walked into the bathroom. He returned with a box of tissues and placed his free hand on her shoulder. "Here," he whispered.

Tanisha took the box and nodded. Her face pinched then, and she hunched, weeping uncontrollably. Her hands balled around several tissues as she cried.

After several moments, Parker softly said, "We need to ask some questions."

Amid her sobs, Tanisha nodded.

"What was your relationship to Raekwon?"

She straightened. She swallowed several times as she fought for control. "Ray was… my brother."

"Your brother?"

"Yes."

"You have different last names."

"We aren't related by blood."

"Then how were you related?"

"His sister was my friend." New tears started and Tanisha dabbed at her eyes. Parker cocked his head as he studied the woman.

Tanisha continued. "Simone died after high school. She got into heroin. Started messing around with it because of some boy. She OD'd one night. After that, Ray and I sorted of bonded. He needed a sister, and I needed family."

"Did you know what Ray did?"

"You're asking if I knew he was a pimp?"

Parker nodded.

"Of course, I knew."

"It didn't bother you?"

She shrugged. "Life's hard."

Looking for the connection to Junior, I asked, "You never worked with him?"

Anger flashed in her eyes. "My brother wouldn't do that to me."

Parker lifted a hand in a conciliatory manner. "Detective Nash knows you're a barista." He flashed an angry look at me. "It was in my report."

She turned her head back toward Parker, but her gaze lingered on me.

"Why did you lie to Detective Nash about Raekwon?" Parker's voice was gentle and caring.

Her eyes returned to him. "He wanted to get Ray in trouble."

"He's investigating the murder of—"

"I knew what he was doing." Her voice took on an edge.

"Did you know—"

"*Junior*," she said. She opened her mouth to say something further, but quickly bit it off.

"What happened between you and Junior?" I asked.

Fury burned in her eyes, but she remained silent.

Parker shifted his sitting position. "Have you ever put together a puzzle?"

Tanisha muttered, "Yeah."

"That's what we're doing," he continued, "except we don't know what the finished picture is supposed to look like. We have all these pieces, some of them aren't colored in yet, others are upside down, and we're trying to click all of them together. Sometimes you find pieces that don't belong to your puzzle, but you won't know that until you flip them over, study them, and decide they're in the wrong place. But we can't get rid of a piece until we're sure it doesn't belong to this puzzle. Do you understand?"

She remained quiet for several moments. "Junior wanted Ray's territory. Ray told him to keep on the other side of Division where he belonged or there'd be hell to pay."

Parker slowly nodded. "And?"

"Junior didn't take Ray's threat seriously because he sent one of his girls down there to work. Ray found her, but made his girls take care of it. Sort of psychological warfare if you will. I guess they beat holy hell out of her."

Parker glanced at me, and I nodded.

Tanisha wiped her nose. "Supposedly, Junior took the whole thing as an affront. He demanded a parlay and wanted a girl in retribution."

"What did Ray do?" Parker asked.

She rolled her eyes. "What do you think he did? He told Junior to fuck himself. Ray said the man caused the problem when he sent a girl into his neighborhood. You should have seen Junior's face."

I scooted forward to the edge of the couch. "You were there when that happened?"

"That's when Junior saw me, yeah. Ray and I were having lunch at Subway—the one on Third."

"Did he think you were working?" I asked.

She pulled back slightly. "Did he think I was a whore? No, he knew exactly who I was. He even came by the coffee stand to show me he knew where I worked."

"The rape," I said, and her eyes snapped to me.

She stayed quiet as her jaw muscles flexed. I caught Parker watching me from the corner of my eye.

"Junior did it," I said.

Tanisha didn't look away, and Parker's attention returned to the woman.

I continued. "It was payback for what Ray did to one of his girls."

Her eyes lowered now, but still no admission.

"He knew who you were and where you worked. You already admitted that."

Tanisha looked up. Her lips parted, but she remained silent.

Parker froze now. Not wanting to disturb the moment.

Softly, carefully, I asked, "Where did he grab you?"

"Out there," she said, thumbing toward the street, "as I was coming home."

"Why didn't you tell the responding officer this? Why be uncooperative?"

She eyed both of us and her jaw hardened. "What would you have done?"

"Arrest him," Parker and I said in unison.

"And let him sit in a cell? Maybe he gets convicted, maybe not."

"He would have been convicted," Parker said.

"I wanted him dead."

Dead men don't rape.

"After I left the hospital," she continued, "I went to Ray and told him what happened. He said he would take care of it, but somebody got to Junior first."

"So, Ray didn't kill him?" I asked.

"Somebody got to him first," she said emphatically. "That's the truth. What difference would it have made had he killed him? Ray's dead now, too."

She lowered her head, but the tears had stopped.

Scooting to the edge of the couch, Parker asked, "Do you know anyone who would have wanted to kill Ray?"

Tanisha said, "There were probably some out there, but I don't know who they are."

Parker glanced at me and shrugged. We both stood. "Thank you for your time," Parker said and then stepped by me.

"Ms. Kreshel," I said. "One more question."

She lifted her eyes.

"At the hospital, when you spoke with the advocate, did you tell her about Junior?"

She shook her head. "If I did, she would have told you guys. Then I couldn't have…" Her words trailed off, and she looked out the window.

Parker tapped my shoulder and jerked his head toward the door. I followed him out.

"I've always hated this area," Parker said and waved his hand.

"Why's that?"

"Look at it."

After the interview with Tanisha Kreshel, Parker and I went down to the East Sprague corridor. We stood at the corner of Sprague and Perry and surveyed the people walking by.

"This whole street—from the other side of downtown to Freya—is just, I don't know, what's the word I'm looking for?"

"Nasty?"

"Mean. This whole street is *mean*. Don't you feel it?"

Across the street, a homeless man slept in the doorway of an antique store. Shawna Brown smoked a cigarette as she walked by him, motioning toward passing vehicles until she saw me. A twitchy white male with long hair stepped out from behind a building and held onto a traffic sign as he swayed.

Parker continued. "Down here, people destroy each other to get by. Drugs, guns, whores. Life isn't worth anything beyond that. But go further that way," Parker pointed east, "you get to the used car salesmen. Different type of mean, same street, but people are still eating people. Fucking gross."

The rant surprised me. He seemed the type of cop who would love this type of corridor—where evil lived and thrived. However, there was something underneath

Parker that wasn't seen by most. Maybe this was what the brass knew when they promoted him to Major Crimes.

"Anyway," he said with a dismissive flick of the wrist, "you said you interviewed some of the girls down here?"

"When we get back to the department, I'll give you a list that Crime Analysis pulled together. I've identified those who worked for Junior, Tiger, or Damon."

"Damon?"

"The other pimp running girls in this area."

"Think he had a thing out for Junior and Tiger?"

"It didn't seem that way."

"If that's so, maybe he has a bullseye on his back. Two out of three are dead."

"Maybe."

"What's he look like? In case I run across him."

I gave a quick description, then added, "Morgan described him as The Great White Hope."

Parker's lip curled. "Fucking Morgan. You think he has the pulse down here?"

"Suppose so."

"Too bad."

"Why?"

"I don't want to ask him for any intel. Guy irritates the hell out of me."

Down the block, a girl exited a car. She waved goodbye to the driver as the car moved back into traffic. She had on the same heavy winter coat and pom pom hat she did from a few nights before.

"Damn," I muttered.

The girl stuck a vapor pen in her mouth as she walked. Every few steps, she turned to face traffic, dipping slightly to make eye contact with drivers.

"You know that one?" Parker asked.

"Yeah."

"What's so special about her?"

"She's sixteen."

We picked up our pace as a red Ford Taurus pulled to the side. Chanel leaned into the open passenger window.

As I made it to the car, I smacked the trunk several times. "Police!" I yelled.

The girl jumped away from the car, and the vehicle accelerated, slipping back into traffic.

"What's your problem, man?" she said.

"You're my problem. You were supposed to stay off these streets."

Chanel eyed Parker.

"Detective Parker, this is Chanel Nelson."

"What's up, kid?"

She pointed at me. "This geezer is busting my balls."

Parker fought back a smile. "Geezer. I love it."

"You're out here working," I said, "when you should be home doing stuff sixteen-year-old girls do."

A salacious grin spread across her lips, and she dropped her coat down over her bare shoulder. "I am doing what sixteen-year-olds do. Only, I'm getting paid for it. Most girls at school do this with their boyfriends and get nothing except bad reputations and abortions."

Parker's eyebrows lifted. "Wow."

"I'm going to walk her home."

"No, you're not," Chanel said.

"Then I'll book you into juvie."

She sighed.

"Where's she live?" Parker asked.

I thumbed in the direction where Marlene had indicated. "I want to meet her grandmother."

"All right, geezer," he said with a chuckle. "I'm going to walk around a bit, maybe head back to the West End. If we don't catch up again, I'll see you on Monday." He stuck out his fist for a bump.

I did so and said, "See you Monday."

As he turned, I said, "Hey Parker."

"Yeah?"

"Nice work with Tanisha."

He nodded, then headed off.

***

"Why are you out here?" I asked.

"What else am I supposed to do?"

"Go to school."

"It's Saturday."

Feeling slightly stupid, I said, "How about hanging with your friends?"

Chanel sucked on her vape pen, then blew out a cloud of peppermint-scented vapor. "I don't have any. Besides, the kids from school are stupid."

"There's got to be something you'd rather be doing than this."

Her face pinched. "Why?"

The kid had a fantastic way of making me feel old and out of touch. "You're telling me this is what you want to do—selling yourself?"

"What I want is to be left alone. I don't need an old, white man to tell me how to live my life." She remained by my side, though—a child in need of a guardian, regardless of her words.

We turned a corner and passed a dilapidated home. It seemed that's all we passed. Rundown homes with debris, car parts, or garbage in the front yards. This part of town wasn't experiencing the gentrification that many other neighborhoods were.

"This journey you're on," I said, "is it because of your mom?"

"Huh?"

"Are you trying to connect with her in some way?"

"She was a junkie. Why would I want to reconnect with any of that?"

"So, you're not using?"

"Only pot, but that's legal."

"When you're twenty-one."

Chanel chuckled. "Don't be a prude."

"Who was your mom's pimp?"

"Junior."

I stopped, and she turned to me with a furrowed brow. "What?"

"You don't think that's—" I wanted to say revolting, but instead I said something she might understand "—creepy?"

"What's creepy about it?"

"He pimped out you *and* your mom."

She inhaled deeply on her pen. As she spoke, vapor escaped from her mouth. "He was sort of a father figure, so I figured I could trust him."

I stared at her in disbelief.

"What? He looked out for me."

"Did you and he…?"

"Sure."

"Oh."

"Stop shaking your head. Some fathers do that with their daughters. It's life."

"Not a good one."

"I had to pay someone, so why not someone who took care of me?"

"You don't have to be on the street."

She stuck the vape pen in her mouth but didn't inhale. "You come down here and tell me how it should be, but you have no idea that this is what I want. I'm good with it. So, what if I gotta pay a tax? You gotta pay taxes. Everyone pays a tax to someone. No different down here.

So, it's gonna be Junior or Damon, and I made sure it was Junior being family and all."

"Besides, Damon doesn't take underage girls."

Her lip curled. "So he claims."

"Are you saying he does?"

She shrugged. "A man says one thing until he's given a better choice."

"Did you hear about Tiger?"

She shot me a sideways glance.

"Word travels fast."

"It's the street, and I didn't kill him."

"Why did you go to him?"

"I may be young, Detective, but I'm not stupid. With Junior gone, Tiger was coming in. If that happened, all the girls better get in line. Everybody knows what happened when Nessa tried to push into his territory."

Recalling a name that I heard a couple of times now, I said, "Vanessa Bolkan."

"Uh-huh. She just now got the nerve to come around the way."

"You saw her?"

"She's not working, but I saw yesterday. She said she was only visiting."

I pulled the folded list from my back pocket. It was creased and wrinkled from many days of wear. Chanel leaned over the paper and tapped the paper next to Vanessa's picture.

"That's her."

There she was—the woman in the army jacket, jeans, and running shoes who stood in the crowd at Gaskin's murder scene. She was the same woman who had walked out of Marlene's office when we first met.

Chanel flicked the paper. "That's why I wanted to make nice with Tiger. So, I wouldn't end up like Nessa. She got busted up bad."

We started walking again, and I tucked the paper away.

"With Tiger gone," I said, "you don't have much choice now. Damon's not going to allow you to run around independent."

"Fuck Damon. If he won't allow it, I'll..." Her thought trailed off.

"You'll what?"

"Nothing. I'm blowing off steam. I'll figure this out, and I don't need you telling me what I can and can't do."

We turned south on Helena Street.

When I was sixteen, I worried about learning how to throw a curve ball and wondering if I'd ever get a girlfriend. When it came to worldly knowledge, this kid was light years ahead of where I was at that age. Hell, she probably knew more than I did today.

"That's my house." She pointed at a beat-up Craftsman.

We shuffled up the sidewalk, and Chanel entered without knocking.

I stopped at the front door. "Your grandmother—I'd like to meet her."

"Help yourself. She's watching TV."

"What's her name?"

"Doris."

Seated in a large recliner was an overweight, elderly woman in a sleeping gown. Her gray hair was tousled, and her lower jaw hung slack. She stared at a flat screen television perched on top of what I assumed was an inoperable console TV. On the screen was a black and white Western.

"Doris?" I said.

She blinked several times but didn't bother looking in my direction.

"I'm Detective Nash with the Spokane Police Department. I'd like to talk about your granddaughter."

Doris licked her lips, then rubbed them together. Her attention remained on the television. "What's she done?"

"She's walking the street."

"That a crime?"

"As a prostitute."

She scratched her breast and muttered, "Hmm."

"Chanel's putting herself into extremely dangerous situations."

"I'll talk to her."

"When?"

"When what?"

"When will you talk to her?"

"About what?"

"About walking the street."

"Ain't no crime in that."

I backed away from Doris and left her watching the television. Chanel watched with amusement. "See? Everything's cool."

"It's not cool. What about your dad?"

Her face scrunched. "What about *him*?"

"Can you go stay with him?"

She clucked her tongue. "I don't even know who he is. He's never been in the picture."

"Did your mom ever talk about him?"

Chanel shook her head. "Never. Doris never says shit about him, either. He could be you for all I know."

I straightened.

"Relax, old man, I'm not accusing you of anything. Besides, we've got plenty of food, so settle down."

Thumbing toward Doris, I asked, "She goes shopping?"

"Someone brings it for us."

I cocked my head.

"The agencies and don't ask which ones because I don't know. They show up with groceries and then they leave. We'll be fine."

"This place isn't healthy. You need to go somewhere safe."

"I'm fine."

"Get your stuff. I'll take you—"

"No." Her face purpled.

I motioned her toward me. "Please, let me—"

"I'm not going anywhere with you."

"I'm trying to help."

"I don't need your help."

"Yeah, you do," I said. "Look around."

"What are you gonna do? Drag me out of my house? Kidnap me?"

"I'll call CPS."

"Do what you want." She walked into the back of the house, and I followed.

"Listen, kid."

She spun around, surprised I was in her room.

Anti-prostitution posters covered the walls. I'd seen many of them in the offices of Her Freedom. The disconnect between her actions and these posters didn't make any sense.

"I didn't invite you back here." Her voice rose with anger.

I pointed at the images adorning the walls. "What are you doing? I don't under—"

"Get out!" she yelled. "Get out!"

I turned to leave. Above the light switch was the same *Dead Men Don't Rape* sticker I'd seen in the lobby. I touched it and looked back at her.

"Out!" she hollered.

45

"She's a lost kid," Marlene Anderson said.

We were at the Starbucks on East Sprague, across from Costco and Home Depot. It was a retail oasis, a couple miles from the strip where I'd picked up Chanel.

After leaving the teenager's house, I called Marlene and requested a meeting. I wanted to follow up on last night's discussion and apologize for the confrontational nature of my visit. Doing so at her office seemed too formal.

Marlene sipped her coffee. "She let you into her room?"

"I walked in uninvited."

"I'm sure she loved that."

"She most certainly did not. Have you ever seen the room?"

"I haven't."

I described what I saw and the teenager's reaction. "The dissonance was shocking."

Marlene removed the lid from her cup and a small burst of steam rose. "You better than anyone should know people's actions never align neatly with the image they portray to others."

"But the image she's portraying to others is a prostitute."

She shrugged. "And?"

"Her room suggests she hates it."

"You find that difficult to process? It's simple, Detective."

"Dallas," I said.

"It's simple, Dallas. She hates her mother for who she was, and she's punishing herself for who she is."

I shook my head. The whole concept baffled me.

"She's a messed-up girl, living her mother's life—same neighborhood, same house, same room even."

"Same pimp."

Her gaze met mine. "Yeah."

"I'm sorry."

"For bringing up Junior? Don't be. He's dead. He can't get at me or her ever again."

"But why connect with her mother that way? Why not be something different? Something better?"

"Look who she has guiding her."

"The grandmother was something. Fully maxed out, just blinking and breathing."

"Chanel only has memories of her mother, and she's trying to understand why her mom did certain things and made certain choices."

"It's so destructive."

"Of course it is. You'll never comprehend what she's going through, so stop trying to place her into a box that fits your paradigm of backyard barbecues and band camp. Trying to understand her choices won't make it any better. Accept that she's screwed up—period. When you do that, maybe you'll be able to reach out and she'll respond."

It sounded like she was describing herself. I sipped my coffee and studied her. She had applied a light amount of make-up today and wore her reading glasses. She also had on a knitted cap and simple earrings.

Marlene asked, "Did you find Tiger's killer?"

"Not yet, but we will."

She raised her eyebrows.

"What?"

"Nothing."

"It's obviously something, or you wouldn't have made that face."

"Are you working as hard to find his killer as you are Junior's?"

I didn't want to go into how Gaskin was officially Parker's case, so I simply said, "Yes."

"Too bad."

"Why?"

"Because Tiger was another leech on society. Somebody did us another favor."

"How's that? There's a power vacuum now. Another pimp will step in and fill the gap."

"Maybe not."

"How can you say that?"

"It's changing down there. Development is occurring. The girls are getting pushed off Sprague. Most of the drug trade is gone. It's not the same as it used to be."

"It will go elsewhere. Damon described it as squeezing water."

"Damon," she said. "Why don't you think he did it?"

"Maybe he did."

"You don't sound convinced."

"I'm not. He had an agreement with Junior to split the territory, so he didn't need the man out of the way. Also, the murder weapon was a small caliber—not exactly what we would expect in a man's gun."

"A *man's gun* is sexist thinking."

I considered her accusation before answering, "Perhaps, but it's based on experience."

"What experience is that?"

"Men tend toward higher caliber weapons."

"You're expecting the killer to be a woman. You've already made your decision."

"I have no expectations."

"Which is why you wanted to look inside Chanel's room."

"Could she have killed Junior?"

"Anyone *could* have killed Junior. He was an evil man."

Iron Maiden's "The Evil That Men Do" burst into my consciousness. The pain was overwhelming. I shut my eyes and pushed my thumb against my temple. When that didn't help, I shoved a knuckle into my eye. The pressure alleviated some of the pain. I remained like that for some time.

When I opened my eyes, Marlene watched me with intense scrutiny.

The chorus whipped around my head as the drums and guitars continued their feverish pace.

She said something I couldn't hear.

I closed my eyes and inhaled deeply, held it for a couple of seconds, then forced it out. I repeated this a few times until the music lessened.

"—you okay?" Her voice wasn't panicked.

I nodded. "I'm fine."

"No," she said. "You're not."

"I am."

"You're coming down."

"What?"

Her disappointment was obvious. "You're a junkie."

"I am *not* a junkie."

"You act like one who's kicking a habit. Sudden weight loss. Crabby. You passed out in my office. I bet you're depressed. Are you depressed?"

I sipped my coffee.

"I'm a recovering addict," she said. "Once an addict, always an addict. Did you know that? You probably did. Are you getting help?"

"I'm seeing a therapist."

"For your habit?"

"I don't have a habit."

"Then what is this?" She waved at me.

I slowly turned my cup and stared at the coffee inside. "My wife died."

"When did that happen?"

I was taken aback. She'd offered no platitudes. Not an "I'm sorry for your loss" or "That's terrible" or even a sappy, silent look of dismay. Instead, she stared at me and waited for an answer.

"A year ago."

"Twelve months. And you loved her?"

"Of course."

"It's not a stupid question, Detective. Most men don't love their wives. Trust me. I know. What was her name?"

"Bobbie."

"A boy's name."

"Roberta Ann."

"Would Bobbie want you like this?"

"Definitely not."

"Then maybe you should straighten up and fly right."

"Easier said than done."

"Why?"

I tapped the side of my head.

"You're depressed."

"More than that."

"You're getting headaches."

"I do, but it's something else."

"I can't read your mind, Detective," Her voice softened, but her eyes remained keenly focused. "You'll have to explain it."

I slowly turned my coffee cup, watching the green Starbucks logo disappear, then reappear. I already knew her secret. It seemed easy to share mine now. "I hear music."

"Music? Like songs?"

I nodded.

She leaned forward. "Are you hearing something now?"

"Yeah."

"Is that why you pressed your head? Put the finger in your eye? Does it hurt?"

"Very much," I muttered.

"And at my office, is that why you passed out? You had one of these… episodes?"

"Uh-huh."

She folded her arms. "The music started after she died?"

"Yes.

"How long were you with her?"

"Since high school."

"High school sweethearts? I didn't think that was such a thing."

"It was with us."

Marlene picked up her coffee and sipped it. Her eyes drifted out the window to the passing traffic. Her face seemed to soften further as she thought about something. When she turned back, she said, "You've never been alone."

"No."

"And here you are."

"Here I am."

"Life isn't fair."

"I knew that from my work."

"It's different when it comes home."

It wasn't meant to be cruel, but the words cut through my heart. Tears filled my eyes.

She reached out and covered my hand with hers. "I'm sorry, Dallas. I didn't mean—"

I pulled my hand from under hers and wiped my face. "It's fine. And you're right. It's different when it comes home."

"You need to leave the past where it is. She's dead and you're alive."

"It's not that simple."

"If the roles were reversed, would you want her suffering the way you are?"

"Never," I said, and I meant it with my entire being.

"Then why are you doing this to yourself?"

I rubbed my hand over my mouth. "I'm not doing this to myself."

"Of course you are. You're a junkie. Your wife is the drug you won't kick."

My hands balled as I fought back more tears. "Where do you get off?"

Marlene's shrug was subtle. "You seem like a decent guy who's whipping himself because the woman he loved is gone."

"It's time to go."

I stood and loudly scooted my chair back.

"Dallas," she said. "The past is a killer. Carry it around for too long, and it's eventually going to get you."

I headed toward the door, not bothering to look back.

46

When I awoke on Sunday morning, I sat upright on the couch and put my face in my hands. There was no song in my head. There was, however, one thought that looped over and over.

The past is a killer.

Marlene had said that.

She also called me a junkie.

I shuffled into the kitchen, started a pot of coffee, then took a shower. While the hot water scalded my skin, my head remained mostly clear. Occasionally, Marlene's words returned.

The past is a killer.

In the living room, I shivered as I picked through the few remaining wrinkled clothes in the laundry basket. I'd need to do some laundry today—probably the dishes, too.

After slipping into a loose pair of jeans and a baggy T-shirt, I returned to the kitchen for a cup of coffee. From the inside of the refrigerator door, I grabbed my bottle of creamer, leaving Bobbie's where it was. Mine was nearly empty, and I shook it. I poured the few drops into my cup and realized it wouldn't be enough to make my coffee the way I liked it.

I considered the container of creamer I kept in the fridge for Bobbie. In the year since she'd been gone, I'd never used any of hers. I didn't like the flavored stuff, so why did I keep any of it around?

Why not just put an empty bottle in there and act as if it were always full?

Was that any less crazy than pretending she was going to show up and share a cup of morning coffee with me?

I stared at the bottle of Bobbie's creamer and remembered Marlene's full admonishment.

The past is a killer. Carry it around for too long, and it's eventually going to get you.

The flavored cream ran slowly down the sink. When the bottle was empty, I ran water through both containers and tossed them into the recycle bin. Then I washed out my coffee cup, removing the remaining cream from it.

I poured myself a cup of black coffee and stepped into the hallway.

***

Six cardboard boxes—for almost a year, I avoided our bedroom because of them.

When I initially packed her clothes, I thought about donating them. Then I considered storing the boxes in the basement, but she didn't belong down there.

I wanted to keep her close. The rational side of me knew that was impossible—she was dead and not coming back.

As I carried the first box to my truck, a headache formed. There wasn't any accompanying music, so I imagined it as pent-up emotions escaping. The second box seemed lighter, but the tears started then.

I tripped while carrying the fourth and landed on it. Crushing the box didn't matter, as it only contained clothes. I stood, wiped the tears from my face, and continued outside.

When all the boxes were in the truck, I thought about where they should go. I wanted them to go someplace important, somewhere they could make a difference.

Why should that matter? They were clothes. They were stuff. I should have been able to throw the damn things away and move on with my life. The tears flowed as I struggled to make up my mind.

It was stupid to cry over clothes.

***

"What are you dropping off?" the man asked before jumping down from The Salvation Army's loading dock.

He wore an orange vest over his sweatshirt. Large leather gloves covered his hands. A dirty Green Bay Packers baseball hat sat cockeyed on his head.

Lowering the tailgate, I said, "Clothes and a TV." I grabbed the television on the way out. I figured if I was going to make a change, I should make it a big one. I'd spent too much time sitting in front of the tube over the past year.

When he reached for the TV, I said, "It doesn't have the remote anymore, but the set works fine."

The worker gently placed it on the dock and said, "Don't matter none. People will still buy it. Or they'll go buy one of those universals."

He then slid the first box to the rear of the truck bed. "Looks like you're cleaning house." He hefted the box to the dock, then shoved it away to allow room for those to follow.

I dragged the second box to the edge of the truck, lifted it, and placed it on the loading dock. Briefly, I wondered what clothes might be inside. Then I pushed it and the remains of those memories away.

"Watching the games today?"

I motioned toward the TV. "Got no way, now."

He grabbed the third box. "We listen to them here." His voice strained as he hefted the largest box onto the dock. "Gotta find ways to enjoy your time."

I hopped into the truck bed and pushed the remaining boxes toward him. The guy must have got the hint I wasn't in a talkative mood because he snatched the last boxes without further chatter.

After I jumped to the ground, I slammed the tailgate closed.

"You sure you want to get rid of this?" He studied the television. "Looks like a nice one."

"I'm sure."

He turned to me with a satisfied nod. "Well then, we appreciate it. Need a receipt?"

"A receipt?"

"For the donation. You can deduct it from your taxes."

The past is a killer. Carry it around for too long, and it's eventually going to get you.

I shook my head. "No, thank you."

"Have a nice day."

He clambered onto the dock as I drove away.

***

Back home, the room smelled stale. I stripped the bed and put the sheets in the washing machine. I carried the cover outside and flapped the dust off it.

For the next couple of hours, I cleaned the bedroom and the house. I put several CDs into the player and let them shuffle. It was nice to have music playing again.

When the laundry finished, I folded my clothes and put them into the dresser in our room—*my* room.

I stared at her empty closet. I wasn't sure what to do with it. Cleaning it out a year ago seemed like enough. There was no rush to decide. I closed the doors.

With the house put back together, I turned off the music. The house fell silent again, but it was different than before. It would only be a temporary silence this time.

It had been almost a year since I read a book. We had a collection of them in the room we used as an office. There were her books and my books. Separated mostly by topic. Mine were crime fiction novels, police research textbooks, and Viet Nam war biographies. Hers were spiritual titles.

My finger tracked the various titles, landing on one that had been hers—*The Secret* by Rhonda Byrne.

I pulled it out and returned to the living room.

MONDAY
NOVEMBER 11th

47

My eyes fluttered open, and I rolled over. The alarm clock showed several minutes past six. I reached over and clicked on the lamp. Yesterday, I went a full day without a song. Could the end of them have come with the removal of the boxes and the return to my bedroom?

A sadness hung in my heart, but something else was present inside. I couldn't put my finger on it. Hope, maybe. It was a lighter feeling than I'd had in quite some time, and it felt good. I hurried through my shower and got dressed. The sensation of putting together the day's outfit in my bedroom felt odd. I had been a vagabond in my own home for most of the year.

Instead of making coffee at home, I wanted to stop for something on the way in. Breakfast sounded good today—maybe hash browns and eggs. Bruncheonette, a little restaurant near the station, had a great plate.

I checked my watch. There was plenty of time to swing by and say a quick hello to Bobbie and still grab breakfast.

In the car next to me, a small boy waved. I smiled and waved back.

I wanted to laugh with joy. It was a beautiful morn—

A guitar screamed inside my head, and I slammed the brakes. Cars honked and swerved out of the way. Guns N' Roses' "You're Crazy" squealed into my consciousness. The volume blasted inside my head, and I fought back an overwhelming nausea.

I forced my eyes open to see cars moving around me. Several drivers looked my way, curious as to why an unmarked police car was sitting in the middle of the road.

The manic pace of the lyrics and guitars whipped around my brain. It felt like a knife was being pushed inside my head.

I activated the car's emergency lights, spun the wheel, and accelerated into a nearby parking lot. When I cleared the street, I stopped the lights, pulled behind the building, and slammed the car into Park.

The song looped its screeching guitar refrain. I pounded on the steering wheel and yelled in anger.

"You're Crazy" provided the soundtrack for my tantrum.

* * *

"You okay?" Glenn asked.

"Fine," I said and hung my coat at the end of my cubicle.

"You look like shit."

I dropped into my chair and started my computer.

"Don't get comfortable."

"Why's that?"

"Lynn Slater's at the Heart."

"What happened?"

"He was involuntarily committed. He tried to kill himself Friday night. His three-day hold ends today."

I pushed wearily back from my desk. "Let's go."

Glenn and I introduced ourselves to a nurse behind the intake counter for the psychiatric ward. She stopped typing on her computer and looked up. Her scrubs consisted of a multicolored top and pink pants. Her crew cut was salt and pepper.

"We'd like to speak with Lynn Slater," Glenn said.

She faced her computer and entered the man's name. While she read, I looked down the brightly lit hallway. A constant mechanical hum seemed to be coming from somewhere.

The nurse eyed us. "Your people brought him in on Friday. He's under observation."

"Were you working that night?" Glenn asked.

"I work days," she muttered as her fingers continued tapping the keyboard. "Hence, the daylight."

Glenn lifted his eyebrows.

She stopped typing. "I'm sorry." She accepted a file from a passing orderly. "It's busy and we're overworked and understaffed, but that's not your problem." She forced a smile. It looked practiced. "Mr. Slater is under observation."

"We heard, but we have some questions for him."

She sighed. "Can it wait until tomorrow when he's out?"

"It's related to a homicide."

Her features hardened. "A homicide?"

"That's right."

She tapped a couple of keys and consulted her screen. Without looking our way, she said, "We can ask him. If he becomes upset, you'll have to leave."

"We can work with that," Glenn said.

The nurse led us to Slater's room. Before we stepped in, she held out her hand, stopping us. "I'll check back in a few minutes. If he gets upset, this is over."

We nodded. The ground rules were set.

"Mr. Slater," the nurse said.

Lynn Slater sat upright in his bed. He wore a hospital gown and bandages covered his wrists. His once carefully combed hair was messy. The hospital lights washed his skin color out. After he recognized us, his pallor worsened.

The nurse allowed us to pass by. "These men are with the police department," she said. "They would like to ask you some questions. Is that okay?"

Slater glanced between Glenn and me.

"If at any time you feel uncomfortable," the nurse continued, "you can stop. Will that be okay, Mr. Slater? This is a safe place."

He nodded, and she left. We took opposite sides of the bed.

"Mr. Slater," Glenn said, "Lynn. You're not in our custody."

"I know." His voice was soft, and he seemed ashamed. Not for any action other than being seen in this condition.

"And you can ask us to leave at any time. Do you understand?"

Slater's brow furrowed slightly, but he nodded.

"If you tell us to walk, we'll turn around and leave right now."

The immigration agent's eyes floated from Glenn to me and back to my partner.

"Lynn," Glenn said, "there were some things we'd like further clarification on."

The man bowed his head and clasped his hands together.

We had to be careful here. Neither of us had read Slater the Miranda Warning. Technically, he wasn't in our custody, but he wasn't free to leave the hospital either due to his involuntary hold status. With two detectives standing at the end of his bed, it could give him a perception of something completely different. However, we hadn't established any level of guilt. We were still seeking to tie him to Carlotta's death, but all we had was conjecture.

"Why did you go to her apartment at night?" Glenn asked.

Slater didn't answer. Instead, he picked at the bedspread.

"You've already admitted to going there at night. We don't believe it was for follow-up. Would your supervisor believe it?"

The man's head remained bowed as he fiddled with the bedding.

Glenn bent slightly to get a better view of Slater's eyes. "Are you going to answer my questions?"

The man refused to look up.

"Patrol officers brought you in on Friday night. Should we talk about that instead?"

Slater's hands wrung together.

When he didn't respond, Glenn eyed me. "According to the report, the apartment manager discovered him."

Slater leaned slowly back, resting his head on his pillow to stare at the ceiling.

"Seems Lynn started filling the bathtub and got in," Glenn continued. "Patrol found a bottle of Ambien and a bottle of wine. Both bottles were empty."

"How many pills?" I asked.

He shrugged and turned to Slater. "How many pills, Lynn?"

When the agent didn't answer, my partner resumed the narrative. "The drugs must have done a good job because he cut himself," Glenn pointed at Slater's wrists, "and settled back for the inevitable."

"But something happened," I said. "Because he was found."

"He forgot to turn off the faucet." Glenn glanced at Slater, whose eyes were scrunched closed.

"The bathroom flooded."

The man's hands curled around the thin hospital blanket.

"There was a drip into the apartment below, and he lived above the apartment manager. From what the responding officer wrote, the manager reportedly knocked and announced several times, then entered the apartment."

"What did she find?"

Glenn thumbed toward Slater. "Him. Asleep in a bathtub. Blood everywhere."

The man opened his eyes.

"I can't believe she made it in time," I said.

Glenn bent down. "He wasn't in risk of bleeding out, though. Were you, Lynn?"

Slater looked away.

My partner straightened. "The cuts were superficial. Several on each arm. The pills, though, they might have got him." Glenn eyed Slater. "They pumped his stomach. Bet that hurt."

Slater closed his eyes and relaxed his hands.

"And here we are," my partner said.

Both of us watched Slater, waiting for him to respond.

"Why did you try to kill yourself?" Glenn asked.

Slater remained still.

We were going to have to find a way to get him to speak, or we'd need to pull the plug on the interview. He could outwait us in the hospital room. The staff would not allow us to spend all day questioning him.

"Here's our read on things," Glenn said. "We stopped you on Friday and said we believed you were linked to Carlotta Winkler's death. That night you attempted suicide. How do you think that makes you look?"

He glanced between the two of us.

"Guilty," I muttered.

Glenn said, "That's my thought, too."

Slater held his hands together.

"What happened, Lynn? Why did you do it?"

Wetness formed at his eyes but still Slater remained silent.

"I can see you're carrying a lot inside," Glenn continued.

Slater shook his head, refusing to talk.

Glenn straightened and looked at me. He shrugged, then dragged his hand across his throat, indicating it was time to tap out. We'd come at him again later. Maybe when we didn't have to worry about upsetting the man and getting ourselves kicked out by worrisome nurses. He moved toward the door.

But I wasn't ready to leave—not yet.

Slater had not wanted to die. The bandages on his wrists proved it. He had tried to kill himself, but it was half-hearted. If he really wanted to die, he'd have been as deliberate as Carlotta. He must have seen no other way out of the trouble coming his way.

Someone had to show him a way.

"I've thought about killing myself," I said.

Glenn faced me and mouthed, "What are you doing?"

I stepped closer to the end of Slater's bed. "Every time I consider it, something holds me back."

Slater's eyes darted around the room.

"That thing, whatever it was, kept me from doing it. Like it wasn't supposed to be my time. Does that make sense? Maybe that's what happened with you. You wanted to kill yourself, but there was something, some reason, that kept you from not going completely through with it."

He nodded a couple of times then mumbled, "Maybe."

Glenn's head jerked toward Slater. He studied him briefly, then turned back toward me. His palms opened in a questioning manner.

I continued. "My wife died a year ago. She was the love of my life. That's cliché, isn't it?"

Slater shrugged.

"We fell in love in high school and never looked back. After she was gone, there was a hole in my life. Like half of me had disappeared. That's when I started hearing the music."

Slater cocked his head, and Glenn's eyes narrowed. Both men seemed to search for the truth in my statement.

"It's inside my head." I tapped my temple. "No one else could hear it. At first, it was nice. A novelty if you will. I even enjoyed it, but now—" Glenn leaned toward me "—I hate it. Some days it's so loud, I can't hear anything else, not even people talking to me. Sometimes it's so loud, I can't go to sleep. It's been so loud I've puked."

Glenn's face slackened, and he swallowed. Slater's eyes widened.

"I was afraid to tell anyone because I could get in trouble for it. But I finally agreed to see a therapist. It wasn't my idea, but I'm glad I spoke with him. After that, I even told a—" I thought about Marlene. "—a friend. It felt good to let someone else know what I was going through."

"Still want to kill yourself?" Slater asked. His voice was low and his words careful.

"Not really."

"The music sounds nice. Better than the thoughts that I have."

"What thoughts are those?"

He stared at me.

"That I need to end it to make it all go away."

I shook my head. "You don't have to do that."

"But that's what I feel."

"If you want to feel better, you need to share. Tell us what happened."

He wrung his hands.

A line from a song came to me—it was about Pontius Pilate washing his hands while the world burns on Judgement Day. No music blasted in my head. The silence was startling. I tried not to think about the tune, afraid it would blare to life, but Megadeth's "Elysian Fields" was one of my favorites. Thinking about the band and the song in that moment hadn't caused the music to burst into my consciousness.

Was this a breakthrough? Had cleaning out the boxes of clothes really helped—

"I forced her," Lynn said.

"Huh?"

Glenn eyed me with disapproval. My thoughts hadn't been on Slater—they'd been on the missing music. His admission caught me off guard.

Slater's gaze dropped to his hands. "I forced her," he repeated.

"To do what?" I asked.

"To be with me."

Dead men don't rape.

From inside his jacket pocket, Glenn pulled a Miranda Warning card. "Before we go any further, I need to read you something."

***

"I regret doing it," Slater said. "If I could take it back, I would. Please believe me."

I stood and leaned against the wall. "What happened?"

He inhaled deeply, looked to the ceiling, then exhaled. "I'm in the middle of a divorce. Ever been through one?" Both Glenn and I shook our heads. "My wife left me for my best friend."

"I'm sorry to hear that," my partner said. I doubted he was. To build rapport, we say those sorts of things now and then.

"Sixteen years and she left me for the guy she always said she couldn't stand. Isn't there a song about that?"

"Lots of them," I said.

"What she did, it made me mad, you know? She's the one who stepped out and I'm getting taken to the cleaner. I guess I sort of lost my mind after that. Started drinking more than I should. Even started smoking again. It had been years since I quit, but I lit up without thinking twice.

"I've tried to meet women. I'm not exactly a catch, I know that. I'm realistic enough to know my weaknesses. I can see it in a woman's eyes when we go out. They aren't interested. They've got apps where you can meet women. I guess I look better in a picture than I do in real life. I get lots of first dates, but never any seconds. They show up, make their decisions over the entree, then they're gone before dessert. It's happened so many times I lost count. No matter what I did I couldn't find someone who liked me *for* me."

He fell silent as he thought.

"Then there was Carlotta," I suggested.

"Yeah."

"Young and pretty," Glenn added with his head down. He was jotting in his notebook.

"She smiled a lot," Slater said. "No matter what I asked, she answered with a smile. She was sweet."

"Some women are that way," I said.

Slater ran his fingers through his hair, mussing it further. "When I told her I needed to inspect her apartment, she never hesitated."

"Is that where you…"

"Yeah."

"What happened?"

"I kissed her."

"What did she do?"

His cheeks reddened. "She didn't stop me."

"Is that how she responded?"

Slater's shrug was half-hearted. "She didn't say no."

"Did she kiss you back?" I asked.

He shrugged again.

"Is that all that happened?"

"That time—yeah."

"When you left, what did you say?"

"I told her I would be in touch and left."

I imagined him running out of her apartment—scared and ashamed. He had to be afraid of her calling the police or telling his employer. When she didn't, it probably emboldened him.

Glenn was concentrating on Slater's words, noting the immigration officer's words in his notebook.

"How many times did you go back?" I asked.

"Several."

"Each time under the pretense of working on her file?"

"It seemed like a natural reason for contacting her."

"That couldn't go on forever," I said. "At some point, you'd have to close the file."

"Yeah."

"So, you kept it open until she told you no."

He didn't answer. Instead, he rubbed his hands together.

Pontius Pilate, I thought. Still, the song didn't show up.

Glenn said, "That's when you denied her citizenship."

A frown creased Slater's face. "I shouldn't have done that."

"Because she killed herself or because it was wrong?"

He sat silently for a while and studied his now clasped hands. "I didn't know she would do that."

"What was her behavior when you came around?"

He brightened. "She dressed up."

I asked, "Was it for you or for your position?"

Confusion crept into his eyes. "What?"

"You were the one who held the ticket to her citizenship. It would be natural for her to respect your power."

His face darkened. "She enjoyed our relationship."

"Did she know it was a relationship?"

Slater swallowed with some difficulty. "I would have made it a relationship—if she wanted."

I moved toward the end of the bed. "When it was becoming clear you were holding off on approving her citizenship, did she refuse to see you?"

"Yeah." The word was barely audible. His hands started moving again, and he looked away.

"Did she threaten to tell your supervisor?"

"No. She wasn't that kind of girl."

"If she had, what would you have done?"

"I don't know." He shrugged, but his hands didn't stop rubbing. "Probably reversed my decision and approved her."

Glenn and I both silently watched the man.

"What's going to happen now?" he asked.

I forced a genial smile. Glenn did the same. It felt dirty, but we were building a case, not making friends.

"That's enough for today," I said.

Glenn added, "We'll have some questions for you later, but for now, you need to get better."

Slater nodded. "Thanks." The simple word was filled with relief.

***

As we walked to our car, I said, "That went better than I thought it would."

My partner stopped and pointed at the front of the hospital. "The hell was that?"

"What?"

"The confession you made." Anger cascaded over his face. "You hear music? Are you hearing something now?"

"No."

"Besides the shrink, how many other people know?"

"Glenn—"

"The chaplain? Did you tell the hand of God?"

"Glenn—"

"If both the shrink and the chaplain know, that means the entire administration knows."

"It doesn't work like that."

"Yes, it does. It most certainly does. Who else knows?"

"What?"

"You told a friend. Who was that?"

"Glenn, relax."

"What friend did you tell?"

I looked away.

"This is serious, Dallas. Who else knows?"

"Marlene."

"*Who?*"

"She's the counselor at the—"

"You told *her*?"

"Listen—"

"Why in the hell would you tell her? Who is she to you?"

I shrugged.

"You know how you sound?" He twirled a finger around his ear. "Three fries short of a happy meal."

"Maybe I am."

He threw his hands in the air. "You're my partner! I don't need a madman backing me up."

"I'm not crazy."

Glenn put his hands on his hips. "Everything makes sense now."

"What does?"

He flicked a hand toward me. "Your distractions. The fact that I need to repeat myself all the damn time. It's the music, right? You can't hear me because the music blocks me out."

"It's not that bad," I lied.

"Then there's your appearance."

"I'm cleaning it up."

"*Now*. But for most of the year, you've looked like a ragbag. People have been worried, man."

"So, I've heard."

"You have? You can hear it over the music in your head? Then why didn't you do something about it sooner because they've been coming to me with their concerns, and I've covered for you. Oh, poor Dallas, I say, he's going through a rough patch. Give him time and he'll be fine. You know what, man? You made me a liar. You're not going to be fine—are you?"

"I *am* fine."

"It doesn't sound like it when you've got a Blaupunkt inside your head."

"Stephen thinks I'm okay."

Glenn threw his hands into the air. "You're taking the shrink's word?"

"He's a doctor."

"Now, you have faith in the guy."

"He's the department's psychiatrist."

"Why did you tell him and what's her name before you told me?"

"I don't know. I kept hoping it would go away."

"But it didn't."

"And then the one-year mark came and went—"

His anger subsided slightly. "One year? Ah, shit. I'm sorry."

"It's fine."

"No. I should have remembered." His face scrunched. "But you should have told me what was going on."

"It's not something I could easily share. Look how you're reacting."

"Because I found out during an interview of a homicide suspect." He pointed at the building again. "During an interview, Dallas!"

I rubbed my forehead. "Probably not the best place to break the news."

"This music—what kind is it? Don't tell me it's that heavy stuff you like."

"Normally, yeah."

"Too bad you don't like John Mayer. At least, that would be good music."

"Not when it's blasting inside your brain all the time."

"And Stephen doesn't think you're crazy?"

"He said they were musical hallucinations."

"You're hallucinating?" He threw his arms into the air once more. "Great. You're seeing little green men, too."

"It's not like that. It's only sound."

Glenn stopped and crossed his arms. "What are you going to do about this?"

"What do you mean?"

"Are you going to tell Brand?"

"Why should I?"

"And Stephen doesn't think you're a harm to yourself."

"He cleared me for work."

"He doesn't think you're a danger to anyone else—specifically, me?"

"Definitely not."

"Are you still going to see him?"

"I have to—to stay on the job."

Glenn nodded while he thought.

"What about you?" I asked. "Are you going to tell anyone?"

"Why the hell would I rat you out?" He moved toward the car. "You're my partner."

***

Glenn spent the ride back to the station lost in thought. I didn't bother him with chatter, figuring it best to keep my insecurities to myself.

When he dropped into his desk chair, he said, "After he's out of the hospital, what are we going after Slater with?"

"He didn't push her off that ledge, so murder is off the books."

"Manslaughter? We'd have to prove he was somehow reckless or criminally negligent in her death."

"Which he wasn't. She jumped."

"But his actions led her to that action."

"Did it?" I asked.

Glenn frowned.

"There's what we know—"

"Yeah, yeah, yeah." Glenn leaned back and looked at the ceiling. "And there's what we can prove."

"So, maybe she jumped for a reason we're unaware of. Maybe she jumped because she missed home. Maybe she jumped because she missed her ex-husband."

"Maybe she jumped because a little voice told her to," Glenn said.

I thought about the story he told me on top of the Western Bank Building. "Or maybe she heard a song telling her to jump."

"Might as well," he said. His chair dropped back into place. "So, we can't prove he had anything to do with the actual act of leaping from the building."

"I don't think so."

Glenn crossed his arms and dropped his chin to his chest. "And we can't prove rape."

"No, we can't."

My partner's brow furrowed while he thought. "Indecent Liberties?"

It was a Class C felony and sort of a catch-all charge when sexual contact is made through forcible compulsion. It was an easier charge to prove than rape, but it still wouldn't work in this situation.

"There's no chance we could prove it," I said. If Carlotta were still alive, we could likely prove it. She was dead so there was no victim and no evidence. The only statement of forced sex was Slater's, and he could easily retract it. Besides, we didn't have him on video confessing to it.

Glenn shifted in his chair and the look on his face intensified. We were digging into charges we rarely worked with. We could go a year or more without ever discussing indecent liberties. They were on the books for a reason, though. When the bigger charges failed to do their job—when they didn't catch a bad guy—the net widened slightly. We just had to remember what those charges were.

"Coercion," Glenn muttered. It was a gross misdemeanor, so the longest prison term associated with that crime would be one year. "Big whoop. She dies and we might hang three-sixty-five on him."

"Hold on to that thought. It's a starting point and a good one at that. We've got his letter terminating her application of citizenship. That's actual proof he retaliated. If we can get him on record saying he used the threat of denial as a way for him to have sex—"

"Harassment?" Glenn interrupted. It was another misdemeanor.

"Maybe."

"We could stack them."

"But it's still just a year. It feels like we're missing something."

Glenn tapped the edge of his desk while he thought.

I racked my brain for another charge. Something I hadn't used in some time.

Eddie Van Halen's guitar masterpiece, "Eruption," began playing inside my head. It wasn't loud nor painful. It was wonderful. I felt my body relax and let my mind drift away on the rising and falling licks. There were no words to the song that introduced the band's first album to the world.

"Eruption," I thought happily. The music had tortured me for so long, I forgot what it was like to have a moment when I enjoyed it. And then the charge came to me. "Extortion."

Glenn dropped forward into his chair. "Oh, that's it. Beautiful. He threatened her with revocation of her application."

The music faded inside my head.

My partner turned toward me. "If I remember correctly, the code specifically includes sexual favors."

"And it's a felony."

My partner grinned. "We've got him."

49

Andrew Parker and Jessie Johnson stood in the hallway outside the Major Crimes office. Both were in suits. Johnson's looked professionally cut and, as usual, Parker's appeared to be a size too big—a result of his bodybuilder physique. They laughed and looked down the hall toward me.

"Parker," I said, "got a minute?"

Their chuckling faded, and Johnson eyed me suspiciously.

"This about Gaskin?" Parker asked.

I nodded.

Curiosity flashed in Johnson's eyes when Parker patted his shoulder. "I'll catch up with you in a few."

We walked and talked, meandering through the hallways of the department.

"What am I missing?" I asked. "What are we missing?"

"I don't follow."

"Everyone says they're better off with Junior dead."

"I'd guess most folks would say the same about Tiger. A pimp's not a philanthropist."

My brow furrowed.

"I know big words, Dallas."

"It's not that. I was thinking about what you were saying. Junior and Tiger weren't going to win friends with what they're doing."

"The opposite of that. They used intimidation and violence to make a living off the backs of women. No one would call them good men."

"So, we've got two dead pimps connected only by their chosen vocation and Tanisha."

"Who insisted we look at Damon Warfield as the shooter of both?"

"I don't see it," I said. "I think if Damon was going to kill a man, he'd be smart about it." The image of him reading the newspaper and talking about détente came back to me. "Maybe even get someone else to do the killing for him. What are you doing now?"

Parker cocked his head. "Talking with you."

"Maybe you should meet Damon. Let's get your thoughts on this guy."

"I'll grab my notepad."

***

Our first stop was Ironsides. It was mid-afternoon and only a couple of patrons were seated at the bar. A reserved sign was placed on the booth in the back.

"That's his," I said.

"He gets reserved parking?"

"The spoils of the life."

"I guess."

The morning's newspaper was spread out on the counter and the bartender was perched over it, slowing moving his lips as he read.

"Where's Damon?" I asked.

Not looking up, the bartender shrugged.

"What time's he usually get here?"

"When he does."

I turned around to see Parker shaking his head. He muttered, "You got a way with people, Nash."

"What can I say?"

Parker pushed me aside and stepped to the bar. He placed his hand in the middle of the newspaper. "Afternoon."

The bartender refused to make eye contact, but his lips stopped moving. Parker balled his fist, crinkling the newspaper.

"I was reading that."

"You were being a jerk is what you were doing."

"Seems like you're being one, too."

"You calling me a jerk?"

"You just called me one."

Parker glanced back. "This guy called me a jerk."

I shrugged.

"You started it," the bartender said.

The customer next to Parker, an older man with a long ponytail, slid off his stool and started to slink away.

"You see that?" Parker asked the customer.

"I didn't see nothing," the older man nervously said.

"How did you not see anything? You're sitting right there."

The customer swallowed before pointing at his bottle. "I was staring into my beer."

"You taking his side?"

"Listen, Officer," the bartender said.

"Stay out of this." To the customer, Parker said, "Let me see some ID."

"What?"

"Hey!" The bartender reached across the bar to put his hand between the detective and his patron.

Parker slapped his hand. "You tried to assault me."

"No, sir."

"You reached out and tried to assault me. That's a felony."

The bartender lifted his hands in surrender. "Hey, now, this whole thing is spinning out of control."

"Then tell us what we want to know."

"I have! I don't know when Damon'll be back, but he will. He always comes back. Maybe an hour."

"An hour?"

"Yeah. Chill out, man."

Parker eyed him, then the customer. "Was that so hard?"

The bartender's face was ashen.

"I see you have a way with people," I whispered.

"It's a talent," Parker said. "You just have to know how to talk to them."

The door to the bar opened and two large men walked in, blocking most of the sunlight. Both wore jeans and winter coats. As they parted, Damon Warfield entered. He still wore his puffy Dodgers jacket, and his baseball hat sat askew on his head.

His eyes darted around the bar. When they settled on me, he murmured, "Aw, shit."

The two goons, hearing Warfield's expletive, hunched slightly and their hands darted inside their coats. Their eyes careened around the bar.

Both Parker and I reached for our hips.

"Relax," Damon said. "Five-oh."

The two men saw us, and their hands slowly reappeared with nothing in them.

Stepping forward, the pimp said, "Wait outside." The two men retreated out of the bar.

Damon spread his arms wide. "Detective Nash, I would have hoped you'd be out catching a killer."

"That's what we're doing. Damon Warfield meet Detective Parker. He's investigating the murder of Tiger."

The two men wearily studied each other.

"What's with the muscle?" I asked.

"I could ask you the same thing."

Parker crossed his arms and cocked his head.

"It's a damn war zone out here, Detective. Two men down. I might be next."

"That's why you hired the goons?"

"I need someone to watch my back. Junior and Tiger got got because no one was watching their backs." He tapped his temple. "I learn from the lessons of others. Nobody's getting close until you find the shooter."

"When did you get them?

"Yesterday. When do you think?"

"How do you hire a couple thugs like that?" Parker asked.

Damon interlinked two fingers. "Connections. I know people who know people. This is how shit gets done in the real world."

"I know how the world works."

"We all can't suck on the government tit, Detective."

"The government—" Parker started. "Man, why do you say something stupid like that? You don't pay taxes."

Damon motioned toward the smaller detective. "I don't like you."

"Takes two to tango."

The pimp's brow furrowed, then he looked at me. "The hell does that mean?"

"It means," I said, "we're here for some follow-up questions. Got any ideas on who might have killed Tiger?"

"How the fuck should I know? I didn't want either man dead."

"You didn't?"

"Hell no! We already talked about this."

"It was suggested by others maybe you did."

"Who would say some stupid shit like that?"

"It doesn't matter."

Damon rolled his eyes. "Hell, yeah, it does."

"Where were you when Tiger was killed?" Parker asked.

The pimp's lip curled.

I repeated Parker's question.

"Happened on Saturday, right?"

"Yes."

"I was down here. Taking care of business."

"Down here?" I said. "That's wide open."

"You know what I do, Detective Nash. Ain't no secret, but I didn't kill Tiger. There wasn't any bad blood between us."

"People seem to think there would be when he started to move in on the territory."

"But he hadn't. No reason to get up in arms until then. What you're implying is a nuclear option before we had even tried to reach a diplomatic resolution."

Parker's nose scrunched. "Diplomatic reso—"

I interrupted. "Were there any witnesses to where you were on Saturday?"

"Depending on the time of night, there would be all sorts. You name it. I've got him." Damon pointed at the bartender. "Got some girls. Even got that underage bitch."

"Chanel?"

"Relax, man, I didn't do nothing with her. Like I said, I don't want jailbait—"

"You go after underage girls?" Parker said.

Damon held up his hand. "Let the big kids talk."

Parker's face reddened.

"What were you doing with her?" I asked.

"I wasn't doing anything with her. She approached me."

"What did she want?"

"To negotiate."

"What did she want?"

"To work. She said she would be independent, work only one corner, but I told her that wasn't going to happen. Only one girl gets to do that—" He glanced at Parker, who frowned in return. "—and there wasn't a chance I would allow another girl to get away with it."

"How'd she take that?"

"She wanted me to be her daddy then."

My face hardened. "You better not even think about it."

Damon waved his hands as he chuckled. "Settle down, Detective. I told the bitch no way—I wasn't interested—but the girl insisted. Even offered me a taste." The pimp tapped his temple. "But that bird is damaged, no matter how fine she is."

"Stay away from her."

The pimp raised his hands in surrender. "You don't have to tell me twice. I want her off the street as much as you do—until she's eighteen. Then she's fair game."

***

"She ain't here," Doris Nelson said.

It had taken repeated knocking to get the grandmother to come to the door. Parker had impatiently kicked the bottom of the door while I knocked. We were loud and obnoxious, and it still took several minutes to roust Doris from her recliner.

Her hair was disheveled, and her nightgown was gray from lack of washing. Being this close allowed us a whiff of her body odor.

"When did she leave?" I asked.

Chanel's grandmother shrugged. Her eyes drifted back toward the television. Her rounded shoulders slumped further. "You made me miss it. Aww."

She shuffled back toward the recliner.

I looked at Parker, who shrugged in return. We entered the house without invitation. Doris didn't seem to mind.

Chanel's room remained as messy as before. I studied the rape and prostitution posters on the wall. Never having a teenage daughter, I was unsure what one should have as decoration, but I'd been in enough kids' rooms to understand it wouldn't be this.

"Damon was right," Parker said. "This bird is damaged."

"Her mother died of a heroin overdose a few years ago. She'd been on the stroll the kid's whole life."

Near the light switch, my fingers ran over the *Dead Men Don't Rape* sticker.

Parker saw my action and examined it further. "Sort of a final solution."

"Yeah."

"Not wrong, though."

I hoped to find a journal, some writings, anything that would help me understand the mindset of a sixteen-year-old who puts herself in harm's way to reconnect with a mother yet hates it enough to display the anti-sex trafficking messages in her room.

But there was nothing.

There were clothes tossed about. In the trash can was an opened pregnancy kit. I lifted the box out. Underneath was a used strip. I pulled the instructions from the box and unfolded them.

"What have you got?" Parker asked.

I showed him.

He walked over, reached in, and pulled the strip out. "Ever read one of these?" he asked.

"No."

It took less than a second for him to say, "Not pregnant." He tossed the strip back into the can and continued his search.

I dropped the box and instructions into the can.

Parker studied the posters on the walls. "Her mom was a prostitute. Now, she's on some sort of vision quest to find her mother. So, this isn't actually about being a whore."

"She's an underage prostitute. I can't tell you what's going on inside her head."

"You think she might have been the shooter?"

My eyes flashed to the *Dead Men Don't Rape* sticker. "Maybe."

Parker lifted the pillow on her bed, then heaved the mattress upward. "And you got to this conclusion how?"

"Junior ran her mom."

"Was the girl around to see it?"

"When she was little, she saw Junior as a father figure. Even said so."

Parker let the mattress fall. "So, her father figure was pimping her out?"

"And assaulting her."

"Did she know Tiger?"

"She went to him."

Parker eyed me. "So, she knew them both."

I nodded.

"We need to find this girl."

50

The phone rang while I was in bed, reading a book.

"Detective Nash?"

"Yes."

"This is Officer Hoffman. I'm at Sacred Heart with a shooting victim. He's refused to talk with me. Said he'll only talk with you."

"Who is it?"

"Damon Warfield."

I sat upright. "How bad?"

"A round through the shoulder. They're working on him now. I was told it shouldn't take long. Then he'll be—"

"Has another detective been dispatched?"

"Not yet. We don't know what we're dealing with. My supervisor said to call you first. Get your read on it."

"I'm on the way."

***

He was in the recovery room when I arrived. His two goons weren't anywhere to be found.

"Bitch shot me," he said.

"Who?"

"The little bird you told me to stay away from."

"You said you didn't want anything to do with her."

"I didn't. I *don't*."

"Then how'd she get close enough to shoot you?"

"She didn't get close."

298

"I don't understand."

Damon cocked his head. "She came back again. Said she was going to give me one more chance." His laugh was hollow. "I told her to come back when she was eighteen and I would be happy to work her. Until then, I wasn't touching it. Bitch got irate and threw a tantrum. The boys pushed her down the block. I thought that was the end of it until we were heard the shot. I thought it was some shit going on down the block until I felt the stinging. One of the boys said he saw her running a minute later."

"Where are the boys now?"

He shrugged his good shoulder and winced.

"Did you send them after her?"

"I'm not stupid."

I stared at him.

"Why would I ask for you and tell you all this just to send my boys after her? I'm smarter than you're giving me credit for, Detective. I tell you about this bird, you got to go get her. Not me, not the boys. It's our tax dollars at work."

"Your goons weren't in the waiting room."

"Maybe they're outside. Once the nurses brought me back, I don't know what happened to them. I figured they'd be waiting out there. Maybe they're getting something to eat. They're some big boys. It's always feeding time with them."

"You're lying."

"To what end?"

"To create an alibi."

Damon frowned. "Listen, man. I take care of my own problems, but killing a kid, even a bird that shot me, that's a problem I don't need. Understand? This game we play is chess and the whole board is laid out before me."

"That makes you the king?"

"And you're my knight. Why should I move myself into harm's way when I can use you to achieve the same goal?"

"If your goons are hunting her—"

"Then they're doing it without my authorization and I'm not paying for it. I'm going to let our tax dollars do my heavy lifting."

"Did you see her shoot you?"

"She was too far away, but that's what the boys said. Besides, you should have seen the bird when I told her no. I thought I tore her heart out."

***

Officer Hoffman stood near the intake counter, chatting with a nurse. He saw me exit, ended his conversation, and stepped over. I jotted Chanel Nelson's information in my notebook, then ripped off the page.

"This is the suspected shooter."

"Sixteen?"

"Call it in and get a unit out to her house."

"Will do."

"And get the round they pulled from the victim's shoulder and put it on property."

Hoffman nodded.

***

The lights were on in the home.

I parked near the small park, walked up the sidewalk, and peered into the window. The television flickered with activity. It was almost midnight, so I was surprised to see a child jumping on the couch, a game controller in her hand.

I knocked on the door, and a moment later, the door opened. The little girl smiled. Six years old. Ten years younger than the girl suspected of shooting a pimp. Her right hand held the door, and her left hand gripped the controller. The game was paused on the television.

"Hi, Sadie."

She tilted her head, and her smile vanished into an exaggerated frown.

"Remember me? I'm Dallas. Is your mom home?"

She ran back to the couch, hopped onto it, and yelled, "Mom!" The game returned to life.

Marlene stepped around the corner. She wore jeans and a sweatshirt. Her coat was on, and a beanie cap pulled down to her ears. Her focus was on her purse as she searched its contents.

"The man," Sadie said, which caused Marlene to look up.

She froze. "Detective."

"Heading out?"

Marlene swallowed and said, "Uh—"

"Excuse me," a female voice said.

An elderly woman walked up the sidewalk. She passed by me as she entered the house. I followed her inside and closed the door.

"Everything okay?" the woman asked Marlene.

Marlene's surprise at my being there melted into a forced smile. "Mrs. Dryden, this is Dallas."

"Is he helping you tonight?"

"Um… yeah."

"How long will you be out, sweetheart?"

"I'm not sure."

"How long has Sadie been up?"

"She hasn't been to bed yet."

The woman held a hand to her chest. "Marlene, this child needs a better schedule."

"I know, Mrs. Dryden, but can we talk about this when I get back?" She kissed the older woman on the cheek and pushed by me out the door.

I followed Marlene out and down the sidewalk to the street. "Where are you going?"

"Out."

"You're going to find Chanel." I ran alongside her. "She shot Damon tonight. There were witnesses."

She walked to her car, a dented Toyota Corolla, and stood near the driver's door. "She's scared."

"Did you hear what I said? She might also be responsible for Junior and Tiger."

"I don't care. I'm still going to her."

"Then come with me. We'll take my car."

The locks to her car clicked, and she opened her door. "No. You might try to take me somewhere else."

"I wouldn't do that."

"Then arrest me. Otherwise, I'm going."

It was probably the wrong decision, but I walked around the passenger side of the car and opened the door.

***

The offices of Her Freedom were dark, but the back of the building was brightly lit. Marlene parked in the furthest stall from the rear entrance. Above the door was a camera.

Before we left her car, I asked, "How'd she get in?"

"She has the code." Marlene pointed at the door. "There's a numbered lock."

"Do you do that for all of them?"

"It's for emergencies."

"Won't that get abused?"

She shrugged. "If it does, we'll change the code, but we have to show them some trust. Somebody has to believe in them."

At the door, Marlene's fingers moved over the keypad. When it opened, she reached inside and clicked on the light. I drew my gun.

"Is that necessary?"

"She shot Damon."

"She's sixteen."

"It's necessary," I whispered.

Marlene disapprovingly shook her head and started to move. I reached out and touched her. "I'll lead."

"No, you won't. She's a kid."

"She's armed."

"Chanel!" she hollered. "I'm coming in."

"What are you doing?" I whispered.

"Detective Nash is with me," she yelled into the building.

I stared at Marlene.

A small voice came from inside the building. "Why'd you bring him?"

"He insisted," Marlene shouted. "And he's armed."

"Tell him to stay outside."

"I can't do that," I hollered.

Marlene cupped her hands around her mouth. "Did you hear what I said? He has a gun."

She pulled free from my hand and walked into the building. I followed closely behind.

It violated every officer safety protocol. The shooter was locked inside a building. The prudent thing to do was call for additional units and secure the premises. If Marlene hadn't been here and walked in, I would have done just that.

As we moved deeper into the office, Marlene said, "Chanel, everything will be okay."

"No," the young woman said. "It won't be. He's here."

"We can work it out," I said, but my words sounded fake.

Marlene glanced back with evident concern.

There was sobbing now. I touched Marlene's shoulder, hoping to slow her down, but she slipped away and continued toward the noise.

Chanel Nelson sat on the kitchenette floor with her back against the wall. She wore the same winter coat I'd first seen her in along with the volleyball shorts and Converse tennis shoes. Between her legs, she held a small revolver in both hands.

I pointed my gun at her. "Put it down."

Marlene said, "Do it, Chanel. *Please*."

"I'm going to jail," she said.

"We'll get you help."

"No one can help me."

Marlene stepped forward.

"Don't," I whispered.

She ignored me and continued forward. "Everything will be okay. Trust me."

Chanel continued to cry.

The counselor sat on the floor and put her arm around the girl. Chanel rested her head on Marlene's shoulder.

"I don't want to go to jail."

"Maybe you won't have to."

"How?"

"You're sixteen. And we'll get you help."

"Who?"

"The agency. We'll find you an attorney."

Chanel cried.

"But you need to give me that."

The girl stared at the gun in her hands.

"Then you're not going to say anything to the police. Understand?"

"Marlene," I said, and both women looked up.

The counselor hugged the younger woman closer. "No matter what Detective Nash asks you, say nothing. Keep your mouth shut until we get you a lawyer."

I wanted to tell her she was interfering with a criminal investigation, but Chanel still held the gun. The most important thing was to disarm the kid. The ramifications of the counselor's interference could be dealt with later.

Marlene looked at Chanel. "Do you understand what I'm telling you?"

She nodded.

"Because we won't move until you do. This is important. Don't say anything to him."

"I understand."

The counselor hugged her again. "When you're ready, hand me the gun."

"Don't touch it," I told Marlene. "Slide it to me, Chanel."

"No," Marlene said emphatically. "You give it to me."

The girl gently handed the gun to her. Marlene placed her hand around the grip.

I lowered my gun a little further but kept it pointed in her direction. "Do you know what you've done?"

"I've saved a girl's life." She moved the gun to her other hand and made sure her fingers wrapped around the barrel. Then she laid it on the ground. With a shove, she slid it across the floor. "Now, you don't have to kill her."

Without hesitation, I picked it up and put my fingerprints on it as well. It was a .38 revolver. I slipped it into my jacket pocket.

Chanel rested her head on the counselor's shoulder.

"Congratulations, Detective," Marlene said. "You got your woman."

51

"Heard you were out late last night," Glenn said. "Get your girl?"

"No," I said.

"I thought you arrested her."

"She's in juvie, but she's not the killer."

Glenn slid his chair over to mine. "You found her with a gun."

"Wrong caliber for the Everson Wiley homicide. The kid had a thirty-eight. Wiley was killed with something smaller. We're still waiting for the ballistics to come back on the Gaskin murder. If I had to bet, I'd say that it was the smaller caliber as well."

"Where did the kid get the gun?"

"Don't know. The counselor muddied up the arrest."

I laid it out for Glenn then.

When I was done, his eyes were soft. "That's the woman you told about the music?"

"Yeah."

"Think she'll use it against you?"

"I don't know. Maybe. She was trying to help the kid. I get that. But the girl also shot a guy."

"Were you able to interview the kid?"

"She refused. Took the counselor's advice."

"So, what's the plan now?"

"I believe Warfield's shooting is a standalone crime. Since it doesn't fit with the Wiley murder, linking it will only cloud that investigation."

Glenn leaned back in his chair. "But this Warfield is a suspect in the other shootings. Getting shot doesn't absolve him of suspicion."

"Except I didn't think he was involved in the first place. What did he stand to gain? He already had détente with Junior."

"Détente?"

"His word. Basically, a tentative peace between the two men since they shared the same territory."

"I know what détente means."

"And Damon knew better than to push into the West End where Tiger was operating."

"If Tiger moved into East Sprague with Junior, would Damon stand for that?"

"I doubt it, but I think he would have tried for a peaceful solution first."

"So, Damon *could* have killed Tiger to stop his expansion."

"I don't figure The Great White Hope as that type of guy. He called himself a finesse player, a chess player. He might have put the pieces into place for someone else to do it, but he wouldn't do it himself."

"The war between Junior and Tiger?"

"I think he fanned those flames, but Junior was using Oxy. His decision-making became suspect. His bottom confirmed that."

"Hence, raping the girl as some sort of payback."

I tapped my desk. "The man was off the rails. He started to lose girls because of it. His bottom, his most loyal girl, questioned his actions."

"What for?"

"For sending a girl into Tiger's territory—"

And that's when I finally put the pieces together. I opened my notebook and found her business card. They patched me into voice mail.

"Marlene, this is Dallas Nash. Call me. Please."

***

"Who are we looking for?"

"Vanessa Bolkan."

Glenn eyed me. "Who?"

"The woman Junior sent into Tiger's territory."

"And you think she's the shooter?"

"Maybe."

We raced down East Sprague looking for anyone I knew, anyone I had recently met.

"This is a wild goose chase," Glenn muttered.

A woman lingered near a bus stop, making eye contact with passing drivers. When she saw my car, she turned around and casually walked away.

I yanked the car to the curb. Both Glenn and I hopped out.

"Scrimmy!" I yelled.

She threw her hands in the air. "What did I do now?"

"Come here."

"I wasn't doin' nothin'."

We hurried toward her.

"When's the last time you saw Nessa?"

Suspicion clouded her eyes. "Why?"

"Please. It's important."

"She in trouble?"

"We need to talk with her."

She frowned and looked away. "Haven't seen her."

"C'mon, Scrimmy, we don't have time for this."

She stepped back and thrust a finger at me. "Screw you. I'm telling you the truth when I say I haven't seen her. Word is she's back, but I haven't seen her."

I lifted my hands to calm her, my mind hurrying for another way to reach my goal. "Who would know how to find her?"

"Try DeeDee."

"She get a new phone?"

Scrimmy shrugged.

I handed Scrimmy my business card. "No screwing around. Call her. Tell her I'm looking for Nessa. Now!"

Her lips pursed as she reached into her back pocket for her phone.

"Call everyone you know. We need to know where she's at."

***

For another thirty minutes, Glenn and I searched the Sprague corridor before heading to the West End. We didn't find anyone there either.

Perhaps Scrimmy's phone calls and text messages spooked everyone off the streets. Two detectives were looking for a former prostitute and would harass the current girls to find her. That wouldn't make walking the streets attractive right now.

After an hour, we returned to the department. Glenn left for a face-to-face with a prosecutor to discuss the Carlotta Winkler investigation.

I sat at my computer to enter an Attempt to Locate on Vanessa Bolkan. I didn't hear him walk up until he was behind me.

"Heard you were looking for Vanessa Bolkan."

Jim Morgan crossed his thick arms over his chest. His ever-present baseball hat was pulled tightly down to his eyes.

"I won't bother asking how you heard."

"Scrimmy told me. Is Nessa the shooter in the Junior and Tiger murders?"

"How do you figure?"

"I did the math."

"It's possible."

"More than possible. The girl got busted up badly by Raekwon's girls because Junior sent her down there. She grew up in Wyoming where guns are like water."

"Rumor was she went home for a while."

"What did I tell you about believing rumors? Girl never left."

"Who told you that?"

"Who do you think?"

"If Nessa was so familiar with guns, why use a small caliber weapon? We're waiting for confirmation, but it appears to be a twenty-two, maybe a twenty-five."

"Twenty-twos can kill a man as easily as any other gun. Maybe it was the only gun she could get her hands on. Felons can't be choosy."

"Why are you here, Morgan?"

"To square things."

"Things will never be square with us."

Morgan glanced up to the ceiling. When his gaze returned, he said, "Fair enough." He put a piece of paper on the desk. It was an address.

"What's that?"

"That's where you'll find Bolkan."

"How?"

"I told you before. My girl's an informant. This is what she does for me. Nothing more."

***

The Sundowner Motel sat at the corner of Second Avenue and Washington Street.

Glenn hadn't returned to the department before I left.

The desk clerk—a heavyset man with a wheezing cough—confirmed Vanessa Bolkan had been in room 202.

"She's checking out today," he said before coughing.

I stepped back from the counter.

The clerk consulted a clipboard. "But we haven't turned the room yet."

"So, she might still be here?"

"I saw her leave."

"You're sure?"

He leaned over and selected a room key. That simple action brought another coughing fit. "Help yourself, Detective. I don't need to do the stairs—" another cough "—my asthma is flaring up something fierce."

A patrol car pulled into the parking lot, and Leya Navarro climbed out. I waved to her, and she hurried over.

On the second-floor landing, we took opposite sides of the door to room 202.

I knocked but got no answer. The second time, I pounded louder.

With the key, we opened the door. "Spokane Police," I yelled.

Inside, there was no movement.

Leya and I nodded to each other and moved forward. It took less than thirty seconds to clear the little hotel room.

"Clear," she said.

"Yeah," I muttered. "Clear."

On the small bathroom counter, among candy wrappers and empty beer cans, was an empty box of .22 shells.

"Let's step out," I said.

***

I leaned a hip against Leya Navarro's patrol car. She sat in the driver's seat with the engine running. The patrol radio squawked with periodic updates from officers on traffic stops.

Leya asked, "You want me to watch the room?"

"I do, yeah. This is a suspect in two recent homicides. I'll head back to the station and prepare a warrant."

"Sounds good. It'll allow me some time to study for the detective's exam."

"Done with patrol?"

"Guess that depends on my test-taking ability."

"Request another unit, so you're not alone. She's killed two men. Probably wouldn't hesitate to kill a cop."

Leya nodded and turned to her in-car computer. "I'll send dispatch a message to let them know what we're doing. Keep it off the air in case anyone is listen—"

A piercing tone came through the radio. Both Leya and I instinctively leaned in.

"*All units,*" a female dispatcher called, "*shooting in progress in front of the Lamplighter, corner of First and Madison. Suspect is described as a white female. Red hair. Baseball hat. Green Army jacket.*"

I smacked the roof of the patrol car. "That's her."

Leya looked up at me.

"Go!"

She dropped her car into gear and squealed out of the parking lot.

I removed my cell phone and called dispatch. "This is Nash. If I'm right, the shooter at the Lamplighter is Vanessa Bolkan." I then phonetically spelled the last name.

"Vanessa Bolkan, copy."

"She's staying at The Sundowner. I'm on scene here."

"I'll direct additional units in your direction."

"Copy. Also, contact Ida twenty-four. He should still be at the department. Let him know where I'm at."

***

The Lamplighter was nine blocks northeast of my location. I moved to the western edge of the Sundowner to watch for her approach. This seemed the natural way she would come.

Cars drove northbound on Washington Street.

If a person were running at a full sprint, how long would it take to cover that amount of ground? Several minutes? If they were hiding to avoid incoming patrol units, it might slow them down.

I glanced over my shoulder into the parking lot of the motel.

If she ran past the building to double back, she could approach me from the rear.

I was overthinking it now.

Things were simple. She was on the run and if she were coming back to this location, she would head from—

A block to the east, a blur of motion appeared from behind one building before it disappeared behind the next. Alleys ran along those buildings before opening into a large parking lot. Unfortunately, a retail building running parallel to Washington Street would hide her if she exited the alley in this direction.

Ratt's "I'm Insane" burst into my head. My world tilted, and I fell against the building. Bile rose in my throat. Drums pounded and guitars squealed as I strained to see. It was as if I stood in a wind tunnel.

Against the music, my thoughts thickened. If that blur was indeed her, she got back to the motel quicker than I calculated. How did that happen?

I'd forgotten the time delay for the call to 911. No call is immediate. There would have—

Guitars wailed inside my head.

—been a loss of minutes. She could have already been on the run by the time dispatch relayed the call.

I pushed off the wall and drew my gun. My heart pounded and my mouth watered as I wanted to vomit. The pain in my head was excruciating. I pushed my left hand into my right eye to ease the pressure—

Drums pounded a frenzied rhythm inside my head.

—but there was no relief. The ground swayed, and I awkwardly stepped back to stabilize myself.

A blur came around the building across the street. Vanessa Bolkan was at a full sprint when she saw me. She stopped and her head swiveled as she searched for an escape route.

The chorus looped loudly through my head. "I'm Insane."

I lifted my gun.

"Police!" I yelled.

Vanessa aimed and fired. She turned northbound and ran toward the train overpass.

I sprinted after her with the music blaring in my head. Northbound cars slammed on their brakes as I crossed Washington Street. Many skidded to a stop. If horns blared, I couldn't hear them.

Vanessa was at the front of the overpass. She turned and fired again, but I wasn't struck. Instead, I stumbled, windmilling my hands to keep my balance and fell.

The chorus spun in on itself, mocking me. "I'm Insane" repeated, coming at me faster, throwing off the rhythm of the song.

I righted myself and vomited. Struggling for breath, my world remained on a seesaw.

From down the street, Vanessa must have seen me straining. She slowly walked back toward me, exchanging magazines in her gun as she did.

There was nowhere to hide. We were under the overpass. My world rolled wildly as the song in my head mocked me. I dropped to a knee.

She lifted her gun and fired.

The song sounded as if it were circling a drain, picking up speed and ridiculing me with the repeated chorus of "I'm Insane."

I raised my gun and cupped it with my left hand.

Vanessa stopped walking and fired again.

I held my breath.

Another flash from the end of her gun.

The front sight on my gun bounced wildly as the world swooned.

The pain from the furious music was excruciating.

She fired again. I don't know where that round landed, but it didn't hit me.

When the sights were on her center mass, I squeezed the trigger.

She fell to the ground and clutched her leg.

I hollered, "Stay down!" but couldn't hear the words above the music in my skull.

Then I retched.

A patrol car raced south onto Washington Street, driving against the one-way traffic, its emergency lights whirring. I imagined its sirens were going, but I couldn't hear them.

Something touched my shoulder, and I turned to see Glenn standing next to me. His gun was drawn, and his attention was on Vanessa.

He said something and patted my back. Then he moved slowly forward.

As Glenn and Leya Navarro handcuffed Vanessa Bolkan, I sat on the sidewalk, listening as the sounds of the city slowly returned.

52

When Captain Ackerman arrived at the scene, Glenn said, "You ready for this?"

"As I'll ever be."

He patted my back and moved several feet away, nodding at the captain as he went.

Ackerman assessed me when he neared. "You okay, Nash?"

"Yes, sir."

"Did you already talk with the union?"

"They advised me of my rights."

Following an officer-involved shooting, protocol dictated an interview wouldn't occur for seventy-two hours. The Spokane County Sheriff's Office would conduct the investigation. One of our detectives would be assigned to shadow their detectives.

He noticed the vomit on my shirt. I had tried to brush most of it off, but it was a futile gesture. "Feeling okay?"

"I might have the flu."

"First shooting?" Ackerman asked.

"Yes, sir."

He leaned in. "I did the same thing after mine."

The captain then glanced towards Vanessa Bolkan while emergency personnel tended to her. An ambulance was parked in the middle of Washington Street. Patrol redirected traffic at Second Street. "You sure she murdered the two pimps?"

"We'll know for sure when we get lab results back on her gun. Glenn confirmed it was a twenty-two so we're a step closer."

"Regardless, we've got her on what's happened today. She killed a woman in front of the Lamplighter."

"Who was the victim?"

Ackerman opened his notebook. "Diedre Dodd."

"DeeDee," I said.

"You knew her?"

"She was Everson Wiley's right hand. This was a revenge tour."

"Burkett and Delaney are on that now. You'll be able to tie all the shootings together?"

"I believe so. Yes, sir."

Ackerman nodded. "Nice work, Nash."

"Didn't do it by myself."

He looked toward my partner, who was talking with Navarro. "We never do, do we?" He patted my arm. "Let me know if you need anything, Dallas."

53

"I saw you on the news last night," Stephen Yoder said. He crossed one leg over a knee and interlaced his fingers.

I scratched the back of my neck. "I'm still trying to wrap my head around it. Not sure how I feel about it."

"We can talk about it another day."

"I'd appreciate it."

"What about the music? Still hearing it?"

"Yeah," I muttered.

"It's only been a week. It's not going to go away overnight. It will take time."

"What if it never goes away?"

"What if it doesn't?"

I didn't want to think about it.

Eventually, he asked, "Did you make any changes over the week?"

"I moved back into my bedroom."

"Your bedroom?"

"I've slept on the couch for most of the year."

He crossed his arms. "You didn't want to sleep in the same room?"

"I had boxed up her clothes. Going into that room… with those boxes… meant I had to do something about it."

"Something final."

"I gave the clothes away this week."

"How did it feel?"

"Good, I guess."

"Like you were removing a weight."

"Something like that."

"But not as good as you hoped."

I tried to force a smile. "Unfortunately, not."

"That happens. Things that are good for us don't always feel good."

"Yeah," I muttered.

"Do you keep a list of the songs?"

"I did. Haven't for a while."

"Will you start again and bring it with you to the next meeting?"

I shrugged.

"I'd also like you to note what you were doing or feeling when a song started. Will you do that?"

I stared at the man. I wasn't going to get better by myself.

"Sure. I'll do that."

***

"My supervisor wanted to charge you with obstructing an investigation."

"Are you going to arrest me?" Marlene Anderson asked. We were in her office at Her Freedom.

"No. You saved her life. It was better than the alternative."

Her eyes searched mine.

"You told Chanel not to talk with me, which means I'm no closer to the truth of why she shot Damon."

"You have witnesses. That's enough."

"But I want to know *why*."

Marlene shrugged. "I don't know what to tell you."

I stared at her.

"She's messed up."

"I knew that."

"She's searching for something she's never going to find." Emotions played out over the counselor's face.

"But why shoot Damon?"

"I don't know. Maybe because he told her to get off the street. Maybe because she didn't like the way he rejected her. Who knows?"

"Where did she get the gun?"

"Where couldn't she have?"

Not having Chanel's story cleanly wrapped up pissed me off. It also frustrated me. "The prosecutor notified us Wanda Acosta is defending her."

Marlene nodded.

"How could she afford Wanda?"

"She's doing it for us—pro bono."

I lowered my head and thought about Wanda. What would she have to work with? Damon's bodyguards witnessed the girl running from the scene of Damon's shooting. I saw the girl in possession of the gun. Following her arrest, the forensic team did a test for gunshot residue on her hands, which came back positive. We were still waiting for lab results on the bullet from Damon's shoulder to the rounds still in the gun. Even if they matched, a conviction wasn't a foregone conclusion.

Chanel could say she found the gun and accidentally fired it away from the scene. If she didn't speak to an investigator, Wanda would sow enough doubt it wasn't inconceivable the girl could walk.

"I'm sorry, Dallas."

I looked up. "For what?"

"Getting on the wrong side of you. You're a nice man. There's not many of you out there."

I turned away.

"You're still in love with her, aren't you?"

"Yeah."

"She's lucky."

"How so?" She was dead. I didn't see how that made her lucky.

"Some of us have never known love like that."

***

"You don't have to do this," Marci Burkett said.

"I'm not good with my feelings. I figured this was the best way I could apologize."

I slipped the mouthpiece in. The molded plastic hurt my teeth and felt as if it were cutting into my gums.

We were in the department's training room with its padded floor and walls. Officers practiced their fighting skills in the room or occasionally solved grievances. Years of blood stains and black smears were on the mats and it reeked of sweat.

Marci Burkett wore the traditional white pants of a karate uniform and a black T-shirt. I wore running shorts and a tank top. Both of us wore mixed martial arts gloves that left our fingers open and exposed for grappling.

I was on my self-imposed 'Dallas Nash Apology Tour.'

I'd already made up to Debbie in Crime Analysis by bringing her a box of donuts. She graciously took them and shared them with her team. She listened as I said I was sorry for being such a heel and asked for her forgiveness.

When I apologized to Glenn, he told me to shut up. He said friends don't have to say they're sorry. I argued that they did, but he ignored me. We went for a cup of coffee and talked about how screwed up the union was. He's about as good at sharing his feelings as I am.

I thought about apologizing to Parker, but I figured I'd done enough by wrapping up his homicide case. We weren't friends, so saying sorry to him would be a sign of weakness. He already considered me soft due to my age, and I didn't need to add fuel to that fire.

Marci put her mouthpiece in and slapped her gloved hands together. She moved her jaw and her eyes narrowed.

The only time I ever trained with Marci was during in-service classes. Those were controlled environments, and I appreciated her martial arts expertise. I was a brawler who'd gotten by in my career with the intimidation of the uniform and the stubbornness of not wanting to lose a fight.

But this was Marci's natural habitat. She was a warrior woman who longed to test herself against all challengers. I'd never taken her up on her invitations to go onto the mat. When I did this morning, she jumped at it without hesitation. She knew it was a way for us to get back to being friends—a way to press the reset button.

Her height dropped—a wolverine preparing to strike.

I settled into a fighting stance, lifted my hands, and prepared to strike my friend. I mumbled through my mouthpiece, "All right. Let's see what you've got."

She punched me in the mouth.

***

"I heard another one this morning," I said. "Took me a while to recall it. Do you remember that band, Zebra?"

Bobbie's headstone stared silently up.

"Couple moderate hits." The wind gusted, and I lifted the collar of my coat to protect my ears. "The song was 'Tell Me What You Want.' It doesn't have any significance. At least, I don't think it does. You didn't send it to me, did you?"

I smiled at the block of marble.

"Just kidding. I know you didn't."

I knelt next to the slab.

"I'm not going to come back for a while. It doesn't mean I don't love you. Quite the opposite. I think I love you too much. I haven't learned how to let go. I need to start."

I kissed the tips of my fingers and then touched her name.

DID YOU LIKE THE BOOK?

I love when friends and family recommend a book for me. I'll often give it a read just because the recommendation came from someone I trusted. That's probably how we all are.

If you enjoyed this story, I'd truly appreciate it if you would tell your friends and family or leave a review at where you got the book.

All writers need feedback on their work—not only to help other readers discover them, but so they know they're delivering the goods with their stories.

Thanks for reading and hope to see you again!

About the Author

Colin Conway is the creator of the 509 Crime Stories, a series of novels set in Eastern Washington with revolving lead characters. They are standalone tales and can be read in any order.

He also created the Cozy Up series which pushes the envelope of the cozy genre. Libby Klein, author of the Poppy McAllister series, says *Cozy Up to Death* is "Not your grandma's cozy."

Colin co-authored the Charlie-316 series. The first novel in the series, *Charlie-316*, is a political/crime thriller that has been described as "riveting and compulsively readable," "the real deal," and "the ultimate ride-along."

He served in the U.S. Army and later was an officer of the Spokane Police Department. He has owned a laundromat, invested in a bar, and run a karate school. Besides writing crime fiction, he is a commercial real estate broker.

Colin lives with his beautiful girlfriend, three wonderful children, and a codependent Vizsla that rules their world.

Find out more about Colin at colinconway.com.

9 781961 030107